Trudy's Awakening

OTHER BOOKS BY CAROLYN CURRY

Suffer and Grow Strong: The Life of Ella Gertrude Clanton Thomas, 1834–1907

Sudden Death: A Novel

Trudy's Awakening

A Novel

CAROLYN NEWTON CURRY

MERCER UNIVERSITY PRESS
Macon, Georgia

MUP/ H1059

Published by Mercer University Press
1501 Mercer University Drive
Macon, Georgia 31207

29 28 27 26 25 5 4 3 2 1

Books published by Mercer University Press are printed on acid-free paper that meets the requirements of the American National Standard for Information Sciences—Permanence of Paper for Printed Library Materials.

Printed and bound in CANADA.

This book is set in Adobe Caslon.

Cover/jacket design by Burt&Burt.

ISBN 979-8-89736-003-1 (Hardback)
979-8-89736-004-8 (eBook)

Cataloging-in-Publication Data is available from the Library of Congress

This is a work of historical fiction. While the book is inspired by real events and includes references to historical figures and people who actually existed, the story and characters are in substantial part products of the author's imagination. Any resemblance to actual persons, living or dead, is either coincidental or used fictitiously. Historical events, locations, public figures, and other actual people are portrayed in a fictional manner for literary purposes and do not necessarily reflect the actual conduct or characteristics of the real people or events. Rather, the author has taken creative liberties with historical facts, timelines, and people to serve the narrative. Readers are encouraged to consult historical, nonfiction sources for accurate information about the period, events, and people depicted in this novel. These sources include *Suffer and Grow Strong: The Life of Ella Gertrude Clanton Thomas, 1834–1907*, this author's nonfiction biography of Ella Gertude Clanton Thomas, which was drawn from, among other extensively researched sources, the detailed personal diary that Thomas kept for more than forty years.

With love and gratitude

To my daughter Kristin,

my granddaughters Evelyn and Claire,

and my daughter-in-law Kelly

Introduction

Trudy's Awakening is a historical novel about three real women whose lives intertwined in 1899 Atlanta, Georgia. I have reams of information about one of these women and very little about the other two. But what I do know made me curious enough to want to fill in the gaps and tell a story about the three of them.

The first of the three women is Ella Gertrude Clanton Thomas. I wrote my doctoral dissertation about her and, in 2014, published a biography about her life. She lived through the horrific events of the Civil War, survived, and prospered late in her life when she became president of the embryonic women's suffrage movement in Georgia. She was born in 1834 in Augusta, Georgia, into one of the wealthiest families in the state, but her family lost everything during and after the war. Her story is one of determination and transformation in the face of great odds.

When Gertrude was only fourteen years old, she started keeping a record of her life that she continued off and on for forty-one years. A treasure trove of information, it is composed of thirteen volumes and 450,000 words. After she stopped keeping her journals, she kept scrapbooks with articles she and others wrote that describe what she was doing and thinking. There are also voluminous legal records about the family's rise and fall housed in the Richmond County courthouse, Augusta, Georgia.

This material outlines how Gertrude's life was turned upside down by a war and all its accompanying hardships. But it was her response to that change that has always interested me. She was able to work through her problems and, finally, to be happy at the end of her life. How was she able to do that? Why can some people survive horrific events and others cannot? Where did she get her grit and determination?

I have written Gertrude's biography, made speeches about her, and talked about her often. I know her so well that even when I don't have her exact words, I can imagine what she might have said. But I will use her words when I can.

I have even chosen to use a more informal name for her. I know that close friends and servants occasionally called her Trudy. In a direct quote in the journal that Gertrude recorded, she is called "Miss Trudy." She was an inquisitive, active, and adventurous woman. Somehow, I imagine her being called Trudy or Miss Trudy later in her life. It fits her.

In this book, Gertrude—or Trudy—tells her own life story. She is looking back from the age of sixty-five, remembering her life and sharing it with a portrait artist named Lizzie Jeter. In 1899, Lizzie did paint a beautiful portrait of Gertrude, so it is easy to imagine a deep conversation between the two of them. I do not know as much about Lizzie as I do about Trudy, but I do know some things from census figures and newspaper articles. She was only twenty-six years old when she painted Trudy's portrait. At that time, she was listed as the sole breadwinner for her mother, her sister, and her sister's young baby. It was fascinating for me to imagine the life of a young, struggling, female artist in Atlanta in the 1890s.

I am the fortunate owner of Gertrude's portrait today. It is evident that Lizzie Jeter captured the spirit of this strong woman with piercing brown eyes and snow-white hair. Set in its original gold-leaf frame, it hangs in the entry hall to my home where friends and family see her every day.

The third woman in my story, a slave named Amanda, is mentioned frequently in Trudy's journal. Amanda was Trudy's age and her constant companion growing up. In the journal, Amanda's name appears with those of sisters and cousins, so it was difficult to know who was enslaved and who was free. They played together, talked, and probably slept in the same room. They shared an obvious connection, a bond. What was it, exactly? Their apparent friendship was interesting and made me want to add a life story to the tidbits I had.

All three of these women's lives were connected. It was fascinating to unravel the tapestries of their lives. They came from different circumstances, with unique problems, and had their own talents. None of them had an easy life, but they all shared one thing in common. They were survivors—or, as we like to say in the South, they had gumption.

Of course, I hope that my readers will learn some history of Atlanta and what it was like to be a female in this growing, changing world. But more important, I hope they will learn that when bad things happen—and they always do—they can find a way through them and come out to a better place. I also loved giving interesting lives to women who are not remembered today. If they could know this story, I hope they would be happy with what I have imagined.

Part One

Chapter 1

Atlanta, Georgia

1899

Lizzie Jeter lumbered off the streetcar with her paraphernalia. In one hand she held a large carpet bag full of brushes, paints, sketching pads, pencils, and a folding easel. With her other hand she managed the edge of a large wooden frame with canvas stretched over it, trying to keep it tucked under her arm. Her equipment was harder to carry than she had anticipated. And it was an unusually warm day for early November in Atlanta. She was getting hot and didn't want to get her pretty white blouse mussed up. Her goal was to look professional and make a good first impression. She knew she looked young for twenty-six years. Most women would see that as an advantage, but not her. She wanted to look like she knew what she was doing.

She had mapped out her itinerary carefully. The house was on a road off Peachtree Street near the First Methodist Episcopal Church South. She had found the street, but where was the house? She was thinking she might be lost when she suddenly saw 54 Alexander Street. Thank goodness, she had made it. She dragged herself up the few steps onto a spacious porch to the front door, put down her things, smoothed her sandy blonde hair, took a deep breath, and then knocked calmly. She waited a few seconds and knocked again. She wondered if she had gotten the time correct, but the door opened to reveal a grizzled old man.

He asked in a gruff voice, "What do you want? Don't

remember anything about anybody coming. What's that? A carpet bag? You one of those damn Yankees who came down after the war?"

Lizzie was shaken and frightened. What was going on? Did she have the correct address? The old man wore a Civil War uniform complete with hat, knee-high leather boots, and a rifle over his shoulder. He looked like he was ready to go fight. She was searching for what to say when the woman who had hired her came up behind the man.

"Now Pa, be nice. Don't you remember I told you an artist was coming to paint Mama's portrait? Now you go on back down the hall. Weren't you getting ready to go to Piedmont Park? Something going on over there today, you said."

"Yes, I'm going to a meeting over there of the Sons of Confederate Veterans. We got important things to discuss. Anyway, this woman don't look like an artist to me. She's too young. And she's got a carpet bag just like those carpet baggers, those sorry folks who came South after the war trying to fleece us for everything we had."

"Pa, just go on. This young woman is definitely an artist. I've seen some of her work. I invited her here today." She guided him a little way down the hall.

Once the old man was out of earshot, the woman came back to the door. "Don't mind him. We all know it's been over for thirty years, but he's still fighting the Civil War. He was never the same after he came home. But he's harmless really. I'm so sorry if he frightened you."

The pleasant middle-aged woman motioned for Lizzie to come in, greeting her warmly with a big smile. "Hello, Miss Jeter, I'm so glad you're here. I'm Cora Ferrell, Mrs. Thomas's daughter. Mama and Pa live here with my husband Patrick and me. It was such a pleasure to meet you at the

State Fair and talk about you doing a portrait of my mother. So glad we could work it out. Let me help you with your things. My goodness, you do have a load."

Lizzie calmed down a little, caught her breath, and said in a weak voice, "Thank you, I didn't think my things would be so heavy. But I do like to paint my subjects in their homes." She turned to gather her supplies from the porch floor.

"I must say you are an energetic soul to manage all these things. Leave them here at the door for a second. I want to show you a portrait of Mama that was done the week she married in 1852." Cora led her into a lovely dining room to the left of the front door. There was a fireplace opposite the windows with a portrait hung over the mantel. "We all love this beautiful portrait of Mama with her delicate jewelry and beautiful white blouse. She always loved pretty clothes. I don't know why she always wears black or gray these days. Of course, no jewelry. Always looks like she's in mourning. But here she is when she was young and carefree."

"It's wonderful, and she was so pretty." Lizzie wondered if Cora was telling her how to paint her mother now. More pressure.

"Let's get your things, then we'll go to the parlor and I'll get Mama. She's in her office down the hall. She loves to read and write and spends most of her time there. She's working on an important speech and doesn't like to be interrupted. She may be cranky." Cora helped Lizzie with her tools and then left to fetch her mother.

After encountering the old soldier with the gun, Lizzie wondered just how "cranky" her subject would be. What had she gotten herself into? She would have to pull herself together. She desperately needed the money from this job.

As she studied the room Cora indicated, she began to feel better. It was a pleasant room with a red velvet settee, several chairs, and a game table to one side with a chess set. The best feature was a window letting in the afternoon light, perfect for painting a portrait. She was setting up her easel in front of the window when Cora returned.

"Miss Jeter, I'd like you to meet my mother, Gertrude Thomas."

Lizzie looked up to see a small, elderly woman with silver-white hair walk into the room. She stood ramrod straight and had an aura of authority about her. Her dark brown eyes were glued to Lizzie as she spoke. "Hello, I'm your subject. Not that I'm excited about it. Where do I sit?"

"Well, hello, Mrs. Thomas. I'm Lizzie Jeter. Pleased to meet you," Lizzie managed to say with a smile on her face. "Would you please come sit in this chair facing the window?"

"Excuse my manners. I'm pleased to meet you, too. It's not your fault I was tricked into having this portrait painted," Mrs. Thomas blurted as she walked over to the window.

This was not a good start. This woman would be difficult. And would the old man be around a lot? Mrs. Thomas was not happy. As Lizzie lifted up the smock she always wore to protect her clothes when she painted, she realized Mrs. Thomas was talking.

"I can't sit still. I have never been able to sit still. Who wants a portrait of a sixty-five-year-old woman anyway? Whose idea was it for me to sit here for hours and have my portrait painted? I have a lot of other things that I need to be doing." She fidgeted with her high silk collar. "It's 1899, for heaven's sake; we're about to enter a new age. I sure hope women in the next century will wear more practical clothes. These long skirts and high collars can be very uncomfortable."

"Yes, our long skirts are difficult, particularly on a day like today. That's why I like to wear a lightweight cotton blouse when I work," Lizzie said, trying to agree with Mrs. Thomas and hopefully get her in a better mood. "Oh, and I heard that you agreed to do this long ago. Your family and all the women you have helped in your life are proud of you. You are still an attractive woman. Look at those beautiful brown eyes. I'll make sure you look good." Lizzie smiled as she tied her smock.

"Now you're flattering me. I don't know how good you can make me look. See my wrinkles and gray hair—I'm certainly not a spring chicken," Mrs. Thomas fired back. "But I guess you're right; I do seem to remember agreeing to allow someone to paint a portrait. But I didn't think about having to sit here so long. I guess I can't get out of it now. What do you want me to do?"

"Now that is more like the feisty, brave woman I have heard about. I'm just happy to be able to spend time with you and get to know you." Lizzie took out her sketching pencils. "I've been doing some research. I know you sign newspaper articles 'Mrs. J. Jefferson Thomas' or 'Gertrude Thomas.' But family and friends call you 'Miss Trudy.' May I call you Miss Trudy?"

"Of course, friends and family have always called me Trudy or Miss Trudy. It's a Southern thing to put a 'Miss' in front of a woman's name when she gets older, whether she is married or not. Call me what you want. Now let's get this portrait started."

"Yes, let's get started. Sit up straight, please."

"You don't have to remind me to sit up straight. I always do. But what will I do while I sit here? I can't just waste time.

I've never been able to be idle. I love to read. Can I read while I sit here or maybe write something? I always have writing I need to do."

"No, I need to see your face. I study your features and make sketches before I start to paint. Sit here and look out the window. No city in America is prettier than Atlanta in the fall. There are so many beautiful colors. Look at that gingko tree ready to drop its yellow leaves any day now. And look at those children playing down the street. You can talk to me. I want to hear your life story. I heard you kept a diary of your life. Did I hear forty-one years? Not many people can do that. If you can keep a journal for that many years, you can surely sit still and talk for a few hours." Lizzie gently adjusted Miss Trudy's face to catch the light.

"Okay, if you put it that way. Miss Jeter, you're a very persuasive woman, and I like that."

Lizzie breathed a sigh of relief. Something seemed to have come over her subject just in time. Mrs. Thomas had become Miss Trudy, and Miss Trudy seemed to like to talk about her story. Lizzie felt calmer, too. She would be fine as long as she could keep Miss Trudy talking about the past and, of course, if that old man didn't come back and charge into the room.

Miss Trudy began talking with a new softness in her voice. "Now it's a long story, and I have lived through some things you may have a hard time believing, but they are all true. My journals are right here on this table. I keep them handy and read them occasionally. They keep the past alive to me, especially the people who have died. I miss them very much, but they are all remembered here in these pages. They are never far from me."

While Lizzie lined up her sketching pencils on a small

table by her easel, Miss Trudy sat and thought for several minutes before she began to talk.

"A good place to start would be a fall day in early October of 1848. I'm sure of the date because I started my journal on September 29. Look at this, Lizzie." Miss Trudy held up her first journal for inspection. "It begins, *Rochester, September 29, 1848. I sent for this paper to form a journal. I will write what happened on Monday Tuesday & Wednesday.*"

Miss Trudy gently stroked the page. "That statement makes me laugh. I had no idea I would keep a record of my life for forty-one years. And to name the plantation 'Rochester' is just like something I would do. Why do you think I chose that name?"

"I have no idea." Lizzie began to sketch.

"Because I had just read *Jane Eyre* by Charlotte Brontë. Remember that was the mysterious man Jane eventually married. I was such a romantic young girl—only fourteen—and took everything I read to heart." Miss Trudy stared out the window with a distant look in her eyes as if she were suddenly somewhere else long ago. "That day I remember vividly. I went horseback riding with my dear Pa to check the cotton crops. It was harvesting time. My life changed forever that day."

Chapter 2

Augusta, Georgia

1848

"Look at this gorgeous day, Pa. I love riding horseback with you more than anything in the world. Tell me again how Grandpa brought you down from Virginia when you were just a boy, looking for good land to grow cotton."

"Trudy, you've about worn that story out. You've heard it a thousand times."

"Please, I love to hear it. Your Pa didn't have much except what he could carry in his wagons, and he arrived here with a dream to create a plantation. He slowly started buying land and then you continued his dream, and look: as far as the eye can see, there are rows and rows of beautiful white cotton, ready to pick. And now you don't even know exactly how much land you own—hundreds, even thousands of acres."

"Sounds like you know the story well enough to tell it to me. But I'm happy about what we have accomplished. Of course, we have an ideal climate for cotton. And it takes so many to run these plantations. The workers we have acquired are essential."

"That's right, Pa. I know your father didn't have any slaves. You inherited some from Mama when you married, but you had to buy the rest of them. Now you have hundreds. There's no way you could get this cotton picked if you didn't have slaves. But do you mind if I ask you a question?"

"Of course not. I always expect questions from that inquisitive mind of yours."

Trudy stroked her horse's mane and looked up at her father. "I hear folks say the slaves are a gift from God. Do you really believe slavery is condoned by the Bible?"

"Yes, there are many verses in the Bible about slavery. There are even instructions about how to treat them and how they are to respond to their master. I try very hard to be a good master."

"Pa, I know you do. But I just can't help but wonder sometimes. I know you're the only person in the world I can ask."

"You are correct to only express your doubts to me. Slavery is our way of life here in the South. We clothe, feed, and house our slaves and treat them like family. You know that. They have the Christian religion because we allow them their churches and ministers. They learn trades and I believe they enjoy them. Yes, I believe we're doing the right things."

"I'm not accusing you of anything. I just can't help asking. It's the way my mind works. I must try to figure things out—everything. Since I've brought this up, can I ask one other question?"

"My goodness, Trudy. Yes, let's get these things out now and move to another subject."

Trudy hesitated. She looked out at the dozens of slaves bent over chopping weeds away from the cotton plants and gathered her courage. "Why are some of our slaves so light skinned? My Amanda and her mother Lurany are almost as white as I am."

Pa hesitated and stared off in the distance, irritation showing on his face. "That's just the way it is. Do not ask any more questions on this subject. Do you understand?"

"Yes, Pa. I didn't mean to upset you. Don't get mad at me. I'm always reading and trying to figure things out, but I have no one to talk to. Mama would be horrified. She just wants me to go to sewing circle and not ask any questions. It's so boring. I hate it."

"She's just trying to prepare you to be a plantation mistress. That's what you should be thinking about. Not all these questions about slavery."

Trudy twisted in her saddle, agitated. She pulled up close to her father and looked him in the eye. "But what if I don't want to be a Southern lady? It's not fair that boys get to go to college at the university in Athens or at Princeton in New Jersey, while we sit at home doing embroidery. Boring. And I'm just as smart as the boys or even smarter."

"I know you're very intelligent. I'm amazed—should I say shocked sometimes—at the things you say. And I have done something about it. I wasn't going to tell you until I had a chance to discuss it with your mother, but I'll go on and tell you today. Last week I went to Macon to look at the new college for women that was started by the Methodists. It's the first one in the country. I wanted to see if I thought it would be suitable for you to go."

"Oh, Pa, that's wonderful. What did you think?" Trudy asked as she trembled with excitement.

"I was impressed. Most of the classes are taught by ministers, and the young women live in dorms with them and their families. The curriculum is more advanced than I thought it would be. Very much like Emory at Oxford, which is for boys only. History, rhetoric, astronomy. Advanced subjects. Do you think you would like it?"

"Of course, I would. Oh, Pa, let me go. Please let me go," Trudy pleaded.

"Well, I think it would be good for you. You need to be thinking about other things than this plantation. You need a wider world. We'll talk about it with your mother tonight. Now I'm going to stop here at this barn and talk to an overseer. Take the horses down to the creek and let them drink."

"You know Mama won't understand. She has precise ideas about what girls should do. Be quiet, don't ask questions, have good manners, and don't read too much. We will have to convince her. But I think it's an absolutely fabulous idea!"

"Don't be too hard on her. She loves you and wants what she thinks is best for you. And she's right about one thing: you should not ask so many questions. No more questions about slavery."

"I won't, Pa. I promise. I do love you so. Thank you, thank you. This is the best news!" Trudy jumped off her horse and threw her arms around her father's neck. "I love you. Thank you for understanding me."

Trudy took the reins of the two horses and hurried down to the creek, humming and laughing to herself. "I'm going to college. I'm going to college. I'm so happy. Thank you, Pa. No more boring embroidery for me. I'm going to college."

"Amanda, Amanda, where are you? You're going to have to help me get ready for dinner. Pa and I stayed out riding late. You won'tbelieve what he's going to do tonight." Trudy ran into her bedroom where Amanda was sitting, looking at one of her books.

"Of course, I'll help you, Trudy. I always help you dress. Why you so excited?"

"Pa is going to talk to Mama about me going to college. Can you believe it? I'm going to Macon to the new college for women—at least, that's what we're talking about tonight." Trudy began to unbutton her dress, which was damp from perspiration and a little splattered with mud.

"You always manage to get your nice dresses dirty. How you do it? Look here at this hem. When you goin' to learn?"

"Oh, I was taking the horses for water in the creek, and I was hot. I took my shoes off and splashed around in the water. You shouldn't be concerned about what I do. I'll do what I please."

"Hold your dress up next time, and try to keep it out of the mud. Now what's this about college? That's good for you, I guess. But I'll miss you. You and me been together almost every day of our lives. Who'll teach me to read after you gone? I ain't even supposed to know how to read. It's against the law. No one else will dare help me."

"I won't be going for a couple months. You're doing so well. I'll have you reading up a storm before I leave. I promise. I love that we have this secret. It's so much fun. Everybody says slaves aren't smart enough to read. I'd say that's true mostly, but you are different. You're smarter than the others. It's a stupid law to say I can't teach you. I do pretty much what I like to do all the time anyway. When I'm gone, you can come into my room and read all my books while you're supposed to be cleaning. Won't that be wicked."

"I don't know any slaves that's stupid. Plenty could learn to read. You wrong about that." Amanda looked away.

"I don't know. You might be right. But right now, I need to wash up."

"Okay, you clean up. There's a bowl of water on your dresser. I'll get one of your pretty dresses." Amanda started looking though Trudy's large selection of beautiful frocks.

"Get that blue dress. Pa likes it." Trudy splashed water

on her face. "And I need help with my hair. It's a mess." She stood at her dressing table and looked in the mirror.

"Trudy, that brown hair always looks good. I'll just smooth it out a little in the back. How 'bout I pull it back and tie it with a blue ribbon? You sit down on this stool for a second."

"Whatever you want to do is fine, but do it quickly."

Amanda tucked Trudy's stray hair up and added the blue ribbon.

"Pull the dress over my head. I want to be the first one downstairs." Trudy held up her arms. "Thank you, Amanda. What will I do without you? I'll miss you. That will be my only problem. You've always been my companion and helped me do everything." Trudy looked at herself in the mirror and smoothed the front of her dress.

"You'll be fine. I'm sure you'll be able to dress yourself at that college. It ain't that hard." Amanda rolled her eyes.

Chapter 3

Augusta, Georgia

1848

After Trudy dashed out, Amanda began to straighten up the beautiful bedroom. She spread the soft, rose-patterned coverlet on the bed and closed the matching curtains for the night. Then she put Trudy's shoes neatly aside to polish later. As she picked up the soiled dress to take to the basement washroom, she realized she would have to soak it overnight to get the mud stains out. That girl would be the end of her. She wouldn't miss cleaning up her messes.

Amanda took the small back stairs two flights down and entered the laundry room, lit by two small, rectangular windows near the ceiling that let in a little natural light. There were two big washtubs, one for washing and one for rinsing. Two straight-back chairs with woven seats stood by a small table with an oil lamp. A cot on one side was her mother Lurany's bed at night. They used the large table against the wall to fold laundry or lay out patterns for sewing. It was a small, cozy room where she and her mother could sit and talk without anyone hearing them. Amanda had always loved this little room and the quiet time she spent there with her mother.

Lurany was sitting in one of the chairs, bent over doing some delicate handwork on the bodice of a little girl's dress. She was lost in her work, concentrating on each stitch she made.

Amanda broke the silence. "Mama, here's Trudy's dress. We got to soak it and get it clean."

Lurany glanced at the dress as Amanda dunked it into the tub of cold water to soak. "How does that child do it? She's so careless with the pretty dresses we make. She's always getting 'em torn or covered with something we got to scrub out. Lordy me, she's an active child."

"Mama, she's no child anymore. She's fourteen years old and should be calming down. At least, that's what Miss Mary says. And now she talkin' about going to that new college for girls way over in Macon, wherever that is. I don't know what I'll do without her."

"Now you know that ain't so, baby girl. You and me be sewing all the time. We always busy. But I know you two been together since Massa Clanton put you in her bedroom to be her companion. You've always did everything for her. But you always played together and had so much goin' on. It's been fun but it's time for her to move on."

"I know, but I been thinkin' we would always be together. Even when she got married. I'm not just her companion; I'm her slave. Massa Clanton gave me to her. But I wonder if I gets to go with her to that college. What do you think, Mama?"

"Oh, I don't know nothin' about womens goin' to college. We'll see. I know the menfolk takes their man when they travel, usually to help with clothes and such."

"I hope I get to go along. I ain't never been nowhere. But I would miss you, Mama," Amanda said as she put her arms around Lurany.

"Baby girl, I would miss you, too. But I know you would come back with Miss Trudy when she returns from college."

"I ain't never left this plantation. I ain't been nowhere. Sometimes I want to walk down the road out this plantation. Just real casual like. I don't think nobody would notice."

"Child, don't you talk like that—never. They would chase you down with dogs and hurt you bad. On top of that I couldn't live without you."

"Mama, you right. I'm only imagining. I won't go. But if I did, I'd take you with me."

"Well I ain't goin' nowhere ever. All I've ever wanted was for us to be together. When you was born, I was so afraid Massa Clanton would sell you—you bein' so pretty and fair skinned. Looked like what they call Fancy Ladies. I was worried to death until I went to see him. He's a good massa, and he promised me he wouldn't sell you and he ain't. He is a man of his word. I believe as long as he's alive, we be together. Now I don't know what Miss Mary would do. But I also know she needs me to do all her sewing. With them younguns she has, there's always a pile of sewing to do. Make yourself needed, Amanda. That's why I been training you to be a good seamstress. The lady folk can't do without their pretty dresses, and they's got to have lots of 'em." Lurany folded the dress she was stitching. Then she stood and headed toward the stairs. "I got to go. Miss Mary told me to help serve dinner tonight."

"Mama, I think Trudy is different. She treats me special."

Lurany slowly turned back and looked at Amanda. "Child, I know y'all always been together. But we never know how they really feel about us. Always remember that. Be careful. Remember we their property. We just got to hope we won't be separated. I love you. You my baby girl, no matter how old you is. We goin' to sit and sew beautiful dresses together forever. That's what I hope."

Chapter 4

Augusta, Georgia

1848

Trudy rushed down the grand circular staircase and into the large formal dining room. She wanted to get the coveted seat next to Pa, since being close to him might give her courage. Mama would be opposed to this idea of college. Catching her breath, she sat down and began to look around. It was a stately dining room with a huge mahogany table that could seat sixteen people. A large portrait of Pa hung at one end of the room and one of Mama hung at the other end. Trudy liked both portraits. They made her parents look younger and happier. She loved the one of Pa. His dark brown wavy hair and fancy starched shirt made him look so handsome. The one of her mother was pretty, too. Mama was an attractive woman. At five feet, four inches, she was almost a foot shorter than Pa. But she was strong and worked hard at raising her children and helping to run the six plantations they owned. An upstanding Christian woman, she believed her role in life was to be a mother, to be "fruitful and multiply," as the Bible said. She had given Turner Clanton seven children and planned to give him more. Trudy did not feel as close to her mother as she did to her father. Busy taking care of everyone, her mother could be distant. But Trudy loved both of her parents and knew she was fortunate to have them.

On many nights, the dining room was full of Pa's relatives and business associates. Fortunately, tonight only the family would be present: Trudy's four sisters, Anne, three years older than her, and Mary, Cora, and Katherine, who were younger, along with her two younger brothers, Nathaniel Holt and James. All of them would be excited about this meal in the dining room only because Pa was home. Pa was wonderful about telling stories of his travels and asking questions about their activities. He had a way with children and made them feel important. Trudy was daydreaming about meals in the past when her mother walked in the room.

"My goodness, this is a first. You're usually the last to arrive in the dining room for any meal. Always in your room reading, daydreaming, or whatever you do in there," Mama said as she looked around, checking details no matter who was coming to dinner.

Before Trudy could think of anything to say, Nathaniel Holt and James came bounding in, racing to see who could reach his chair first.

"Boys, boys, please slow down. Mind your manners. Your father is here for dinner, and he will be watching you. Be young gentlemen like I've taught you," Mama said as the young girls came walking in with their big sister, Anne.

"Well, well, here you are, Trudy," Anne said as she sat at the other end of the table by Mama's place. "Already seated for dinner after being out and about all day riding a horse with Pa. Why in the world would you be on a horse all day? That's not what women do. That's what men do. Can't believe you've gotten yourself presentable for dinner so quickly."

Thankfully, before Trudy had a chance to respond, Pa strolled into the room and everyone went quiet, looking his way.

"Isn't this a wonderful evening when all of us can be together," Pa said as he sat down. "Trudy and I had a lovely day riding around the plantation looking at the crops. Everyone bow your heads, and I will give thanks for this bountiful meal." As soon as he was finished, he asked, "Now what have the rest of you been doing? Boys, what were you up to today?"

Nathaniel Holt could not wait to tell Pa about the fort he and James had built under the scuppernong arbor behind the big house. "Pa, we stacked up rocks and made a high wall, had big sticks for swords. Those scuppernong grapes are so good. There are still some on the vines. We ate a lot of 'em, though."

"Boys, I've told you not to eat those grapes. They can make you sick. I hope you haven't ruined your appetite," Mama said as the servants began to bring in the food.

As the fried chicken, baked sweet potatoes, beans, and hot biscuits with gravy were carried around the table and served, the room grew quiet again. Everyone was hungry, and the food was delicious.

"Lurany, please tell Tamah the food is especially good tonight. My family is eating a little too quickly, but I will permit it this once." Mama looked adoringly at Pa. "They're excited about their Pa being home. Boys, slow down and leave a little room for apple pie. Now Father, please tell us about your travels. We always love to hear where you have been and what you have done."

"Well, Mary, I had a great trip. I stopped in Atlanta first. I had some business talking about cotton shipments and warehouses, stuff you kids don't want to hear about. Tell you what, let's enjoy our pie and then the younger children can be excused. I'd like Anne and Trudy to come to the parlor with you and me. I want to tell you about my visit in Macon."

The younger children thought that was a great idea and quickly ate their pie. Not the least bit interested in grown-up talk, they went off to their rooms to prepare for bed.

Trudy held her breath as they all settled into comfortable chairs in the parlor and Pa began to speak. "I'm not sure how much you know about the new college for young women in Macon, Georgia, called the Wesleyan Female College. But I decided to stop by there and check it out. Have you heard about it, Mary?"

"I heard some women at church talking about it, but honestly, I didn't pay much attention. I don't understand why we need a college for women. The job of women is to have children and take care of the home. How can college help them with that?"

Pa continued as if he didn't hear her. "I was very impressed. It was started by some businessmen and pastors of the Methodist Church. All the instructors are ministers, and the girls live upstairs in houses with the ministers and their families, who live downstairs. I feel it is a safe and wholesome environment."

"But it isn't necessary. The girls can learn what they need to know here at home. That's what I am trying to do with Anne and Trudy. I don't know a single woman who has ever gone to college. Young men do that."

Trudy kept looking down, anxious to speak her mind but knowing she shouldn't disagree with her mother.

Mary grew agitated. "Don't you remember that woman who stood up in church meeting a few weeks ago and everyone was shocked? Women are to keep silent, as it says in the book of Corinthians: *Let your women keep silent in the churches, for they are not permitted to speak.... If they want to learn something, let them ask their husbands at home; for it is shameful for women to speak in church.* I bet she was one of those college women who have opinions of their own and ask too many questions. She sure did not act like a lady."

"Now Mother, please calm down. I agree that she should not have stood up and said anything. It was not ladylike. But we don't know if she was a college woman. There is nothing in the Bible that says women can't learn new things. Our girls are very intelligent. I have decided that the college is doing a good job trying to educate women in a Christian environment. They will be even better mothers to their children someday."

An awkward silence fell as they all looked around at each other. Finally, Pa said, "I would like to know what the girls think."

Unable to hold back another moment, Trudy exclaimed, "Oh, Pa, I would love to go. I want to learn history, read Shakespeare, and have discussions with professors about astronomy. Please let me go."

Mary was clearly uneasy with Trudy's response. "Trudy dear, calm down. You are not even the oldest girl in this family. If anyone goes, it should be Anne. At seventeen, she is three years older than you are and certainly more mature. I would like to hear what Anne thinks."

"No, not me. I have no interest whatsoever in going to some college. I don't sit in my room and read all day. I had much rather be downstairs with Mama and her friends, visiting and doing cross-stitch. I am not a recluse," Anne said as she glared at Trudy.

"Now Sis Anne, be kind to your younger sister," Pa said. "There is nothing wrong with Trudy's love of reading. I admire it. I know she's curious and wants to know things. She is very intelligent. If you don't want to go, Anne, that is fine. But if Trudy wants to go, I have decided to give my permission. She will start in January at the beginning of the next session."

Trudy almost jumped up and hugged her father's neck, but she knew that was not wise. Anne was already jealous of her relationship with Pa. Too much enthusiasm would only make it worse. She kept calm and simply said, "Thank you, Pa. That makes me very happy. Thank you so much."

As they all sat quietly for a few minutes, Trudy thought how lucky she was to have Pa as her father. Most men and women would agree with her mother. Virtually everyone they knew would probably agree with her. No one thought women were smart enough to go to college.

Finally, Pa spoke up. "Does anyone else have anything to say? If not, then it's settled. Trudy will be the first in our family to go to college. Maybe the first in Augusta. How do you feel about that, Trudy?"

"I could not be happier. Thank you. Thank you, Pa. I will make you proud." Trudy got up and hugged her father. She didn't care what Anne or her mother thought. Pa approved, and that is what mattered to her. She would show them all that she could be a lady and still go to college. What could be wrong with that?

"Trudy, we missed you at sewing circle yesterday," their neighbor Mrs. Phinizy said as she found her spot among the cross-stitch gathering hosted by Trudy's mother. "My girls were looking forward to seeing you."

"I'm sorry I missed it, too. But I went out riding with Pa to check the crops." Trudy looked down and began to remove some of her cross-stitches that she had messed up.

"My dear, you must be careful not to ride horses too much. I've heard that too much riding can hurt your reproductive organs."

"No ma'am, I don't ride too much." Trudy couldn't believe Mrs. Phinizy said this in front of Mama and her friends. She already had to put up with enough from her sister Anne. And anyway, that was only an old wives' tale.

Thankfully, at about that moment Mrs. Wood entered the room and called for Trudy to come get something she had for her. "I just came back from Charleston," she said, "and I picked up this new book, *Wuthering Heights*. Because of prejudice against women writers, the author first claimed her name was Ellis Bell. Now we know it is Emily Brontë. Have you read it?"

"No, but I've heard about it and can't wait to read it."

"I knew you would be excited. I've already read it and would be happy to loan you my copy until you can get one."

"Thank you for thinking of me. You are always so kind to let me borrow your books."

"It's not easy for us to get the latest books from England. I know you like to read the same way I do. Take it and look through it now."

"You can have my seat in the circle, and I'll look at it a minute." Trudy began to thumb through the pages, loving the feel of a new book.

"Mary, sorry I'm late," Mrs. Wood said. "I'm taking Trudy's place. She's looking at something I brought her from Charleston. You have the most gorgeous silver tea service, and look at these scrumptious goodies—cream puffs and strawberry tarts. I love your little tea parties."

Mary glowed. "You may remember this was my mother's tea service. It came from England, and she left it to me. I prize it above all my possessions. And my cook, Tamah, has become so good at making pastries. I'm glad you are enjoying everything."

"Well, I certainly am. I'm worn out from shopping in Charleston, and these gourmet treats are divine. They'll give me a lift."

Mary got so involved in enjoying her friends that she didn't realize that Trudy had not returned to the circle. When she finally noticed, she called to her, "Trudy, my goodness, we're missing you. What in the world are you doing?"

Trudy had sat in a comfortable chair and was lost in the new book when she heard her mother calling her. "Oh, I'll be right there. Mrs. Wood was sweet enough to share her new book with me. I started reading it."

"Please join the circle again. Ladies, I'm sorry my daughter is so rude. She loves to read and does it too much. I'm worried it will have a bad effect on her. Come now, Trudy."

Trudy reluctantly put down the book, thinking she couldn't wait to go off to college. Thank goodness, at Wesleyan she would not have to go to the dreaded sewing circles. And she imagined riding horses any time she wanted, with no one around to fear for her fertility. She couldn't wait to leave for Macon and college, where she would be free.

Chapter 5

Manchester, Georgia

1895

Lizzie met her friend Malorie at Benson's Pharmacy to have one of those new soda fountain drinks they loved so much.

"Lizzie, isn't it great we have finished school? God, I love the freedom. It's such fun to meet you here. And don't you love this drink! What do they call it again?"

"Coca-Cola. I think it's delicious, too. It's taking off all over. Everybody likes it. And it was started right here in Atlanta."

"What makes it so good?"

"It's made from a special formula syrup mixed with carbonated water. It's sweet tasting with a fizz."

"You're so smart. You always know the answer to everything."

Lizzie and Malorie were sitting at a small round table by the window, looking out on the street. Lizzie stirred her drink slowly with her spoon. "I'm not sure how smart I am," she said, "but I do love to learn. I want to go to that new college that has come to town. You know, the LaGrange Female Seminary that is going to be called Cox College. I'm so excited about it. I've even heard we might change the name of our town from Manchester to College Park."

"No college for me," Malorie said, running her finger along the condensation on her glass. "Thomas and I want to get married. I've begged my folks, and they have said since I'm seventeen, I can. Don't you want to do that instead of college and more studying?"

"Definitely not. I've taken a job at LuVee's Dress Shop, and I'm saving every penny. I'll have to convince my folks to let me go."

"Well, good luck. Even though I don't understand, if that's what you want, I hope it works out. Knowing how stubborn you are, I imagine you'll get your way." Malorie laughed as she got up and gave Lizzie a hug. "Got to go now."

"Me, too. It was great to see you. Let's do it more often." Lizzie walked toward the door and swung it open. She knew she was lucky to have such good friends and live in this charming little town. For some reason, she felt so happy and carefree today, like a kid, and almost skipped down the street.

The town had a main street like many small southern towns—with a pharmacy, a general store, a feed store, a café, a lawyer's office, and a women's dress shop. The Methodist church stood across the railroad tracks that ran through town along main street. Of course, she could also see a Baptist church and a Presbyterian church down the street. She was headed for the picturesque depot in the middle of town, proud that her Daddy worked for the Atlanta and West Point Railroad. He ran the depot, and everyone in town loved him. The friendly Jeremiah Jeter kept everything running smoothly, receiving packages, greeting travelers, and doing it all with a smile.

When Lizzie walked in the door, her father was tidying up the office, putting everything in place as he prepared to leave for the day. "Daddy, I'm here to walk you home. Are you ready to go?"

"You bet I am. Been cooped up inside all day. A brisk walk home with you will be great. I'm so glad to see you." He gave her a hug.

"I love to come walk with you. I just saw Malorie at

Benson's for a Coca-Cola. Isn't it great that you get to walk to and from work in this charming little town?"

"It sure is. Now let's get out into this gorgeous fall day."

They walked along in silence for about a block. Then they came to the new, three-story brick building of Cox College. "Look at all the girls out on the lawn painting at their easels. You know, the light is so good at this time of day. Isn't it wonderful? I'd really like to do that."

"Lizzie, you don't need to go to college to learn to draw. You have always been gifted at sketching. I remember when you were seven years old, and I gave you a sketch pad. You filled it up in no time with amazing drawings."

"I remember, Daddy. You and I would draw and paint while Mama and Nellie cooked in the kitchen. Nellie loved her cooking lessons with Mama, and I loved my drawing lessons with you. At the evening meal, we would show them our drawings and they would serve us their cakes and pies. It was fun for all of us."

"Yes, those were joyful days. Time passes so quickly."

"It does, and now I'm ready for college. I want to go and then become a real artist."

"You *are* a real artist. You can enjoy sketching and painting your entire life. What a gift you have."

"Daddy, I mean a real artist who paints pictures and portraits and gets paid for it."

"Girls don't do that. Men are professionals. You will be busy having children and raising them."

"I can get married and have children and be a real artist, too. Please let me go."

"College is expensive. I'm sure it cost a lot of money. We can't afford it."

"Daddy, please. Think about it. I could live at home and

just go take classes. I've been working at the dress shop and saving every cent. I would not be a boarding student. Please think about it."

"You have always been stubborn, too. Once you get your mind set on something, you won't let go." Daddy laughed.

Lizzie laughed along with him. When they entered the house, her mother Julia and her sister Nellie had a lovely roast waiting for dinner. Nellie was so domestic. Even though she was younger, all she wanted was to get married and have a baby. The two sisters were different but loved each other dearly. They all sat, ate, and laughed as they reflected on a good day.

"Daddy, when I graduate from school, I want to marry Joshua," Nellie said, handing the platter of roast beef to her father. "You all know him, and I love him. We want to marry right away and start having babies."

"You are awfully young. Don't you want to wait awhile and be sure this is what you want? Joshua doesn't seem that mature to me. Seems to have a bad temper, too." Daddy served beef onto his plate, handed it down, and lifted the bowl of potatoes.

"He's just excitable. I love his personality. We laugh a lot, and he's so handsome."

"My dear, you need more than good looks to make a marriage work. Take your time."

"I don't want to wait. I'm not the only one, either. Two friends in my class are getting married right after graduation. I know Lizzie talks about college all the time. But that is not for me. I want to be a wife and mother. That's all I want."

Over the coming weeks, Nellie would not let it rest. "Daddy, it's all I want in life. To hold my own baby in my arms will be so wonderful. I was meant to be a mother."

At the end of April, during one of their family dinners, Jeremiah Jeter gave in. "My dear, I don't have a good feeling about it. I wish you would wait. But your mother and I have talked about it endlessly. To get some peace in our life, we have decided to go ahead and give you our permission."

"Daddy, thank you. I love you." Nellie jumped up and threw her arms around his neck.

That June there was a lovely, small home wedding. Julia made a gorgeous wedding cake, and the two families got to know each other.

Exactly nine months later, Nellie gave birth. "Daddy, isn't he a precious baby boy? Have you ever seen a cuter newborn in your life? Look at all that hair and his big blue eyes." She cradled her new son close, looking at him with awe.

"I must say he is precious. I know you're happy."

"And guess what. I'm naming him George after Grandfather. Does that make you happy?"

"That's wonderful. He does sort of look like my daddy." Everyone laughed. It was a joyous occasion.

Nellie grew completely absorbed in taking care of little George. But the responsibility of a wife and baby was too much for Joshua. In only a few months, Nellie came home, crying that her husband had been abusive. Her tears did not last long. She stayed with her parents, and soon everything was fine. Nellie was so happy with her baby that she didn't seem to miss her husband at all. Lizzie thought maybe what she really wanted was a baby and not a husband.

Through all the family drama, Lizzie kept thinking about her dream. "Daddy, I'm more convinced than ever that I don't want to get married until I find the right man. If I wait to marry, I will be more mature. In the meantime, I can go to college and study art."

"I can see you're not going to give up the idea of college," Daddy said with a chuckle. "How did we get two such stubborn daughters? You're going to drive us crazy, too. But you do seem to have your heart in the right place. And I love art like you do. I don't want you to make the mistake Nellie made. Take your time. We'll work it out for you to go to Cox College."

"Oh Daddy, thank you. You'll be proud. I'll learn how to paint well, and I'll paint a portrait of you someday. How do you like that?"

He laughed and nodded. "I can't wait to see my portrait."

Lizzie was in heaven. She purchased all her art supplies. The day she resigned from LuVee's Dress Shop, her father gave her money for new clothes. On the first day of classes, she walked proudly down the sidewalk in her favorite new yellow dress. She held her head high. She was now officially an art student at Cox College.

She enjoyed her classes and new professors. Her English and history classes interested her. But she was there for the art classes. She absolutely loved them. Life was perfect. She especially enjoyed her classes with Lucy May Stanton, who taught portrait painting and watercolors. The first time they went out on the lawn to paint, Lizzie felt grateful for a dream come true. Now she was one of the young women at her easel among the magnolia trees.

By the following spring, she was gaining confidence in her ability. Lucy Stanton had taken a particular interest in her work and complimented her every day. "Lizzie, you have a God-given talent. You are doing things that are just impossible to teach. I'm so proud of your progress." She looked over her shoulder at a watercolor Lizzie had begun.

"Thank you, Miss Stanton. I can't tell you what that means to me."

"Call me Lucy. I'm not much older than you are, and we have become friends."

"I will. At least, I will try to call you Lucy. Thank you." Lizzie had never been so overcome with joy. Now she was certain she had made the right decision. She could be a good artist. A real artist. A professional.

That afternoon she folded her easel, took her art supplies back into the building, and stored them in the classroom. She hung her smock on a hook and floated out of the building, feeling like she was on top of the world.

What a gorgeous, warm day. She soaked in the feel of spring, the new growth on all the trees, the flowers beginning to bloom. But just as she strolled onto the sidewalk, she saw Nellie running toward her.

"Lizzie, come home right now." Her sister grabbed her arm. "It's Daddy. Hurry."

"What did you say?" Lizzie began to run.

"I said hurry, it's Daddy. They say it's his heart. Mama sent me to get you."

Lizzie and Nellie sprinted home. When they threw open the door, they saw their father on the sofa and their mother weeping hysterically.

"Lizzie, your father's dead. It happened so quickly. What do we do? Tell me what to do."

"Mama, calm down. Tell me what happened. Nellie, run next door. Dr. Pickett might be home by now."

Her mother was gasping for air and sobbing uncontrollably. "He was outside working in the garden. He came in complaining he didn't feel well and was going to lie down on the sofa. I went to get him some water and when I came back, he wasn't breathing. Just like that. So quickly. What do I do?" Lizzie took her mother in her arms, rubbed her back, and tried to console her.

After her mother slumped down in a chair opposite the sofa, Lizzie stood frozen and looked at her dear, sweet father. He had brought so much joy to her life. Teaching her things, drawing with her, paying attention to what she thought. No one else did that for her. A numb sadness came over her whole being. She didn't want to move, but she knew she had to get a grip on her emotions. Even if she didn't want the job, she was now in charge. What could she do to get them through this trauma?

At that moment, Nellie and Dr. Pickett came running in the door.

"Nellie, take Mama in the kitchen," Lizzie instructed. "Sit her down and get her some water. I'll be there in a minute." She turned to the doctor. "Dr. Pickett, thank you for coming. Please examine Daddy. Tell us if he's really gone."

He opened his bag and pulled out his stethoscope. He began to check for any pulse.

"I'll go check on Mother and be right back."

When she got to the kitchen, she said calmly, "Try to breathe and calm down. We're not sure what has happened." She sat with her mother and sister, trying to think what to do next. They were both weeping as Lizzie sat almost in a trance. Finally, she could wait no longer. "I'll go talk to Dr. Pickett."

In her heart, she knew before the doctor spoke that her father was gone. She was just trying to soothe her mother and sister. She felt wretched, too, but wouldn't let them see. She had to be stay in control.

"My dear, your father is dead. Probably his heart. I will begin to make arrangements to have someone pick him up and take him to the undertaker. Would you like me to reach out to the minister at the Methodist church?"

"Yes, please do. Thank you for coming so quickly. We were fortunate you were home."

"Lizzie, there will be a lot of decisions to make about the burial and the service. I can see that those will fall to you. I don't think your mother or sister will be able. I'll get something to help them both sleep. Do you know where the baby is?"

At that moment, they heard a baby begin to cry. "I had forgotten all about George. I guess he was asleep and is just now waking up. I'll check on him. Yes, give Mama and Nellie something. I'll stay awake and take care of the baby."

From that moment on, Lizzie became the decision maker. As she was the oldest daughter with a strong personality, her mother and sister turned to her. In an instant, her newly carefree life became a burden. All she could feel now was the weight of that load.

Lizzie was devastated, but she had no time to grieve. The next day, she went to withdraw from school. The first person she approached was Lucy Stanton.

"My life has just blown up. My father died, and I've got to withdraw from college. I can't afford to continue. I have so many decisions to make. I've got to take care of my mother and sister. But I love studying with you. Your classes are wonderful." Lizzie broke into sobs. She had promised herself not to cry, especially in front of her sister and mother. Now, with Lucy, she allowed herself to let go of all the emotion she carried.

"I'm so sorry your father died." Lucy put her arms around Lizzie. The two of them stood and held each other for several minutes.

When Lizzie's tears began to let up some, Lucy said, "You are a very talented young artist. In fact, you are one of my best students. I see great promise for you."

"That's so nice to hear. I love painting more than anything in the world. When I'm painting and sketching, I lose track of time. But I must give it up now. I have to support my mother, and my sister and her baby. I feel overwhelmed." Lizzie wiped tears from her eyes. "I've been happier here in your classes than I have ever been. But no more art for me. I will find a job."

"No, you can't give up your art. Never. You must keep painting." Lucy appeared to think for a few moments. "I have an idea. I was about to open an art gallery, but I'm going to New York for further study. Why don't you open the gallery? I'll let you sell some of my paintings. I'll also get other artists to put their work with you. You'll get a percentage of their selling price. Then you can keep painting and sell your own work. What do you think of that?"

Lizzie's face lit up. "That sounds divine. There's nothing I'd rather do. But I'm not well known like you."

"You don't have to be well known, just hardworking and talented. You are certainly that. And I'll help you any way I can."

Lizzie left campus with new hope. Maybe, just maybe, she could keep painting. It was a risk, but she couldn't help feeling excited.

They buried Jeremiah Jeter at the Methodist church cemetery on a beautiful spring day. Azaleas and dogwoods were blooming. Somehow the lovely flowers and sunshine helped. Everyone in town came.

"Reverend Brown, that was a beautiful eulogy," Lizzie said after the service. "We appreciate your words more than we can say."

"My dear, your father was a great man. Everyone in town loved and respected him. He will be missed."

"I don't know what Mama, Nellie, and I will do without him. He was our rock."

"This community will be with you. Let me know if you need help."

At that moment Lucy walked up. "What a lovely service."

"Thank you for coming. You didn't even know Daddy."

"I wanted to see you one more time. I'm leaving for New York next week. If you need help, get in touch. And let me remind you one more time that you are a good artist, maybe even great. Never forget that."

"That means so much. I must admit to you I'm scared. But the fact that you believe in me has made all the difference."

As everyone walked away from the cemetery, Lizzie felt alone. Now the rest of her life would start. What did it hold? She was afraid to imagine it.

After her father's funeral and the other necessary tasks, she sat down to talk with her mother and Nellie. "I have been thinking hard about what we should do. The only thing I know anything about is art. It's the only thing I want to do.

My friend Lucy Stanton has convinced me that I can start an art gallery. We would have to move and rent a space somewhere. You two would have to agree to it and be willing to help. What do you think about that?"

Her mother put her arms around her. "Lizzie, I have no ideas. Thank God you do. Of course, I'll help you any way I can. But I'm depending on you to make the decisions. I can't."

Nellie clutched little George to her chest. "Of course, I have to take care of this fella, but I'll do what I can."

After talking to her mother and sister, Lizzie felt the pressure more than ever. Their well-being was up to her. It was a huge gamble. Since making the decision, she had not had a good night's sleep. She worried day and night, but she could not turn back now.

Chapter 6

Atlanta, Georgia

1899

Suddenly, Lizzie realized she had stopped sketching, and Miss Trudy was talking to her. "Oh, I'm sorry. I was lost in thought. Your story made me think how I had to beg to go to college, too, then had to quit when my father died."

"We all get distracted at times. I'm sorry about your father's death."

"Thank you. He was a wonderful man. He worked for the railroad, but he was an amateur painter and provided me with paper and pencils. I was close to him, too. We would paint and draw together for hours."

"It's wonderful that you also had a father who was interested in what you were doing and would spend time with you. That's always a rare thing, especially for men involved in business. They usually think women are supposed to stay at home while men go out and work," Miss Trudy said with conviction. "But sometimes that is just not possible. I know very well from my own experience. At one point, I had to try to support my family, too."

Lizzie was somewhat agitated and kept talking. "I went to Cox College, once called LaGrange Female Seminary. I begged Daddy to let me go. He said I didn't need it. I was supposed to get married and take care of children."

"You were persistent until your father gave in. Good for you. You must always stick to your convictions. But losing your father suddenly must have been painful. The day my father died was the saddest of my life," Miss Trudy said.

"Yes, it was the saddest day for me, too. His heart just stopped beating. We were all devastated. On top of the sadness, our family was in financial trouble. But I also realized I was going to have to become the breadwinner in my family. My mother was a widow in her sixties, and my sister Nellie had left an abusive husband and moved home with her baby. Then Lucy Stanton, my art professor, gave me the idea to start my own gallery. She said I was a good artist. I would never have had the courage to do this had it not been for her believing in me. There you have it. That's what I've done. I've taken a huge gamble. I'm working very hard." Lizzie paused. "Oh, my goodness, you're supposed to be telling your story, and here I am telling you mine. I apologize for talking so much."

"No, no. I want to hear. What you have done is wonderful, Lizzie. I admire you. How's your studio going?"

"So far, I'm hanging on. My mother and I sold the house and took the small savings she and Daddy had, and I started looking for space to rent with rooms for the studio downstairs and an apartment for us upstairs. I've moved several times but have now settled on Woodward Avenue in Grant Park. It's a growing area with lots of new homes going up, and folks need art for décor. My mother keeps the shop when I'm away with a commission. I just painted a portrait of Mrs. Joseph Thompson. Do you know her? Is that how you found out about me and my work?"

Lizzie picked up her pencil and began to sketch again.

"No, I don't know Mrs. Thompson. Remember my daughter Cora saw your paintings at the state fair. She said you had some excellent watercolors and a portrait of someone that was prominently displayed near the entrance to the women's exhibition. I should think the fair has helped you."

"Yes, it has. I've also started advertising in the *Atlanta Constitution.* I've had some favorable comments made in the paper. I was thrilled when someone said that I was 'one of the foremost painters in the South.' I think that's an exaggeration, but I'll take it just the same."

"Miss Jeter, I would say that is astounding. You are quite a businesswoman. I am very impressed, my dear. Being the head of your household and supporting three other people is a huge task. I admire you. I'm certainly glad my family picked you to do my portrait. You are a perfect example of the women I have been trying to help. You inspire me to work harder."

"Thank you, Miss Trudy. Sometimes I wonder if I can make it. I work from dawn to dusk every day. Thankfully, I have my mother and sister to help me any way they can. But I see a lot of women running shops or trying to keep their farm going. So many men died in the war that their wives and daughters had to take over their roles. The war changed our world. I keep telling myself if these other women can do it, I can, too."

"Yes, the war did change everything. My life has never been the same. I'll continue to tell you about it. But I'll not complain anymore. If you can be this brave and work so hard to support your family, I'll not be a grump. I'll cooperate and help you." Miss Trudy leaned forward and gave Lizzie a hug.

"Thank you, I feel so much better just talking to you. I didn't know you when I walked in this door, and now you know my life history." Lizzie laughed and returned Miss Trudy's hug.

"Yes, now we are friends. And I think we might be very much alike. I'd say you and I have gumption, and that's a good thing. I believe we can help each other. Now—while we talk—let's get back to this portrait."

Chapter 7

Augusta, Georgia

1849

"Amanda, it's not even light outside yet, and it's such a cold, bleak, gray day," Trudy said as Amanda helped her put on her new coat. "January is always depressing. I'm scared, but I can't let anybody know. I begged so hard to go away to college, and now I'm not sure I'm doing the right thing. I've never spent more than one night away from home, and that was to spend the night at Cousin Emily's. Now I'll be gone for months."

"Trudy, you be fine. You always get over your fear. Just remember how afraid you were of those big horses, and now you ride all over the place. It'll be the same with this college. You will love it before you know it."

"I hope you're right. Oh, this new coat your mama made for me feels so warm. And it's blue, my favorite color. It looks like it was made in New York. Every time I snuggle up in it, I will think of you and Lurany and feel better. Please tell her again how much I like it and the other new dresses she made for me. The only problem is that I need more dresses. I would like to have a new one to wear every day."

"But you already got so many dresses. Mama's been working late into the night to get all these ready for you. How can you need more?"

"I just do. Don't tell me how many dresses I need. I know the girls at school will have a lot of dresses. It's none of your business how many I have."

"Sounds just like something you'd say. You never have enough dresses." Amanda shook her head.

At that moment Pa called up the steps.

"I'm coming. Be right there," Trudy said as she gave Amanda a hug. "I'll miss you."

As Trudy went out the door, she turned back. "I'm sorry I can't take you with me. Pa says girls don't take servants with them to college. He says all the girls don't have servants, but it just isn't allowed anyway. But I would have really liked to take you with me. You would be a big help to me."

"You just go and learn all that stuff and come home and maybe teach me. That'll be nice," Amanda said as she waved Trudy along.

ൟ

The ride to the depot only took a few minutes, but Trudy, Anne, and Pa had to hurry. They ran to the train and climbed up the steps into first class. They were the last to board. Trudy sat by the window with Pa to her left. Anne sat by the window facing her. Why in the world was Anne coming along? She didn't want to go to college. She probably just wanted to make everything unpleasant.

As the train pulled out of the station, Trudy stared out the window and watched Augusta disappear. She put her forehead against the glass and hoped no one saw her tears. Pa had already started reading the *Augusta Chronicle*, and Anne was looking at a magazine. Thankfully, Trudy soon became fascinated with the fields and forests that seemed to glide past them, and her tears vanished.

"Anne, did you notice we are the only women in this car?" Trudy asked her sister.

"Yes, women are at home taking care of their children while their husbands travel on business. That's what I'm going to do," Anne said as she went back to glancing at the pictures in *Godey's Lady's Book.*

Trudy didn't respond. She was mesmerized by the passing landscape and refused to let her sister ruin this trip for her. She was determined to enjoy her ride. It was magnificent. She had only ridden on a train once—to Charleston when she was a baby. She had been too young to remember anything, but not this time. This trip fascinated her. She would remember every minute.

The train stopped often at cities on the route, cities she had never seen: Union Point, Greensborough, and Decatur, until they finally arrived in Atlanta. As they pulled into the station, Trudy exclaimed, "Look Pa, it's snowing. Can you believe it? We get to see snow so seldom. It's beautiful."

The snow only added to the excitement as they moved through the station. All her apprehension was gone. She was soon caught up in the hustle and bustle of people darting around them as they made their way to the train that would take them to Macon.

"Pa, isn't this fun, seeing all these folks dashing around heading for heaven knows where. It's so exciting!"

"The railroad lines coming through Atlanta are making the city grow into a real transportation hub," Pa said, his excitement matching hers. "There are so many business opportunities here. It's going to be great to see what this city becomes in the future."

Trudy walked along in the cold air with snowflakes hitting her face. What an adventure this was. She was so happy.

"Here we are at our train. Climb in and get settled. We'll have lunch in Griffin and won't arrive in Macon until time for our evening meal," Pa said as they took their seats.

As much as she loved to read, Trudy had a hard time

concentrating. Now she couldn't wait to arrive in Macon. After lunch, the train's many stops began to annoy her. Would they ever get there?

"Heads up, girls. Check around your seat to make sure you haven't left anything." Pa got up from his seat and gathered his belongings.

"We're here, finally! Isn't it a charming city. At least, the train station is." Trudy laughed as she began to button her coat and put on her hat.

"I see the carriage is here. Come girls, make haste."

They rode through the dark streets with the wind in their faces. Trudy couldn't see everything, but what she did see was strange and new. She felt a mix of fatigue and excitement. Why was she having such mixed feelings?

When they arrived at Mr. Floyd's hotel, a young man unloaded their bags. They entered an old-fashioned building that looked more like a house than a hotel. As Pa gave them their keys, he said, "Go to your room and freshen up. Meet me back down here for dinner in fifteen minutes. I don't know about you, but a good meal sounds wonderful to me."

"Pa, is it okay if I don't come back down? I'm not hungry. I guess it's because I'm so excited. I want to go to bed." Trudy yawned and rubbed her eyes.

"Of course, do as you please. What about you, Anne?"

"I'd love to meet you for dinner. I'm hungry, too. Are you sure you are well, Trudy? Never have known you not to want to eat. You usually eat like a pig," Anne said in a sarcastic tone.

"No, Anne. I'm not sick. We had a big lunch in Griffin, and it wasn't that long ago. I just want to get some rest, thank you." *Why does Anne always have to be snide and hateful?* Trudy wondered. *She's probably jealous. I just want to rest. I will hold my head high tomorrow. I will not be homesick. I'm a college woman now.*

The next morning, Pa and Anne stood with Trudy in her new dorm room.

"You don't have to leave so quickly, do you?" Trudy asked as she held her father's hand and looked up into his eyes.

"I'm afraid I must. I've got business back home." Pa checked around the room one more time.

"Yes, we must go. I wanted to see what this looked like, and now I know. We'll have to leave you now," Anne said casually. "Are you sure you don't want to go with us?"

"I knew you couldn't stay long, but I didn't know you would have to go so soon." Trudy choked back tears. "But thank you for bringing me."

"Looks like you have everything you need in this spacious room. Your trunks have arrived with your clothes and linens. Plenty of wood for your fireplace." Pa gave Trudy a hug. "I'll leave you with this lovely young lady who's to show you around. Have a wonderful time. We love you."

Pa and Anne walked out the door. One minute Trudy felt brave, and the next minute she was afraid. What was wrong with her? She was even surprised that she wished Anne would stay.

Suddenly, she realized the young woman there to help her was talking.

"My name is Ella Pierce. My father is the president here, and he promised your father that I would show you around. We're happy you have joined us." Ella gave Trudy a warm smile as she led her down the hall. "Your two roommates are already here: Jo Freeman and Lou Howard. They were here in the fall and can help you find your way around to the chapel, the dining hall, and the classrooms."

Trudy had always had her own room with Amanda to help her. How would she manage living with two girls she didn't know? How would she make her own bed and take care of the fireplace with all the other things she had to learn?

"Morning bell will ring for wakeup at 6:00. Then you get dressed and go to prayer and chapel. Breakfast is at 8:00," Ella said.

"Do we really get up that early? I've never done that. I don't know if I can. I usually sleep late." Trudy frowned.

"Oh, you'll get used to it. I promise." Ella continued, "Classes start at 9:00. We have instruction and then recitation for a period of two hours. Then we have classes at 11:00, 2:00, and 4:00 with a break for lunch. Prayers at 5:00 and dinner at 7:00. Lights out at 10:30."

"What is recitation?" Trudy asked, feeling bewildered.

"Oh, we get instruction from our professors. Then we are called on to stand and answer questions. You know, 'to recite' what we have learned. It can vary, but it's something like that."

"That sounds demanding."

"It can be. You must pay attention to keep up."

"I don't know if I can do all of this."

"I promise you'll get used to it. At night, you will fall asleep immediately when your head hits the pillow. Then you will get up and do it again from Monday to Friday. You get the weekend off. As I said, you'll get the swing of it."

"Gosh, I hope so."

“Wake up. Get your clothes on. Got to get going.” Trudy’s roommate Jo Freeman was having to prod her again.

“Okay, okay.” Trudy wiped her eyes as she pulled on her clothes. Jo had told her to keep her dress and shoes right by the bed and put them on first. That was good advice. It was cold in the room. She hated splashing cold water on her face, but she had to do it.

“Come on. It’s almost time for chapel,” Jo urged. “You’ll warm up on the brisk walk.”

Thank goodness, Jo was positive. She had been such a help to Trudy. Not only did she show her where to go, but she was always giving uplifting advice. Trudy had liked her immediately, and their friendship grew every day.

“See, if you walk fast or even run, it gets warmer. Also, it makes you tougher. Trudy, you are doing great.”

By the time they got to breakfast from chapel, she was starved, and thankfully the food was good. She and Jo had begun to laugh about everything—the cold weather, the strange habits of some of the professors, and how Trudy was fumbling along, trying to keep up. Her life at Wesleyan was so much better because of Jo.

“I’m glad we have English together,” Trudy said as they hurried to class. “I love Shakespeare. I’ve read the plays before, but I didn’t always understand them. Isn’t it great to hear Dr. Myers explain things and ask us what we think?”

“I agree. *As You Like It* is such an interesting, fun play to study.”

After class they went their separate ways, and Jo waved. “See you this afternoon in the room. We have some free time, and I’ll build a fire to keep us warm.”

"How was your astronomy class?" Jo asked as soon as they were back in their room.

"I enjoyed it, but I didn't realize there would be so much math. I just want to know about the planets and stars. Guess I'll have to work hard to keep up."

"Yes, but you can do it. You are very smart, and you already work hard."

"Thanks, I'm so grateful I've got you to help me. I'm beginning to think I can make it."

"I'll build the fire this afternoon and we can warm up. The three of us will take turns making the fire. It's my turn today. You can do it next time."

"I've never made a fire. I don't know how."

"You've never built a fire? Even in your own room? How can that be?"

"Amanda always did it for me. She is my companion. She's always with me. She even lives in my room."

"What do you mean she lives in your room? Is she a slave?"

"Yes, but I don't like to call her that."

"I've been wanting to ask you about slavery but haven't until I knew you better. I'm from Philadelphia. Our family moved to Atlanta when my father took a job in the construction business. He's an engineer. We don't have slaves, never have. In fact, my father is opposed to slavery."

Trudy was quiet for a few moments. "Slavery has always been a part of my life. I grew up with a lot of slaves around me. But truthfully, I have begun to have some questions about it. I haven't been able to talk to anyone except my father about my feelings. When I asked him questions, he told me that's just the way it is. I don't know what to think. But I'll be glad to talk to you. I like to know both sides of all issues."

"That's admirable. Folks we've tried to talk to in Atlanta have not been open. There seems to be denial about the evils of slavery."

"My father and most slave owners say it is condoned by the Bible. They can point to verses that tell slaves how to act and how masters should treat their slaves."

"But that was an ancient time. My father says you can find something in the Bible to condone just about anything."

"Well, we can talk about it all you want. I have lots of questions. You tell me what you think. We're friends now, and that's what friends do. But right now, teach me how to make a fire."

Trudy was proud of herself. In no time at all, she was building blazing fires with glorious orange flames. Trudy, Jo, and Lou would pull their chairs in front of the fire to study. It was cozy and warm. They would read and munch on cookies they had brought from the dining room. She was soon over her homesickness and happier than she had ever been.

One Friday afternoon, Ella Pierce popped into their room. "Stop reading, girls. You three are much too serious. We need more players on the lawn. Come on, we'll teach you the rules of baseball."

As the girls hurried outside, Trudy laughed and said to Ella, "Happy to get up and move. I'm so glad you came to get us. What do we do?"

Ella explained positions, and the girls took sides in the game. Trudy loved the way the girls really competed. They hit the ball, ran bases, and cheered their team. Trudy went running through the shrubs, trying to catch a ball. She fell back into a bush, catching the ball on the tip of her glove. Everyone cheered. Laughing, running, and feeling the air in her lungs: everything felt good to her.

"Trudy, you're a good athlete," Ella cheered. "I'm glad we got you out of your room. We go for ice cream downtown when the game is over. You'll love it, too."

As she walked along with her new friends, Trudy felt things she had never experienced in her life. She could take care of herself. She wasn't helpless. She smiled, knowing that Amanda had been right. It wasn't that hard to dress herself. And she had made wonderful friends—especially Jo, Lou, and Ella. Now she knew she had a good mind and could explore new ideas. Wesleyan had been the absolute right decision. She was not homesick at all. She felt her chest swell with pride and self-confidence.

She was so busy that time flew by. Before she knew it, her first semester at Wesleyan was over. How did it pass so quickly?

"Pa, I'm glad to see you." Trudy threw her arms around his neck. "I've missed you. Thank you for coming to get me."

"I would never let you ride the train alone. Of course, I came to get you. Had business in the area anyway. Now get your things and let's get to the train station. I want to hear all about what you have learned."

As soon as they were settled on the train, Trudy began to talk. "I have loved everything about college. Almost everything. I'll admit I wasn't crazy about math but really got into astronomy after a little adjustment. English was my absolute favorite. Since I love to read that makes sense. And my friends Lou, Ella, and Jo are my favorites. But I made a lot more. Have you ever played baseball? You'd love it." She never slowed down until she fell asleep. Pa only nodded and smiled the whole trip. Unable to get a word in edgewise, he was exhausted nonetheless and fell asleep, too.

On her first night home, all the family gathered around the table for dinner, and Trudy could wait no longer. "You would not believe how we must work to keep up. I was standing up reciting in English class, talking about one of Shakespeare's plays when Dr. Myers said I was well prepared. He wanted to know what I thought."

"Wait," Mama said. "You stand up and give your opinion? I thought you were there to be taught by the teachers. You are not to draw attention to yourself. Do you also ask questions?"

"Yes, Mama. That is what we do. We stand up all the time and give our opinions and ask questions."

"That does not sound good to me. I don't want you to be a 'strong-minded' woman."

"Mama, what does that mean—'strong-minded'?"

"That's what they call women who are too smart and have their own ideas about things. It isn't ladylike."

"That's not a bad thing. It's a good thing. I would sure rather be a 'strong-minded' woman than a 'weak-minded' woman," Trudy said angrily.

The room got very quiet as Mama glared at Trudy.

"Now, Mary, I'm sure what Trudy is doing is productive," Pa said. "It won't hurt her to have opinions and state them. I'm sure Trudy will do it in a ladylike way. Won't you, Trudy?"

"Yes, sir." Her mother didn't understand and probably never would, but she thought Pa did. She would not talk about it anymore. Why had she brought up what she had learned with her mother? She couldn't wait to go back to Macon.

Trudy grew close to Dr. Myers, his wife, and their children, who lived downstairs. She would see them in the dining hall and out on the lawn in the evenings. She especially enjoyed the children. They were all excited about the new baby Mrs. Myers was expecting.

"Do you think it will be a boy or a girl?" Trudy asked little Susan.

"I want a baby sister."

Then her brother immediately answered, "No, I want a brother." This went on each night, with everyone laughing as they chased fireflies. They were having fun, never thinking anything could go wrong.

One evening the girls were sitting on the lawn talking when Dr. Myers came out of the house and called them over to him. "Ladies, you have been waiting anxiously for our baby to arrive. I'm sorry I have sad news for you. We lost our baby today. She was a beautiful little girl. Looked perfect." Dr. Myers paused, fighting back tears. "At first, she appeared to be healthy, but she had trouble breathing. We don't know exactly what was wrong. But she only lived for a short time. The Lord giveth, and the Lord taketh away. Tonight, our blessed baby is with God. If you would like, you ladies may come view the body."

As Dr. Myers walked back across the lawn, a couple of the girls mumbled, "So sad. So sad." But no one knew what to do or say. They were all stunned and sat staring into the distance. Suddenly, the night sky seemed gray and dismal. How could this have happened? Mrs. Myers was so healthy. Trudy and her friends sat in silence, unable to speak. Finally, Ella said, "Do you want to go view the baby?"

When Trudy entered the parlor, she expressed her condolences to the family. There on a small table in the middle of the room sat a tiny coffin lined with soft pink fabric. Tears welled up in her eyes, and she felt weak. She wanted to go over and look, but she was fearful. She inched slowly across the room. The baby girl was dressed in a lace gown and had two white roses—one on each side of her head. She looked as if she were only asleep, so angelic. Trudy would never forget that sight. One moment that darling baby was alive, and suddenly, she was gone.

Life changed for her that night. Things were not as simple and understandable. There were hardships she had not known but now began to fear. She did not know what it meant at the time. Babies dying before they had a chance to live was wrong, unfair. This was one thing she had not thought she would experience at Wesleyan. Trudy did not realize it, but the death of this infant was a precursor to what she and the other young women would experience over and over in their lives.

At seventeen years old, Trudy graduated on July 11, 1851. Her composition was titled "Learn from the Lord: Drink from the Well of His Wisdom." It was a lofty title, but she was a wiser person now. She did not know what life had in store for her, but she had a sense of satisfaction and pride in her education. She had also begun the practice of examining her life, something that would never leave her.

She was packing her trunks, getting ready to go home when Jule Thomas, one of her new friends, came into her room. "Trudy, I live in Burke County near Augusta. I want you to come visit and meet my brother, Jeff. He'll be home from Princeton. He loves horses the same way you do. For some reason, I think you two will be just right for each other."

Trudy blushed. She had not given much thought to boys. But she said, "Sure, I'd love to visit." She had no idea how much her life was about to change.

Chapter 8

Atlanta, Georgia

1899

"Miss Trudy, you've been transported to an earlier time. I can tell how much you loved going to college; I can see it in your eyes. They light up when you talk about those years." Lizzie stood studying Miss Trudy's expression.

"Oh, you're right. I did love those years. Except for the death of the Myers baby, they were the happiest, most carefree days of my life. My experiences there changed me. I was never the same again. I know we were too young. It would have been better if we had been older. Nonetheless, after those years, I looked at life differently. I had always asked a lot of questions and was sometimes put down for it. But after my experiences with my professors, I knew it was good to ask questions. I learned to think for myself, examine everything, and not take anything for granted. Lizzie, I hope you will approach life that way."

"I'll try. But I never feel like I'm in control. I'm always being swept along by circumstances. I know I tend to worry too much. I'm always wondering what bad thing will happen next," Lizzie confessed.

"I did that, too. But it doesn't do any good. Bad things happen to us all in life. It's how we respond to them that matters. I know that now, but I didn't know it when I was young. I wasn't prepared for all the bad things that were about to happen to me."

"None of us are ever prepared for the bad things that happen to us," Lizzie responded. "I never dreamed my father would die and I would need to support my family. I'm only twenty-six years old. I don't have a moment of free time. I don't know if I'll ever get married. I don't have time to meet men. I'll be too old very soon."

"No, you won't. Don't say negative things about yourself. You are quite amazing. Look at what you've done. You're a very attractive young woman. You have plenty of time. You never know what or who might be around the corner," Miss Trudy said with conviction. "I will not let you be negative about yourself."

"I hope you're right. Nobody else talks to me the way you do. I appreciate what you're saying. It makes me feel better."

"You should feel good about yourself. I'm quite amazed by you," Miss Trudy said as she began to get up.

"I didn't realize the time. I got so interested in what you were saying. I'm sorry," Lizzie said.

"Don't apologize. You have done nothing wrong. On the contrary, you have inspired me. Now it's getting late. We need to call it a day and start over tomorrow. How did you get here?"

"I took the streetcar. I love riding around in the new streetcars. Aren't they wonderful? Have you ridden one?"

"Yes, you know me. Even at my age, I like to try new things. They are an improvement in transportation. But I don't ride them often."

"I zip all over on them. They're a wonderful way to see the city and meet people."

"Well, see there. That is one good thing you have experienced that is helping you. Another thing: always be grateful for what you have. Always see the glass half full instead of half empty."

"Okay, you're right, and I'll try. Now I must get going. Fortunately, my mother will have dinner waiting when I get home. That's certainly a help and something I appreciate." Lizzie laughed. "I never learned to cook, and I'm exhausted when I get home."

"See, I told you that you have a lot to be grateful for," Miss Trudy said as she gave Lizzie a hug.

"You have made me feel so much better. I believe I've made a new friend today. May I leave my canvas bag here with my supplies? It gets a little heavy."

"Yes, of course, leave your bag here. And we have indeed become friends today. That is what women do. We talk and help each other. We will continue tomorrow."

"Will 10:00 be okay, or do you prefer later?"

"Let's start later, say after lunch at 1:00. I have an important meeting in the morning. Then I will tell you what happened next in my life. It will take all the energy and courage I have. I don't talk about my trials and tribulations often, but I will tell you. Hopefully, in the end, my story will help you."

Lizzie opened the studio at 9:00 the next morning. Since she didn't have to leave until midday, she was enjoying looking around the shop. It was bright and colorful with good art on display. One of Lucy Stanton's watercolors stood in the window along with a portrait Lizzie had painted of her father, signed "E.S. Jeter." She was arranging books and small miniature portraits on a back table, her back to the front door, when the bell rang to signal someone had entered. Lizzie looked up and saw a handsome man dressed in a dapper business suit. She felt a little flustered and was about to ask if she could help him, but he spoke first.

"Hello! This is a beautiful shop. I was admiring the art in the window. I wondered, could you put me in touch with the artist, Mr. E.S. Jeter? I would like to speak to him," he asked in a proper Northern accent.

"Oh, I'm E. S. Jeter. The initials stand for Elizabeth Sherwood. I'm the portrait painter." Lizzie put out her hand to shake. "I'd be happy to talk to you."

"I apologize. I assumed the artist was a man. But I'm pleased you're the artist," he said with a smile.

"I'm glad you feel that way. Some folks think artists should only be men. It might be deceptive to sign my work that way, but I want the viewer to study the painting first without thinking about gender. I advertise by that name in the newspaper, too. Not everyone approves, but I get more inquiries that way. Some work out and some don't."

"I must say I'm surprised but not bothered one bit. I was raised by a woman who did the same thing when she wrote for the newspaper. She would approve of what you're doing."

"That's good to hear. I'm afraid I don't meet a lot of men like you in this area. May I ask where you are from?"

"Certainly, my name is Jonathan Everett Hopkins. I was born in upstate New York in a little town called Auburn. I'm sure you've never heard of it. It's about an hour from Rochester. I'm moving to Atlanta to work with the railroad, and I'm looking for a place to build a house. Grant Park was recommended to me, so I'm here looking around."

"Oh, my father worked for the Atlanta and West Point Railroad all his life and loved it. He was excited about everything that was happening in Atlanta. He saw a great future for the city."

"He was correct. I believe Atlanta will be a major transportation hub for our country. I'm happy to have a part in building it. And I like the weather, too. By this time of year in Auburn, we usually have quite a bit of snow. That's something I'm happy to leave."

"Atlanta does have a good climate—four seasons. You'll like it. Now what kind of art are you interested in?"

"I was thinking about getting someone to paint a portrait of my mother. She has lived such an interesting life, and she's getting up in years. Having a portrait of her would mean so much to our family."

"That's a wonderful thing to do. I'm sure it will make her happy. Is she moving here with you?"

"Yes, she's already here. She was drawn by your good climate, too. We are renting a house until I find a place to build."

"That's good. Should you select me, I like to spend time with my clients making preliminary sketches and studying their features before I start to paint. I usually go to the client's home several times and then bring the work back here to finish it. Here are my prices," Lizzie said as she handed him her price list. "These were published in *The Constitution* in May of this year. I charge $100.00, $300.00, or $500.00 depending on the size of your portrait: head shot, half or two-third shot, or full size. I charge $50.00 for a picture in little, as we call miniature portraits."

"Those prices sound fair to me. I know a lot of work goes into your paintings. I'm impressed with what I've seen in the window. Do you have anything else I can see?"

"As a matter of fact, I'm working on a portrait of a woman now. I should have something to show you in a couple weeks."

"Wonderful. Give me a date, and I'll be back to see that painting."

"I'm meeting her this afternoon. We talk a lot, which slows us down, but I can have something in two weeks. It may not be completely finished. I like to keep looking at it for a while before I let it go. But yes, two weeks will be fine."

"Sounds perfect. It's been wonderful meeting such an attractive, talented artist, E. S. Jeter. I look forward to returning in two weeks." He tipped his hat and walked out the door.

Lizzie stood stone still and watched him walk down the street. He was so nice and handsome: wavy, dark brown hair and tall, too, about six feet or maybe a little more. He walked with such confidence. She hoped he had not noticed how nervous she was. What was wrong with her? He was just a polite customer, for heaven's sake. She was acting like a silly schoolgirl.

Later in the day, Lizzie jumped off the streetcar and walked down the street with a new spring in her step. It was one of those gorgeous fall days she loved in Atlanta, sunny but a little cooler with a slight breeze blowing. Orange, yellow, and brown leaves were gently falling from the trees and piling up against the walls along the sidewalk. She couldn't help herself. She started kicking at them as she did when she was a child. For some reason, she felt playful today. She hadn't felt like this in a long time. She was smiling when she arrived at Miss Trudy's door.

"Good afternoon," Miss Trudy said, welcoming her in. "Young lady, you look happy today. Full of energy. Bright-eyed and bushy-tailed, as we like to say. Come in."

"I do feel good. It might have something to do with the fact that a nice man came in the shop this morning. He was different from most of the men I meet. He was looking for E. S. Jeter. That's how I sign my paintings and newspaper ads. He did not look askance when he realized I was the sole proprietor of the studio as well as the artist. Some men think I'm being deceptive. Do you know what I mean?"

"Child, I am sixty-five years old, and I've gotten those looks all my life from men and women when I do something they think only men should do. But don't be afraid to go on and do them anyway. What did I tell you yesterday when you said you didn't have time to meet young men? Here you are today telling me about some fella you've met. I'd say that is a nice coincidence," Miss Trudy said with a smile.

"It's nothing, really. He's just a nice man looking for an artist to do a portrait of his mother."

"Oh, it is not nothing. You felt something when you saw him and talked to him that you don't always feel. Pay attention to those times. I remember when I first saw my husband—so handsome and nice. Something happens; your heart starts beating faster, you feel giddy."

"Maybe something will come of our friendship. Who knows? I just met him. But he's coming back to see your portrait. When I told him I was doing a painting of a woman, he wanted to see it."

"Well, that's a positive sign. You better get busy and make me look good. Got to have a lovely portrait to show him. But keep in mind, he might want to see you, too."

"I must admit I hope he wants to see me." Lizzie began to set up her easel.

"I have no doubt. Now let's go back to the time right

after I left college. I was only seventeen. But it is a happy memory. Pa gave me a debut party and invited three hundred guests. I think everyone in Augusta came. It was huge. Pa spared no expense. The entire night is stamped in my memory. That was the night Pa met Jeff for the first time. I can still see and feel everything. Another happy memory before the bad ones started."

Chapter 9

Augusta, Georgia

1851–1853

"Amanda, this is the most beautiful dress I've ever seen. The lace with the pearls, these tiny fabric buttons, the delicate tucks. The material is so soft. What is it?" Trudy gently stroked the smooth fabric.

"That's pure silk. Your Pa ordered the most expensive white fabric from New York for Mama to make your debut dress."

"Well, Lurany created a gorgeous dress. I can't believe it. It makes me feel so special." Trudy looked at herself in the mirror.

"You sure are mighty pretty in it. That young man comin' tonight is goin' to be swept off his feet when he sees you. Who's he anyway? Tell me about him."

"He's my friend Jule's brother, Jeff. I met him when I visited her after graduation. No one in the family has met him yet. He's been going to Princeton and plans to be a doctor. He's handsome with dark hair and brown eyes. He's great fun, too. On our visit we had lovely dinners, played cards, and took long rides on horseback. You should see him on a horse—he sits so straight."

"I'd say you smitten. He's a mighty lucky young man."

"I don't know what it means, but I've never felt this way before. I hope this night goes well."

"Oh, it will."

"Before I go downstairs, check my hair. I love the way you put it up in the back with those pins with pearls on the end. So elegant."

"Looks perfect. I'd say you be the most beautiful girl in all that crowd of folks tonight. Your Pa is goin' to be proud, too. He's showing off his daughter, the college graduate, to all his friends."

"I know Pa's proud, but not everyone approves. His friends won't let on to Pa because they do business with him. I know for sure Ma's telling people how I haven't changed a bit—still her sweet, quiet daughter." Trudy grinned as she left the room.

Before she went down the stairs, she stood and looked upon the sea of people. Their family had moved into the twenty-four-room mansion only three years earlier. For the first time, all the large rooms downstairs were full of people, the doors and windows open to let in a gentle breeze. Women in flowing gowns glided along, chatting with their escorts in formal attire. The sweet fragrance of flowers filled the air in every room. A woman played a harp in the parlor. Everyone was talking, laughing, and smiling. When they realized she was at the top of the stairs, they paused and looked up. As she looked down into their smiling faces, she thought of how truly happy she was tonight. Then she saw Jeff, waiting for her. As she slowly took each step, she felt giddy and held the handrail to steady herself.

"You look beautiful tonight," he said when she came close. "I'm honored to be here."

"Thank you. I'm glad you're here," was all she could manage to say. Her heart was beating so fast, she thought her face must be red.

As Jeff began to walk her into the crowd, she nodded and greeted people, trying to get control of herself. Gradually, she began to calm down. Her mother and her sister Anne stood nearby. "Mama and Anne, I'd like for you to meet my friend Jeff Thomas, who is here tonight to be my escort."

"Jeff, we are pleased to meet you. Trudy told us about her lovely visit in your home in Burke County." Her mother smiled and took Jeff's hand in hers.

"Jeff, this is my sister Anne. She is three years older than I am."

"Mr. Thomas, I am pleased to meet you," Anne said with a sly smile. "I hear you like to ride horses the same way Trudy does. I'm afraid she's rather addicted to riding, so watch out."

Trudy could tell they both approved. Anne had to get in a jab the way she always did, but nothing could bother Trudy tonight. She looked around the room. "Come with me. I'd like to introduce you to my father." For some reason, she felt nervous about this introduction.

When Pa spotted Trudy, he came over and put his arm around her shoulder. "My dear, you look beautiful this evening. I'm so proud of you. This party is just for you, and I want you to have a wonderful time. I also want you to meet all my business associates." He wore a huge smile on his face. When he saw Jeff, his smile went away immediately. He gave Jeff a blank stare.

"Pa, it is such a wonderful party. Thank you so much." She hugged her father. "I want you to meet my friend, Jeff Thomas. I told you about him. He's my friend Jule's brother."

"Yes, you told me about him. Nice to meet you, Mr. Thomas. I hope you're enjoying our party for Trudy."

"Yes sir, how could you not enjoy this evening? Everybody in town is here—I'd say everyone in Georgia seems to be here. Yes, I'm enjoying myself, and I'm happy to be with your lovely daughter." Jeff smiled at Trudy.

Trudy caught her father looking at Jeff with a strange

expression. Why would Pa have reservations about Jeff? She had noticed some hesitation when she had asked her father to invite him. At the time, she thought it was probably her imagination. But maybe her nerves were warranted. Obviously wanting to show her off, her father began to introduce her to his friends and left Jeff standing alone.

After she had met practically everyone in the room, Trudy was happy to work her way back to Jeff. "I'm sorry. Pa wanted me to meet everyone—politicians, businessmen, clergy, distant relatives. Everyone here! I'm glad I've made those rounds." Now, as she strolled around the room on Jeff's arm, she knew she would enjoy the rest of the evening with him. She glowed as she spoke to one guest after another. She was happy to have this handsome man as her escort. Finally, she could relax.

"Are you hungry? Let's get something to eat. I know the food is going to be divine." Trudy took Jeff's hand and led him into the dining room.

A glorious flower arrangement of blue hydrangeas and pink roses stood in the center of the huge table. Tall silver candelabra with numerous candles sent a soft glow over the room. Piled high on silver trays was every delectable party food imaginable—fruits, nuts, cheeses, various meats in little biscuits, and delicious sweet treats. They took small china plates and selected samples of everything. Then they walked out into the garden to sit on a bench and visit with friends. They were tired and happy to sit down. Enjoying each other's company, they laughed and talked into the early morning hours.

Occasionally, Jeff would sneak off to the side with one of his buddies and take a sip from a silver flask he kept in his breast pocket. Trudy thought it was funny and didn't mind.

Pa was a teetotaler and didn't touch alcohol. She knew he wouldn't approve, but Trudy knew Jeff was just having fun with his friends. After all, she was "smitten," as Amanda had said. She found nothing wrong with Jeff. As she would write in her journal later that night, somehow he had stolen her heart.

After the debut party, Jeff began visiting regularly to see Trudy. They would sit in the parlor and talk and sometimes take long walks. They would go to church and to programs at the Masonic Lodge. Their favorite activity was horseback riding, something they both loved.

On a beautiful summer day, Trudy and Jeff rode out to the Tubman Plantation on the Savannah River, one of Turner Clanton's six plantations. That day, more than forty slaves tended its five hundred eighty acres of cotton plants.

"I'm glad we came out here. It's so beautiful," Trudy said. "I love to ride this way with Pa."

"It sure is beautiful. All these healthy slaves working row after row of cotton. This is going to be a great crop."

"I agree with you. I heard Pa say just the same thing the other day."

"Let's stop here and walk our horses for a while. I want to talk to you about something important."

"Okay, what do you want to talk about?" Trudy slid down off her horse.

Jeff walked slowly for several minutes and then began. "I want to talk about plans for my future—I mean, our future. You know I've been saying I want to be a doctor. I've changed my mind."

"Why? I think you'd be a wonderful doctor."

"I've said that I wanted to be a doctor for a long time without thinking about having to go to medical school. I've never been crazy about college, and the thought of going back is awful."

"I would love to keep going, but I'm different from you that way. You have a hard time even sitting still, much less learning while you sit." She laughed. "You can't concentrate very long and have a short attention span."

"You're right. I can't argue with you. But I don't want to do what doctors do, cutting on people and delivering babies. I get a little lightheaded even thinking about it."

"Well, in that case you'd better not be a doctor. What do you want to do?"

"I want to be a planter. If truth be told, I want to be a Southern gentleman like your Pa and not work too hard." Jeff smiled. "Is that terrible?"

"No, Pa is wonderful, and I admire him, too. He's what I'd call a Southern gentleman, but he does work hard to manage the plantations and all his workers."

"But he has overseers to run things and hundreds of slaves. What I want is lots of slaves to do the hard work."

"Gosh, it's taken Pa years to accumulate the land and slaves he has."

"But when we marry, you're going to inherit land and slaves, aren't you? I'll get some from my Pa, but not as many as you'll get."

"Are you marrying me for what we'll get from Pa—or should I say what you'll get?" Trudy said as she hit him lightly on the shoulder.

"Of course not. You know I love you. But now I'm just talking business. He is one of the wealthiest men in Georgia, after all. I just wanted to ask how many slaves you think you'll get when we marry."

"Oh, I don't know for sure. Maybe twenty or so."

"Well, that's a good number. They will multiply and we will buy more. Before too long we'll have hundreds, too."

"Well, maybe. It takes work and time. But you're right about one thing. If you have acres and acres of cotton like Pa does, you must have lots of slaves to pick it."

"Exactly. And they're suited for hard labor in the hot sun, not us white folks. Let them toil in the fields, and I'll ride by and check on them occasionally."

"Jeff, you oversimplify everything. The slaves are human beings and work very hard. I get concerned about the heat and folks thinking it doesn't affect them. Sure it does. You have to be understanding of that."

"Okay, I'll be understanding. Don't get huffy. But that's my plan. I'm glad you go along with me and aren't disappointed about me not being a doctor."

"I do think you would have been a good doctor. And I don't think being a planter—and a Southern gentleman, as you say—is as easy as you think it is. My Pa is a great businessman and a hard worker. There are ups and downs, with bad weather years, and the price of cotton fluctuates. As you go into it, don't forget those things."

"Okay, I won't. But I don't think it will be hard at all."

"I hope you're right."

"I'm going to talk to your Pa this week and ask for your hand in marriage. Would you like that?"

"Oh, Jeff, that's wonderful." Trudy threw her arms around Jeff's neck. "You know I love you. But be prepared for Pa to ask you a lot of questions. He can be difficult."

"I'm ready for whatever he asks me. What would he not

like about someone who idolizes him and wants to be just like him?"

Trudy looked at Jeff. He had no idea how tough Turner Clanton could be. She just hoped Jeff could win him over. She knew Jeff wasn't nearly the businessman her father was, nor did he have her father's innate intelligence. Even though Jeff was naïve, she couldn't help herself. She loved him—flaws and all.

"Amanda, I'm so nervous. Jeff has come over today to talk to Pa."

"Why you nervous? Mr. Thomas is always coming over to visit. You crazy about him and your Pa knows it."

"Yes, I am, but Pa has reservations about Jeff. I believe Jeff is going to ask for my hand in marriage, and I don't know if Pa will agree."

"My goodness, I didn't know he was goin' to do that. You not the oldest daughter. Anne ain't married yet. Oldest daughter usually marries first. I imagine that's something to do with it."

"I know, but she doesn't even have a beau at this point. And Jeff is so nice, from a good family in Burke County. What could be wrong with him?"

"Well, for one thing, I think you're your Pa's favorite. He's so proud of how smart you are and everything. And you only eighteen years old. I know lots of women get married at that age, but I think he feels you shouldn't. That's just what I think, I don't know."

"I know those things. But I think there's something else. I've begged him, but he won't say what it is. He may not even know. We'll just have to wait and see what Pa says. I've never been so anxious in my life. I love Pa and want him to be happy, but I love Jeff, too."

Trudy was so anxious that she got down on her knees at the side of her bed and started praying that Pa would give his approval. She was lost in her prayers when Amanda gave a gentle knock on the door. "Trudy, Jeff just left, and your Pa says for you to come to his office. He wants to talk to you."

Trudy stood slowly, walked into the hall, and went over to the stairs. As she began her slow descent, over and over she said to herself, *Please let Pa say it's okay to marry Jeff. Please, God.* She tapped on his door. "Pa, it's me. Did you want to see me?"

"Yes, dear. Please sit down and let's have a conversation about this proposal of marriage."

Pa was sitting in his big chair, and she sat opposite him in a smaller chair. For once in her life, she saw how tall and imposing her father could be. She thought Jeff must have been terrified when he saw him earlier. All she could do was mutter, "Yes, sir."

"Trudy, my dear, I know you want to marry this young man, and I imagine you can sense that I have some reservations. I think you know what a close relationship you and I have always had, and I want the very best for you in life. I have thought about this a lot. I have heard some accounts of him having a great affection for alcohol, and you know how I feel about that. There was some kind of brawl in the southern part of the county with lots of young men being rowdy. Do you know anything about it?"

"No, I haven't heard anything about that. But he does take sips from a flask sometimes—the same way so many of the young men do these days. I think he just likes to be one of the guys. He loves to laugh and tell funny stories. He is great fun."

"Trudy, that may be true now, but it could lead to more serious drinking later. I can't help but be concerned. But it isn't just that. I don't know if he is ready to take care of a family. I watch people and have a sense of their maturity. You are so intelligent. Do you think he will listen to you and understand your progressive ideas?"

"Oh, Pa, I'm sure he will. Just like all men, he doesn't want me to talk about business or anything that is supposed to be men's domain. But we have great fun together and enjoy talking about everything else. I don't believe I scare him with my ideas." Trudy tried to laugh but couldn't manage humor in the remark.

"Well, because of all my concern, I plan to set up a trust fund for you. I will do one for each of my children. The statute that says a separate estate can be established for a woman only appeared in 1847. It's still new, but I've been working on yours. I plan to give you twenty-three slaves with an appraised value of $23,290.00. There will be additional money also at my death. But that fund will be yours and not liable for any debts your husband may accrue. I want to make sure you and your siblings get a good start in life. I won't always be around to fix things for you."

"Pa, don't mention anything about you not being here. Please. That's a dreadful thought."

"It's reality. None of us get to stay on earth forever. Of course, I hope it will be later rather than sooner," Pa said with a smile.

"I hope it will be much later. I don't know what we would do without you. Please don't bring it up again."

"I didn't mean to upset you. I just want you to think

rationally."

"Okay, I'll try. But it's nice if you plan to help us get a good start. The gift of twenty-three slaves is very generous. Jeff says he will be an understanding master and treat them well. He says he wants to own lots of land and slaves and be as successful as you are. He really admires you, Pa. That should make you happy. I'm sure you'll be a great help to him."

"Yes, he told me all about how he wants to do what I have done. But I can tell he has no idea about what is involved in running these big plantations. It's not just having slaves. You must think about management and equipment. I'm willing to help him any way that I can. I told him I could provide some wagons, horses, oxen, mules, bushels of corn, and fodder for feeding the animals. He looked at me as if he hadn't thought about needing those things. I can tell he doesn't know what he's doing. I guess he will have to learn by trial and error."

"Oh, Pa, he's a dreamer. But he's young and energetic. He will want so desperately to make it work. I'm sure he will do fine."

"Trudy, I hope you're right. But you can never predict the future. I do know that you are very much in love with this young man. I trust your judgment enough to believe you have picked well. But I must be honest with you and tell you about my concerns up front. With all that I have said, and against my better judgment, I will still give you permission to marry. I wish you great happiness." Pa rose to take her in his arms. "Yes, I hope you and Jeff will live happily ever after. Isn't that what they say in the fairy tales?"

"Yes, Pa, that's what they say. Thank you, thank you. I love you so much. We will not disappoint you. I promise we will live happily ever after," Trudy said with tears in her eyes.

December 16, 1852, was a brisk, cool day in Augusta. Clear and sunny, the weather was perfect for a Christmas wedding. The Methodist church was covered in poinsettias and magnolia leaves, with fresh greenery giving the church the smell of the holiday. The sanctuary was packed with family. Jeff and Trudy were pleased that friends from Wesleyan and Princeton had traveled to celebrate with them. Jo, Lou, and Ella, Trudy's best buddies from college, were bridesmaids along with her sisters. Dr. Myers came to officiate, and his whole family accompanied him. The ceremony was lovely. Trudy could not have been happier.

"I must ask. Whose idea was it for us to ride from the church to our home for the reception in an open buggy with bells attached?" Trudy said, laughing.

Jeff grinned. "That was my only contribution. But isn't it fun? All the bells jingling gives you the Christmas spirit. Notice the greenery tied with red ribbons. I think it is a marvelous creation. I even helped decorate it. Had to have lots of bells."

"Leave it to you to make things fun. Yes, I love it, and it does put me in the spirit of the season."

They snuggled under a blanket as they rode down Greene Street, looking up at the canopy formed by huge oak trees. "Even without leaves, these great old trees look magical today." They rode along then without saying a word. It was so peaceful. Trudy closed her eyes and breathed in the fresh air.

As they arrived at the grand mansion, Trudy said, "I'm

so glad you planned that ride. It was wonderful. I hate for it to end."

Candles burned in all the windows and gave the house a welcoming glow. Small branches of evergreen pine were tied together and draped over the front door. Once they entered the foyer, they noticed a huge bunch of mistletoe tied directly over the doorway. They stopped, and Jeff gave Trudy a kiss as everyone broke into applause.

Trudy immediately saw her mother and threw her arms around her neck. "Mama, it's all so beautiful. I know you loved getting ready for this reception. Everything is perfect. Thank you, thank you."

"Yes, I have enjoyed this. Of course, I had a lot of help. But come into the dining room and look at the table. I must tell you that Amanda, Lurany, and Tamah really got into the spirit and worked hard on the food and decorations."

"Oh, they are magnificent. Look at that huge cone covered with bright red apples in the middle of the table. The magnolia leaves and holly branches add to the Christmas feel. And all the food. What a feast—a turkey and a roast, squash casserole, sweet potato souffle, and fruit. And the sweet treats: cookies, tarts, and candies. A Christmas feast to remember."

"Yes, as I said, they really worked hard and did a magnificent job. They are still working in the kitchen now to keep everything replenished."

"Too bad they can't be here with us to enjoy it. But I will thank them when I see them. And thank you again, Mama. I know you oversaw everything."

"You are my first daughter to marry. This is what women live for—to get married and start having babies. Of course I'm happy. I wanted everything to be perfect."

Trudy hugged her mother again and started walking through the crowd, greeting the guests. Everyone seemed to be having a great time except for Pa, who was a little subdued. Her sister Anne had a scowl on her face, probably thinking she should have been the first to marry. Except for those two, the crowd was joyful.

Trudy did not let them dampen her spirits. Her wedding had been so long in coming. She knew Jeff wasn't perfect, but she would help him overcome whatever difficulties arose. She held his hand and led him through the crowd, proudly introducing her handsome new husband. This was the first day of the rest of her life or, as she had told Pa, the first day of her happily ever after. Nothing was going to ruin it—not Pa and certainly not Anne.

"Isn't this wonderful, taking a trip to New York with Mama and Pa before our first baby is born? I'm so excited. They are so generous."

"I imagine they are excited about their first grandbaby. I'll make sure this won't be the last one." Jeff winked as he leaned over and whispered in her ear.

"Oh Jeff, keep your voice down. Pa is so close," Trudy said, giggling. She was flattered by her playful, new husband, but she thought it best to change the subject.

"I love riding on trains. This reminds me of my trips to Wesleyan. I was always anxious to get to the college," Trudy said in a loud voice as she squeezed Jeff's hand.

"Can't say I loved taking the train to Princeton," Jeff added. "I always dreaded getting back in the grind of classes. But the real reason I didn't want to go to medical school was it would take me away from you."

Trudy was smiling at Jeff, enjoying their banter, when Pa handed her his newspaper. "Picked this up in the Washington train station. I've finished it. Big controversies and disagreements everywhere. Would you like to read it?"

"Yes, please," Trudy said as she eagerly took the paper. "I've always loved reading the newspapers you brought home with you from your trips. You get a new perspective on other parts of the country."

"Jeff, you sit over here with me and let's talk about running plantations," Pa said as Jeff quickly jumped up.

Trudy was happy Pa had invited them to travel with him on this business trip to New York. Pa was getting to know Jeff better, and they seemed to be hitting it off. Pa couldn't help but be pleased with the way Jeff hung on every word he said.

Trudy began skimming the many articles. A few short ones on women's fashion caught her eye. There was a report on the slow progress of the Washington Monument, designed by Robert Mills, which was to be a 600-foot-high obelisk but was only in its first phase. Then she saw an article by the abolitionist William Lloyd Garrison. She had heard a little about him and his newspaper, *The Liberator*, but she had never read one of his articles. She held the paper so that no one could see what she was reading. Most Southerners ridiculed abolitionists like Garrison, viewing them as the enemy. But she always prided herself on the fact that she liked to hear both sides of any argument.

She read quickly. Garrison's strong words leaped off the page. The Declaration of Independence said all men were created equal; therefore, Garrison proclaimed himself an abolitionist. He said freedom is of God and slavery is of the devil. Every slave is a stolen man, and every slaveholder is a man stealer. Any church that consents to enslavement is horribly atheistic. Jesus included slaves among those for whom he laid down his life. Trudy realized his words were logical, and she was moved.

She closed the paper, also feeling confused. The Bible condoned slavery. She knew many of the verses by heart.

> Ephesians 6:5: *Slaves, obey your earthly master with respect and fear, and with sincerity of heart, just as you would obey Christ.*
>
> 1 Peter 2:18: *Slaves, submit yourselves to your masters with all respect, not only to those who are good and considerate, but also to those who are harsh.*
>
> Colossians 3:22: *Slaves, obey your earthly master in everything: and do it, not only when their eye is on you to win their favor, but with sincerity of heart and reverence for the Lord.*

Trudy's father was fond of quoting Jefferson Davis's speech in the United States Senate on February 14, 1850, when he said that slavery was established by decree of Almighty God. It was sanctioned in the Bible in both Testaments, from Genesis to Revelation, and it had existed in all ages and been found among people of the highest civilizations.

Feeling even more bewildered, Trudy leaned her head back and closed her eyes. Who was right? What was the truth? No one around her would want to talk about any of this. She wished her friend Jo were here to discuss the

Garrison article with her. She decided to put it all out of her head for now and soon fell fast asleep.

The foursome spent several wonderful days in New York. The weather was warm but not hot. Trudy loved spending time with her mother walking the streets while Pa and Jeff went to business meetings. They visited an elegant women's shop and ordered new coats to be made. Trudy chose a cape that would fit her pregnant body. They laughed and made plans for the baby as they ate in charming restaurants. Trudy thought she had never enjoyed being with her mother as much as she did on this trip.

The two of them could browse for hours at a time. Trudy's favorites were the wonderful bookstores. It was heaven to be among so many books. While her mother flipped through the latest issue of *Godey's Lady's Book*, Trudy saw the new title by Harriet Beecher Stowe, *Uncle Tom's Cabin.* A woman from a prominent, religious family, Stowe had published a number of articles and books. Trudy had never lost her desire to be a published writer. She knew Stowe's new book was an anti-slavery novel. But what harm could come from reading it? She was comfortable with the idea, but she knew her family would not approve. She quickly purchased the book and slipped it into her bag where no one would see it. She would keep quiet about it. It would be her secret.

After the trip was over and they rode the train back South, they agreed that it had been a vacation to remember. Despite all that was going on in the world, their life was good. Trudy and Jeff were about to have their first child, a joyful sign of future hope.

Chapter 10

Atlanta, Georgia

1899

"You were really in love with Jeff. He must have had something special," Lizzie said as she studied her canvas.

"Yes, Jeff captured my heart, and I could see no faults. Pa was much more cautious."

"And what a gorgeous wedding reception. I can't imagine such a wedding being given for me. Then that wonderful trip to New York. Were you able to travel a lot because of your family's wealth? This may sound strange, but did you realize your family was wealthy?"

"No, that's a good question. I knew I always got everything I wanted. I took it all for granted. I was spoiled and naïve. I thought only of myself. It wasn't until Pa died in 1864 that I learned about what he was worth. An inventory was made of his property that revealed twelve thousand acres of land, six plantations, almost four hundred slaves, city lots, and on and on. But to me he was just my dear father who loved me and seemed to care about me more than anyone. I was lucky that way. I'm ashamed today that I was so self-centered and ignorant about how the rest of the world lived."

Miss Trudy began to get up out of the chair. "Lizzie, let's take a break. I'm a little tired from sitting so straight. Let's move over to the settee and rest."

"Of course. I need a break, too. I was getting lost in what you were saying," Lizzie said as Miss Trudy's daughter Cora walked into the room with a pitcher of iced tea.

"That's good timing, Cora. I believe you saw Lizzie

when she was here yesterday."

"Yes, and I'm glad you're here painting Mama's portrait." Cora set the pitcher on the table and added a little tray of sugar cookies. "You two seem to be talking up a storm. Mama does have interesting stories to tell. I'll let you continue to visit. I must run some errands. Good to see you, Lizzie."

"Good to see you, too, and thanks for the iced tea."

"By the way, Cora, did your father come back from Piedmont Park yet? I know he said he was going to spend last night, but I didn't know if he would be back today."

"No, Mama, he's not back. You know him, he may spend another night. He loves camping out with his men, talking about various battles and what went wrong," Cora responded.

"Yes, I know. But since I hadn't seen him, I thought I would ask. Thanks, and I will see you this evening."

The front door shut. Miss Trudy drank a few sips of tea, took a deep breath, and sat quietly for a few minutes. "I know you were frightened by my husband Jeff yesterday when you arrived. I want to explain. Since he returned from the war over thirty years ago, he has never been the same. Before the war he was playful, fun-loving, and not overly serious about anything. He came home completely different. Something happened to him emotionally. I know the fighting was horrific, and he saw men slaughtered all around him. He won't talk about it. Since then, I know he has had bad dreams. Once he said to me that he was so distraught that he was fit for an insane asylum.

"After the war, he could not accept the defeat, the loss of everything he had ever known. Confidentially, I will tell you that he only fought nine months before he bought a substitute and came home. He paid a man from Maryland three hundred dollars to stand in and fight for him. He never mentions it, but that is what he did. I think he was ashamed. I know I was.

"But at any rate, he seems to be reliving the war to this day. I have tried to get help for him, but he refuses. And there really aren't any doctors who seem to understand. Combined with his drinking, I must admit that my father was correct with his concern. But I do not believe in divorce. We have disagreements, but then we go our separate ways. He lives in the past, and I live in the present. I never give up hope that he will snap out of it. That is a simple explanation. Maybe it will help you understand. But he will not harm you. Don't worry about that. I just thought you needed to know since you are visiting in our home."

"Miss Trudy, I'm sure this has been very hard for you and your family. I've heard of other families with similar stories. War is hell. Of all people who could have said that, I've heard it was William Tecumseh Sherman, a man so reviled in Georgia. But I believe it is true. Thank you for sharing that with me. I understand and will not be frightened of him. I might be startled at times, but not scared."

"Thanks for your understanding. I thought you were owed an explanation. Now where were we? Oh, yes, I was going to tell you about my marriage."

She paused for a moment and then began, "I was very young—only eighteen. As a woman, it was my destiny to get married and have children. I accepted that role and looked forward to it. I was happy and believed I was marrying for life. I loved Jeff. At first, everything went well in our marriage. Even the birth of my first child was not too difficult. In December of 1853, I gave birth to a darling little boy I named Turner Clanton Thomas—of course, after Pa."

"How wonderful. I know your father was proud, too."

"Yes, Pa was absolutely fascinated with little Turner. That made me happy. But I knew right away that I was not prepared for running a household. Remember I had no interest in cooking or sewing and had resisted my mother's attempts to teach me these skills. And it was around this time that we began to have financial troubles. We were living on a plantation Jeff had inherited from his father. I wanted help with the cooking and asked for a servant to do it. Jeff said we could not afford one. I also asked for help with the sewing, and again Jeff said we could not afford it. Remember Jeff did not have any experience with running a plantation himself. Combined with hard economic times, we began to really struggle."

She took another sip of tea, sat quietly for a few seconds, and picked up the journal in front of her, opening it to the middle. "This is where I recorded one of the most difficult periods of my life. Financial uncertainty was not my biggest problem. It was my destiny as a woman to give birth often, but I knew the hazards involved. I had seen Mother have children who died, and I had seen friends my age die. Naturally, I had mixed emotions when I discovered I was expecting again when Turner was only eighteen months old. I was apprehensive, as well I should have been. What I'm going to tell you is very difficult for me to discuss. Even though these memories are vivid in my mind, I almost never talk about them. But I will share them with you, hoping they will help you."

Lizzie reached over and took Miss Trudy's hand, dreading what she might say.

Chapter 11

Augusta

1855–1858

"Jule, I'm so glad you're here for a visit. This porch is my saving grace on many days. Just look at the weather. I feel like I've been freed from captivity. Can you believe that I'm pregnant with our second child?"

"That's wonderful." Jule searched Trudy's face. "Right?"

"Of course, I just never imagined that at twenty-one I would be a mother of one and have another on the way."

"Look at Turner," Jule exclaimed. He was a beautiful, chubby, blue-eyed baby. Slow to walk, he still preferred crawling, which—to their amazement—he did vigorously. "He's never still, crawling all over the place and pulling up all the time. He's as active as my brother Jeff has always been. I remember well when we were kids, Jeff never slowed down. How do you keep up with this active baby?"

"It's not easy. That's why I like to have him on the porch. If we put our two rocking chairs here, we block him from getting past us. The railings of the porch give him a big play pen. Rather ingenious don't you think." Trudy laughed.

"Yes, that is a neat idea. And I see he loves horses just like his father."

"Ben, one of our slaves, carved those two wooden horses for him and he plays with them all the time. I'm so thankful they keep his attention. I love playing with him, but I just don't have the energy I used to have."

"Trudy, you are seven months pregnant. You've got a baby inside your belly. That certainly explains your lack of energy. You should take good care of yourself."

"Oh, I do. I have servants to help me. I don't know what I would do if I didn't. I wish I had more help with cooking. You know I have no knowledge of that. But thankfully, I have childcare."

The two of them sat rocking back and forth and looking out over the garden at the newly blooming daffodils and forsythias.

"Your flowers are so beautiful. The yellow jumps out and cheers our souls. Don't you agree?"

Trudy didn't answer. Finally, she said, "Jule, I must admit to you that I'm apprehensive. Even though the birth of Turner went well, I know things can go wrong. Did you hear about the girl we met at Madison Springs last summer, Mrs. William Turpin? Mama got the news that she had died in childbirth. Did you know her?"

"No, but I did hear of someone else named Maggie O'Brien who died. It does happen, but I'm sure you will be fine," Jule responded.

"I hope so. I can't help but think about it and dread the delivery. I've heard some women refer to pregnancy as sickness."

"I think most women are like you. They all have these feelings."

"I am so fortunate that Dr. Eve will come, and Mama is always present to share her expertise. Even though we have our babies at home, we have a good doctor."

At that moment, Trudy felt a sharp pain spread across her stomach and lower back. She kept rocking, hopeful it would go away. A few minutes later, another pain shot over her stomach into her lower back with more intensity.

"Jule, something is happening. I don't feel well." Another

sharp pain struck. "This was a labor pain. Would you get Jeff? He's inside working on some ledgers. Call him. Take Turner with you. I can't watch him."

Jule ran inside to get Jeff and quickly returned to corral Turner.

As Jeff hurried out the door, Trudy cried, "It's way too early. But I'm in labor. Send someone to find Dr. Eve and get him here immediately. Send someone else for Mama."

Jeff went to get help, and Jule lifted Trudy with one hand and took Turner by the other. "Come on, Turner. Let's go inside with Mama. She doesn't feel well and needs to go to bed."

He was fussing and trying to get his toy horses, not wanting to go in. "Jule, just stay here with him. I can manage to get to the bed in the downstairs bedroom."

Trudy slowly made her way to the bed, sat down on the side, and leaned back on the pillow. *Please God, don't let this be happening. Please not now.* She began to sweat profusely, the pains radiating through her body. *Dear God, let Dr. Eve get here quickly. I don't want to die.* Tears began to run down her face. She was feeling much worse than she had felt when Turner was born. What was happening?

At that moment, Jule ran into the room. "I got a servant to take Turner. Trudy, what can I do? I don't know what to do. I'm so sorry. I'm no help. I've never seen a birth or been through it myself." She began rubbing her hands together. "Oh, I'll run get a cool rag to rub your forehead. Maybe that will help."

At that moment Jeff came in shouting. "We'll get help! They're not here yet, but they will be soon. What can I do for you? I know nothing about birthing a baby. Is it coming now?"

All Trudy could do was roll back and forth, clutching her abdomen. She couldn't say anything. She didn't know what to do either. Jule came in with a damp rag and started wiping Trudy's forehead. The minutes dragged on and the pain grew worse. Finally, a servant rushed in and said Dr. Eve was in the other part of the county today and could not come. Jule and Jeff froze. What were they going to do? They were panic-stricken.

At that moment, a tall black woman walked in carrying a large satchel. Calmly she said, "I'm Susan, a midwife that belongs to Miss Mary. She not home today, but I heard what was going on. The driver you sent, Uncle Sykes, brought me back with him. I've delivered lots of babies. I'll take care of this birth."

"Thank goodness you're here," said Jule. "What can we do?"

"I need hot water and clean rags. Miss Jule, you go get 'em. Mr. Thomas, I suggest you go out and find your son. Maybe take him for a walk. We'll be busy here for a couple of hours."

A calm entered the room along with the midwife. Susan helped Trudy remove her clothes and get into a large white cotton gown she pulled from her bag. "Now you breathe in big breaths of air, Miss Trudy." She began to rub Trudy's stomach. "This baby is in the right position with head down. That's good. Now, Susan will take care of you. We'll get this baby out just fine."

Trudy followed Susan's calm instructions. She still had pain—extreme pain—but not the terror from before. Susan had instilled some kind of confidence in her, and Trudy did what she told her to do. She breathed and pushed for about two hours. Then, to everyone's relief, the baby began to come.

A tiny head appeared in the birth canal, and Susan pulled out a baby boy who began to cry immediately. Susan put him in Trudy's arms. All she could do was sob. She was exhausted but so happy. She and the baby had both survived.

Trudy looked at her lovely baby and noticed he was having trouble breathing. Trudy began to pray, "Please God, let this precious baby live. He is so small but so beautiful; please let him live." She held him close and looked at the midwife.

"Susan, I'm so thankful you came today. We were all terrified. No one knew what to do. You saved my life. Thank you, thank you," she said with tears in her eyes.

"Miss Trudy, I's just doing what comes natural to me. It's all God's way. He gave this gift of birthing to me. It brings me so much joy when I help a new baby into the world."

"You do have a gift. You blessed us all today. I'm forever grateful. Before you leave, I'm trying to get him to nurse, but he doesn't seem to want to. What should I do?"

"Just keep trying. I'll send Dr. Eve as soon as he gets back. And keep a close eye on him. He so little," Susan said as she left. "We got to pray for him. You rest now."

Trudy did not rest. She couldn't take her eyes off the baby. She and Jeff had already decided that if they had a boy, they would name him Joseph after Jeff's father. But her body was full of anxiety. She must keep praying. *Dear God, please let little Joseph live.*

In the days that followed, Trudy, Jule, or one of the servants watched the baby constantly.

Everyone in the family came to see him—Mama, Pa, and her brothers and sisters. Even her cousin Emily drove from her plantation out in the county. They were all celebrating and admiring the baby.

"We are so happy for you. I don't think I've ever seen a

more beautiful baby. He is tiny, though, and seems to have trouble breathing," her mother said with concern.

"I know. Dr. Eve came but had no suggestions. I get so frustrated. Why can't Dr. Eve do something helpful? It drives me crazy with worry."

To everyone's horror, the beautiful tiny boy lived only three weeks. They had his funeral for family only, with a brief ceremony in the chapel at the Methodist church and a short blessing at Magnolia Cemetery. Joseph's casket was so small.

It was a sad, gray day without a glimmer of sunlight. Trudy would always remember the gloom. She tried to keep her faith in God, but she was so angry.

She didn't know what to do to make herself feel better. For some reason, putting her thoughts on paper had always helped. Wanting to memorialize the baby in some way, she went home and began to write in her journal.

> *The Lord giveth and the Lord taketh away. Blessed be the name of the Lord.*
>
> *But Oh, it is hard. Nature rebels and turns shudderingly away from the thought*
>
> *That tonight my poor little darling will sleep its first sleep in its grave.*

After writing in her journal, she went to bed crying and sank into a deep depression. She stayed in bed for several days, refusing to get up. Jeff, Jule, her mother, and her father all tried to console her. Finally, she found the strength to get up. After all, she wanted to take care of Turner, and a mantra kept going through her mind: *Be fruitful and multiply. It is your duty as a woman.* She must get strong enough to have another baby.

Maybe it was too soon, but miraculously, in seven months she was again expecting a child. God had not cursed her. Trudy was happy to know she had no trouble getting pregnant. She set about preparing the nursery again. But her joy was cut short by a miscarriage at two months. Horrified, she went back to bed, and this time she made no effort to get up.

Trudy was in bed a week with her curtains pulled shut. She couldn't stand the light. Everything and everyone annoyed her. On a sunny Sunday afternoon, the curtains were suddenly pushed open. There stood Amanda with her hands on her hips.

"Trudy, it's Amanda. Your Mama can't come. She's expecting her baby any day now herself. I been helping my Mama do sewing for you and Miss Mary. She told me to come on back to you. I'm so glad 'cause I been wanting to be with you again. How you feelin'?"

"I'm not feeling well—a bad nervous condition. I'm afraid I'll never have another healthy baby. I don't know what's wrong. I think God is punishing me."

"Now don't say that. You young. This happens to a lot of womens. It's just nature's way. When something's wrong with the baby, it's better if they don't come. I just know God ain't punishing you. You sure ain't perfect. You got a way of saying things you shouldn't, but God don't punish you for that. You tell me to hush up if I say you have enough dresses and when I tell you to take care of your clothes better. Stuff like that. No big deal. If he punished all the womens who said mean things, wouldn't be no babies," Amanda said with a smile. "Look how many babies your Mama's had. Is this ten? She's had four die. It's just God's way."

"I hope you're right. I don't know what to think or believe. I know I pray, and God doesn't answer my prayers. I prayed for him to save my little Joseph, and he didn't. Then when I was expecting again, he took that baby, too. Like I say, I don't know what to believe anymore."

"Well, I don't know much for sure, but I know God ain't punishing you. Now come on up. Take my arm. We goin' to walk around the garden and out into that field."

It was an overcast day, but Trudy liked the fresh air, even though her legs felt weak from lack of use. "Amanda, it's so good to be out walking with you. I'm sorry Mama kept you sewing so long and away from me. But if she asks me to let you help your mother, I can't say no to that. How is Lurany doing?"

"You know Mama. Fit as a fiddle. Never complains. She happy when she's sewing. I have to admit that I don't love it like she does, but I like it fine. Mama is determined that I become as good as she is, but I think that's impossible."

They walked arm in arm and talked. "Lurany is an expert seamstress. Remember those clothes she made for me when I went off to Wesleyan? And the lovely debut dress that I ended up using for my wedding dress, too. I was so happy then."

"You be happy again. I'll have to ask Mama to make you a new pretty dress. Will that make you happy?"

"Oh, you know me. I've always loved pretty clothes. I'll have to get Mama to give her a nice fabric."

"Glad we thought of a new dress. That is the way to your heart. Now are you feeling a little stronger?"

"I am. No one on earth can get me to do things the way you can." Trudy laughed as they finished their walk. "Do you think we walked a mile?"

"Definitely. Maybe more. You gettin' your sass back, too."

Before long, Amanda had Trudy smiling and remembering good things from the past. She teased her the way she always had, and Trudy liked it. In the following days and weeks, Amanda and Trudy walked and visited regularly. Gradually, Trudy's nervous condition began to fade.

❧

"Amanda, just look at our precious new baby girl," Trudy said as she threw her arms around Amanda's neck. "I must say you were correct. After I had that miscarriage and was so down, I thought God would not let me have another healthy baby. But look at her. She's perfect."

"Well, it took a little while. But not too long. And God done blessed you with this sweet baby. What did you name her?"

"We named her Anna Lou. It's a happy name. Fits her, doesn't it?" Trudy said as she lifted the baby from her crib. Here, hold her. She will steal your heart."

"Yes, I'd say. She is a pretty thing. I like her name, too."

"Hold your finger out to her. Look how she wraps her little fist around it. She's smart and strong. Now we have a healthy boy and girl. We are truly blessed."

"Yes, and you goin' to have a little christening in the Methodist church. Mama and I have a gift for you." Amanda held out a small wrapped package.

When Trudy opened it, she was overjoyed. "Look at this gorgeous little christening gown. It's so beautiful. All this delicate trim."

"Yes, it's lovely. Mama did all that lace. See that collar. That's called tatting. She makes it with tiny knots somehow. I can't do it, but I love it, too. It's real sturdy. Should last for several chillun."

"She will wear it for her christening. And I want you and Lurany to be there. You two should see her in this gorgeous dress."

Anna Lou was born in September, and Trudy and Jeff planned her christening for November around Thanksgiving, when all the family would be home and could attend the service. Trudy couldn't wait for everyone to see their precious daughter.

The day of the ceremony in the small church chapel, the baby was so calm in her christening dress. Everyone said she looked like an angel in the delicate, soft white lace. The family sat on the front rows, while Amanda and Lurany sat in the back, proud to see little Anna Lou in the dress Lurany had made. After the service, they all went home for lunch.

It was a beautiful, sunny fall day. Leaves fell on Greene Street as they pulled up to the mansion house. Mama had worked with her servants to plan the traditional feast of turkey, dressing, sweet potato casserole, green beans, and two kinds of pies—pecan and pumpkin. Everyone ate too much and laughed and talked. Of course, they all admired little Anna Lou. Trudy could not have been happier.

One day during the first week of December, Trudy sat in the parlor with Anna Lou in a cradle at her side. She noticed that the baby seemed to have a little cough. Her mind began to race. *This can't be happening.* She picked up Anna Lou and offered her breast. Trudy's milk did not seem to be coming the way it should. Maybe Anna Lou wasn't getting enough to eat. Was that the problem? But then Trudy saw that she was having trouble breathing just like little Joseph had.

"Amanda, send for Dr. Eve immediately. Something is bad wrong."

It seemed like it took forever for him to get there that afternoon. By the time he arrived, Trudy was panicked.

"Dr. Eve, what is wrong? Please tell me what's happening."

He examined the baby for several minutes. Finally, he spoke. "I'm not sure what's wrong. I suggest we use some hot plasters. The baby may be uncomfortable and get some blisters, but that should help her."

"What do you mean? Won't that hurt her?"

"My dear, we can only do so much."

Trudy was horrified and left the room. She could not watch. It seemed that he was making Anna Lou worse. When the doctor left, he said they should watch to see if her fever went down. Trudy began to cry. What was wrong with her beloved baby girl? The problem was that no one ever knew what was wrong when babies got sick. They could do nothing.

Her concern was justified. On December 21, Anna Lou died. Trudy was devastated. She began to weep uncontrollably. As was her habit, one week later she wrote in her journal.

> *Our precious little Anna Lou is dead. Today one week ago she breathed her last. My child, Oh my child how I miss your sweet smile, your little twining fingers as they clasped mine, even your feeble moan of pain expressive of so much suffering. Would to God, he had blessed you with life and health and you were still here to cheer our heart.*

Trudy found herself in the depths of depression yet again. She didn't know what to do or think. How could this be happening to her? She didn't know if she could bear it anymore. She wept until she had no tears left. Thankfully, the servants took care of the house and little Turner. Trudy just sat and looked out the window at the garden. She was fortunate that Amanda kept coming to see her and could persuade her to go outside and walk. Somehow, getting out in the fresh air and walking helped her begin to come back to life. Jeff, too, tried to console her any way he could. He came back and slept with her, and then the inevitable happened. She was pregnant again.

"The baby should come in November," she told Amanda on one of their walks. "Of course, it all depends on whether the pregnancy lasts that long. I am not feeling well and have no energy at all. In my short life, I have become strikingly familiar with this 'sickness.'"

Amanda squeezed her arm. "You only twenty-four. What is this—the fifth time you with child? Maybe this will be the lucky one. You know I keep telling you not to give up hope. Lots of womens go through these hard times."

"Well, I'm not optimistic, and I'm not enthusiastic. I can't go through another baby dying. I can't spend my life this way."

"It's too late for you to be talking like that. You are into it now, whether you like it or not. You might as well try to cheer up and make the best of it."

"You're right, of course. But I would sure like to have wider intervals between these pregnancies so my body can recover. I think that's what takes all my energy. My body is not ready."

"I agree with you there. Can't you control Mr. Thomas?"

"Amanda, you know men. They are insistent, and it's my duty. And I do love Jeff. I want to give him children. As you said, it does no good talking about it now. I must pull myself together and get ready for what comes."

"Trudy, I'm here to see this beautiful baby girl. Let me have a peek," Amanda said as she came into the bedroom. "Now what did I tell you? I knew you could have a healthy baby. Can't be any prettier or healthier than this one."

"Yes, she is pretty and healthy. Dr. Eve and Susan were both here with me. I insisted we have Susan in case Dr. Eve was called away with some emergency."

"Well, I know you happy and proud. You did it."

"I don't know. I'm going to be honest with you, Amanda. I'm afraid to celebrate or be happy. I'm apprehensive. I've been guarded with everyone and don't say much. I think Jeff is worried about me, but you understand, don't you? I've just lost the last three. I'm holding my breath."

"Yes, I understand. But try to be happy. I have a good feeling about this baby."

"We can't just hope or feel good. We must wait and see. I prayed so many times and my prayers were unanswered. This time I wrote my prayer in my journal,

> *I hope I am grateful to a kind providence for many mercies—Again has he blessed me with a little babe and to make that blessing doubly dear—she is a girl.... Father in Heaven, I pray thee that thou wilt preserve her in life and health, and enable us fully to appreciate the immortal soul thou hast given in our charge.*

The fact she is a girl does make me happy. But I must be honest, I'm afraid of what can happen."

Everyone in the family was overly attentive. Trudy was not in a good mood and snapped at people when they asked her questions. Why was having babies so dangerous, why did women have to have so many babies, why were women dying, and was she or this baby going to die?

One hot summer day, she was sitting by the window reading when she looked up and saw two slaves, Judy and Maria, talking to each other excitedly as they came through the yard. She had visited with them about their pregnancies just the previous week. They did not have long to go before delivery. She immediately felt sympathy for them.

Soon there was a knock on the bedroom door. One of her servants said, "Miss Trudy, Maria and Judy want to see you."

"Fine. Show them in." The young women came in, their bellies full and round. "Hello, you both look like you are about to deliver any day," Trudy said. "And how do you feel?"

"Ma'am, you know how it is when you get big like this. We mighty tired. Dragging."

"Yes, I certainly understand how you feel. Take a seat and get off your feet." Trudy motioned to two chairs nearby.

"Oh, thank you, ma'am. Good to get off our feets."

"What did you want to say?"

"Ma'am, as you see, we's 'bout to give birth. You know what it's like. Massa Thomas says we got to go to the fields tomorrow to work. It's so hot. Kills our backs to lean over. We don't know what will happen to us 'cause we so big and tired. We afraid. Can you get him not to send us out?"

"My goodness, you are in no condition to go out into the

fields at this stage of your pregnancies. Of course, I will speak to Mr. Thomas right away. You go now and try to get off your feet as much as possible. I do know how you feel. Bless you."

Trudy was waiting when her husband returned from his ride around the plantation. "Jeff, please come in the bedroom. I have something to discuss with you."

"Of course. I hope you're having a good day," he said. "I would lean over and give you a kiss, but I'm hot and covered in dust. It is hot out there today. Almost unbearable."

"Yes, I know. That's what I want to discuss with you. Two of our slaves, Maria and Judy, came and talked to me this morning. I'm very concerned."

"Why in the world would they come talk to you? They're supposed to be working."

"Jeff, you know many of the slaves talk to me regularly. They come to me about their ailments. I've talked to Maria and Judy about their expected babies. Now they're about to deliver. They said you wanted them to go into the fields to work. You can't ask them to do that in their condition."

"Trudy, they'll be fine. The blacks are different from us. They're used to this heat."

"How can you say that? They are women about to have babies. They can't be doing back-breaking work in the fields at this stage."

"Stay out of this, Trudy. I know what they can and can't do. I am the manager of this plantation and not you."

"You may be the manager, but you are a man. You know nothing about the demands on a woman's body when she is about to give birth. Remember these women are human beings, not some brute animals!" Trudy screamed as she slammed down the book she was reading. "They are humans just like us, with the same feelings."

Jeff stared at her, turned, and walked away. He stopped at the door and said, "These are not your decisions to make. They will go to the fields tomorrow. End of discussion."

She would not let Jeff have the last word. "Knowing you, I would think you wouldn't want them to lose their babies. That would be money out of your pocket."

Trudy sat and glared out the window as Jeff walked across the yard. She had never seen him like this before. What did he know about women being pregnant? She knew the horrors, not him. The nerve of him to talk to her like that. She had never been as furious with him as she was now.

After sitting quietly for several minutes, she tried to collect herself. And as she did so often, she picked up her journal to record her true thoughts.

> *All women in their condition should be favored.... I know that had I the sole management of a plantation, pregnant women should be highly favored. A woman myself, I can sympathize with my sex, whether white or black.*

The shared suffering in childbirth had brought her closer to her slave women. Susan had already saved her life once. From this day forward, she would always feel more compassion for them. No matter how those around her felt, her views about slavery were forever altered.

Thankfully, Trudy's new baby, named Mary Belle, did survive and brought the family great joy. But the price was high. Pregnancies and dying children had changed Trudy from the carefree girl she had been when she first married. She and Jeff began to have more differences of opinion, especially concerning slavery. What did the future have in store for them? Life was turning out to be very different from her earlier expectations.

Chapter 12

Atlanta

1899

After Miss Trudy finished telling Lizzie her heart-rending story, the two of them sat quietly for several minutes. Tears rolled down the older woman's face, and she was unable to speak. Finally, she said, "The pain is always with you. It never goes away."

"Miss Trudy, that's the saddest story I've ever heard. I can't imagine going through all of that suffering when you were younger than I am."

"I don't know that a woman is ever prepared for the death of a child, no matter her age. And I must say, on top of my youth, having the deaths happen one after another almost drove me mad."

"I'm sure each death was its own nightmare, but having them stacked on top of each other was horrific."

"All deaths of loved ones are hard. But Lizzie, I want you to think about something. Because you're older and have not had these traumas in your life, you have been able to devote your time and energy to your education and painting. I know you didn't plan for your father to die, but our parents are supposed to go before we do. Our children are not."

"I've never thought about that. But I understand what you're saying. My father's death was difficult, but I think it was also the added responsibility it created for me. I certainly had no sense of security in my life. I guess I should be grateful that I haven't married too young and had your heartache. My problem is the opposite—fearing that I'll never marry.

I'm too old."

"Not true. You are the perfect age," Miss Trudy said with a smile.

"I hope you're right." Lizzie smiled back. "But I must ask you a question. You were constantly pregnant or getting over the loss of a child. Couldn't you refuse Jeff's desire?"

"The simple answer is no. I often got mad at him like I did about Judy and Maria. My attitude toward slavery was changing, but his was not. We had both been raised in a slave culture where everyone around us believed the slaves were inferior beings. Mutual suffering in childbearing had changed the way I thought about the slave women. How could I not feel different? Jeff never had that change. We argued often about it. But we always made up and went about our life. Of course, I was so indoctrinated that it was my duty to have children that he could get in bed to comfort me, and before long, it was happening."

"I apologize for such a personal question. But I was thinking that there was no concern about your health."

"No, I don't believe there was any thought for my health. I got resentful and angry, but so much went unsaid in those days. We couldn't even use the word 'pregnant.' We talked around things, referring to pregnancy as 'sickness' or simply 'that way.' I know now I should have spoken up more, but I was too young. And I was doing my duty 'to be fruitful and multiply' as the Bible told women to do."

"Miss Trudy, let me ask you about something else. It seems women were expected to have babies from the time they got married until they were past childbearing age. That was their primary job and duty. As females, they were to think of nothing else other than giving birth and raising children. You and your mother were pregnant at the same time."

"Yes, that is the way it was. Women were not to think about anything like being an artist or running a gallery for profit. We were not supposed to have professions."

"I guess I would have had a hard time back then. I can't imagine the stress it put on you and all women to be 'fruitful.'"

"Yes, for me it started out joyfully with my first child and went down from there."

"Well, I must say honestly, I don't see how you survived without dying or losing your mind. Such highs and lows. You went from one extreme to the other." Lizzie put her hand on Miss Trudy's shoulder.

"I did almost lose my mind. Since that time, I have had other children die, and I have had others live and be healthy, but those early years in my life were brutal. For the first time, I knew pain and heartache. I would never look at life the same way again. I was far more realistic and, at times, depressed. I have worked to be happy again. I have survived, but it has not been easy."

"I think your story is quite miraculous," Lizzie said. "You have helped me to think in a new way and believe more in myself. Maybe I haven't had it so bad."

"If I've been able to help you, that makes me happy. I hope in the future medical science will improve women's lives, especially where childbirth is concerned. And I want young women today to know what we suffered and be grateful that things have changed." As she wiped a tear from her eye, Miss Trudy added, "We must always keep working to protect women and their sacred duty and privilege of giving birth."

Suddenly, Miss Trudy rose. "Lizzie, let's get busy and stop talking about childbirth and children dying. We must get to work on the portrait again. You've got to have it ready on time for that young man to see. We can talk more while you work. I haven't even begun to tell you about the war. I can still vividly remember all that happened during those tumultuous years."

Chapter 13

Augusta

1861–1862

"What an exciting day!" Trudy looked out on the parade field on a hot August morning. The entire town had come to see the men who were about to leave for the war. "Amanda, look at Jeff. Isn't he the most handsome man? Sometimes he drives me crazy, but we must put hard feelings aside on such an important day. These men are marching off to war."

"You always been smitten by his looks, Trudy. He does look nice on that horse, but so does lots of the other men."

"But his uniform looks so much better on him than on the others. Of course, most of the credit goes to Lurany. I'm grateful she made his uniform. It fits him well. And the blue trimmed in yellow is so pretty. Don't you think?"

"Oh, Mama did a good job. That's for sure. But I don't know about this war stuff. Don't seem mens ought to be excited about going off to try to kill each other. I don't understand exactly what it's about either."

"Oh, it's about states' rights. It's just like the revolution we had with England. The states should be able to make their own laws, and if they can't, they should be able to secede. The North is always trying to tell the South what to do. That's what it's about."

"I don't know. I hear lots of talk. I hear they want to free us. Is that true?"

"Amanda, you're happy here. Why would you want to be free? I know all slaves don't have the best living conditions, and some are treated harshly. But you are part of our family.

We'll always take care of you and Lurany. You know that, don't you?"

Amanda stood quietly as Trudy jumped up and down when Jeff rode close by. "I know this has always been our home," she said after he passed. "Still, it would be nice to be free. I don't know where Mama and I would go. That's scary. But the more I think about it, the more I want to be free, fo' sure." She saw that Trudy wasn't listening. Or maybe she just couldn't hear. With everyone cheering, the noise was deafening.

Trudy leaned over and shouted into Amanda's ear, "Doesn't Jeff have the prettiest horse? Stanley is a gorgeous stallion. I'm so glad Daniel will be going with Jeff to help him with his clothes, meals, and Stanley, too. So much will be happening. I'm sure Daniel will be essential."

"I guess so, Trudy. I just know all this seems like a crazy time."

Trudy shrugged. The laughter and shouts were so loud. People were thinking only of their loved ones who were leaving, sure that the war would be over soon and the South would be the victor.

Jeff left on August 18, 1861. It did not take long for Trudy's cheers to turn into tears. She grew distraught, wondering when or if she would ever see Jeff again. Silently, she prayed that God would take care of him and bring him home safe.

In the beginning, Jeff's service went smoothly. He joined the famous Cobb's Legion under the command of Thomas R. R. Cobb and was made captain of Company B. He was away for nine months, and Trudy felt apprehensive not knowing where he was or if he was in danger. But when she received a rare letter, she opened it with trembling hands.

> *Dearest Trudy,*
> *There has been a travesty of justice. I have been passed over. Instead of first captain in command I have been made 6th. I cannot tolerate this insult. I have resigned my commission and hired a substitute. Paid a Maryland man $300.00 to stay and fight for me. I will be returning home to join the local militia, The Wheeler Dragoons.*
>
> *All my love,*
> *Jeff*

After Trudy caught her breath, she read his explanation again. She was shocked. The war was so important. Of course, she was thankful Jeff would be out of danger, but she was also embarrassed. When so many men risked their lives, her husband was coming home to the relative security of the local militia. She couldn't help but wonder if his explanation was the true reason for his departure. What should she do?

On a warm day in May, Trudy and Amanda were out in the yard. Trudy watched the children play while Amanda snapped a mess of beans. "You and Lurany will not believe this," Trudy said, "but I have joined the Ladies Sewing Society to make shirts for the troops." She couldn't help laughing when she said it.

"You right about that. I don't believe it. You can't sew a straight stitch."

"I know, but I must do something to help the war effort. I've also volunteered to make cartridges. I find that work far more agreeable."

"Trudy, stick to making cartridges. That sounds more like you. Ain't no hope you be sewing no shirts."

"You're probably right. But this Friday morning, I want you to go with me to take food to the soldiers down at the train depot. There's no food service for them on the trains. We're taking soup, fried chicken, tea, and biscuits. We'll set up tables and benches for them to have a place to eat. We need to get some other servants and the kids to help. Doesn't that sound good to you?"

"Yes, that's good, but you gettin' carried away. You trying to do everything the women folks is doing."

"I sure am. We must all do our part. After we go to the train station with the Ladies Lunch Association, on Friday afternoon we'll go to the Third Georgia Hospital to visit the wounded."

"Lordy, we be dragging by then. But I go with you, I guess."

Friday was hot with high humidity. Feeding the troops went well, but it required a lot of effort from everyone. There was no breeze to help cool them off—a typical late May day in Augusta. Trudy would have liked to go home and rest, but she was determined. When she and Amanda entered the hospital, they were wiping sweat off their faces when a sudden odor hit them. Spread over the large room was cot after cot with wounded men, some moaning and others with blank stares. The scene was immediately horrifying.

"Dear God, I didn't know it would be this bad," Trudy said quietly. "So many of them have dreadful wounds. What can we do or say?"

"Miss Trudy, it sure be awful. Let's leave now. Ain't nothing we can do. You gonna have bad dreams after seeing all these mens' wounds and hearing their crying."

"I know, but we have to try to do something," Trudy said as a delirious man grabbed her arm. His leg was missing, cut off. He struggled to get up.

"Ma'am, I got to get home to my wife and kids." His grip was tight.

At first Trudy froze, panic spreading through her chest. She took a deep breath and steeled herself. "I'm sorry, but you can't go right now. Amanda, could you get some cool water and a rag from that table for his forehead?" She turned back to the weary soldier. "Let me help you smooth out this pillow. Lay back and try to relax. That's it. Now let me see what I can do for you. I tell you what, while Amanda wipes your brow, I'll write to your family and tell them you're in the hospital. They will be happy to hear from you." Trudy held her breath, hoping he would calm down. When he did, she breathed a sigh of relief and took a pad and pencil from her pocket. "Now tell me your wife's name."

"My wife's Jane. Beautiful. Kids Joey and Jenny. Good kids."

"I know you're proud. What's your name?"

"I'm Samuel Jenkins. Tell 'em I'm alive. Coming home to them as soon as I can. Tell 'em I love 'em."

"Where should I send the letter?"

Samuel mumbled an address in Atlanta and drifted off to sleep. Trudy said a prayer that he would make it home. She folded the note and tucked it in her pocket to mail later. They moved to the next cot, where another man held out his hand to them, crying.

Trudy and Amanda stayed at the hospital comforting the wounded, writing letters, and having conversations until it began to get dark. "Come on, Amanda, let's go home." Outside, Trudy said, "I'm glad we stayed. I'm exhausted, but somehow I feel like we've been useful. Maybe what we did will make a difference."

Chapter 14

Augusta, Georgia

1862–1864

It was a pleasant day in December 1862. Trudy sat on a bench in the garden, a light shawl draped around her shoulders. A slight breeze blew, and the cool air felt good on her face. Maybe it would soothe her a little. She was nauseated and had no energy. Naturally, since Jeff returned home in September, she was again "expecting to be sick," as she referred to yet another pregnancy. She did not view it as a blessing. She was angry. At the beginning of the war in 1861, she had given birth to little Jeff. She now had three living children, three dead children, and another on the way. She did not feel up to another birth. Thankfully, baby Jeff had survived, but it wasn't because of her. She could not produce milk for nursing. If Georgianna had not given birth to little George at the same time and been a wet nurse for Jeff, Trudy was sure he would not have lived.

Just then, she spotted Georgianna in the yard and waved her over. "I was just thinking of you. What are you doing out here today?"

"Picking up dead sticks from the storm. Also looking for some Christmas holly. You know I take care of this garden. Like to be outside."

"I was so sorry to hear that little George died. When you brought him to me, I hoped that Dr. Eve could help him. But it has happened to me before, too. No one ever seems to know what is wrong with the babies. They all seem to die so frequently."

"Thank you, Miss Trudy. I've cried and cried. He so sweet. Melted my heart. I know you tried to help."

"The death of so many children is something we share. Whether black or white, children die all the time, and we grieve. Sometimes we don't know if we can go on. But with time, we manage. I want you to know I've been thinking about you."

"Thank you, Miss Trudy." Georgianna wiped away a tear.

"And I want to thank you again for nursing my little Jeff. I believe you saved his life. It looks like I'll need another one of you to help me, as I'm again with child. I dread it. I already feel so weak."

"Sorry, Miss Trudy. Hope all goes well. Know Nancy be having a baby next spring. She'll help you."

"Let Nancy know. Would you?"

"Sure, Miss Trudy. Hope you feel better soon. I better get goin'."

Trudy had no expectation of feeling better. She had come to the garden to get away from the noise inside the house. She wrote in her journal that morning, *The fact is my nervous organization is so completely disorganized that I require perfect quiet.*

Not that she was going to get it. She didn't have enough energy to move, and the children irritated her terribly. Her anger weighed her down. She could only pray that she would feel better in the coming months.

Her depression did not let up. Then on June 23, 1863, Trudy went into labor.

"Miss Trudy, me and Dr. Eve both here today to take

care of you. He in charge. I'm just here to help you stay calm. Breathe. Try to calm down. Push when he say," Susan said as she rubbed Trudy's stomach.

"Thank God you're both here. This never gets easier," Trudy said as she felt another pain shoot through her body.

"I have a new remedy that is going to help you today," Dr. Eve said. "You'll like it. Don't be afraid. It's called chloroform."

"If it makes this pain go away, I'll take it," Trudy gasped.

"It's time. I'm going to put this cloth over your nose and mouth, and you take a big breath. Then you'll fall asleep." Dr. Eve covered her mouth and nose, and Trudy had no time to think. Gradually, she seemed to be floating. Dr. Eve's face grew dim and distant. She fell into a deep sleep. Happily, when she awoke, she had a baby girl.

"Thank goodness," Trudy said with a weak smile. "Everything seemed to have gone well. That was the best delivery I've ever had." She was not completely awake yet but knew she was not as traumatized as in the past.

She named her baby girl Cora after her younger sister. Trudy was doubly grateful—for her beautiful, healthy baby and for the new chloroform that eased the awful pain of childbirth.

But in the following months, she still battled fatigue and depression. News of the war was not good. Everyone lived in fear of what would happen next. Would northern troops come and burn Augusta? Would they trample their crops and take the livestock? On top of constant anxiety, the worst possible tragedy occurred. Pa fell seriously ill and was not expected to live.

Trudy received a note from her mother: *Your father is gravely ill. I need help, too. Please come quickly.* When she received the news, she fell to her knees. Alone in her room, she wept and wept. She must go and see for herself. She wanted someone to tell her it was not true. *Please God, don't let this be true.*

"Uncle Sykes, I'm glad you were here to take me over in the buggy. I have to get there quickly. Mama says Pa is gravely ill. She wouldn't say that unless it were true."

"Yes ma'am, we sorry your Pa's sick. He always been strong."

"And healthy. He has always been our rock. I can't believe it, or maybe I just don't want to believe it. Not in these troubling times."

She was so afraid. She could not imagine a world without Pa. As soon as she reached the mansion on Greene Street, she ran to his room. He was propped up in bed, looking like she had never seen him before. He was pale, had lost weight, and didn't seem to recognize her at first.

"Pa, it's not true, is it?"

Pa opened his eyes and spoke in a whisper. "Who is it? Oh, Trudy, my dear girl."

"I can't believe you're sick. You've always been so strong." Tears rolled down her cheeks.

"Yes, I have dysentery. Bad abdominal pain, but I can manage it. Don't worry." Pa began to close his eyes again. "Sit with me, dear. I'll rest."

Trudy sat and looked at her father. She had always adored and loved him more than anyone else. He had put up with her questions and seemed to understand her. She irritated him sometimes, but he never got mad. She remembered how he took her to and from school at Wesleyan, knowing how important it was to her. How could she go on without him in her world?

Just sitting with him was a comfort. She felt his strength. He was the glue that held the family together. He had such a bright mind and vigorous intelligence. As long as he was still alive, she would sit with him and pray. *Dear God, let him live.*

But he could not go on. He grew weaker and weaker. In his last days, he called all the family together and gave them brief instructions that took all his energy. "I don't think I will live much longer, but I am ready. I love you all. Do not despair. I have my will in order. I have taken care of your mother and each of you. I admonish you as a group to please live in peace and harmony."

After he said these words, he closed his eyes. It was only hours before he was gone. After everyone else left the room, Trudy sat and wept. She felt a void in her life. Pa's dynamic spirit had left his body. She was weak and thought of her own death. How could she recover from yet another loss—this one in particular?

Chapter 15

Augusta, Georgia

1864 and 1865

Five months passed after Pa's death in late April, but Trudy still had a hard time thinking about anything else. She found purpose only in her work with the wounded soldiers. Maybe she could help some of them live and go home to their families. She didn't want anyone else to feel the grief that weighed her down.

All summer she and Amanda made it a point to go at least once a week to the Third Georgia Hospital. One morning, they went early and saw more soldiers than usual. The mood in the South was bad. General Sherman had just taken Atlanta and started his march to the sea. Even though Trudy felt despondent, she tried to cheer the soldiers. But it didn't work, and the effort exhausted her. Finally, she and Amanda were able to get their jackets and start for the walk home.

"I'm glad you and I have kept coming here, Amanda. When we talk to the soldiers and write letters for them, I think we're helping. It makes me feel better."

"I think it's a good thing, too, Miss Trudy. But it's been a long day now. It's goin' to be dark before long. We got to get goin'. I'm bushed."

"Let's go, then."

"You got to take care of yourself. You in a weakened state. You done had little Cora, on top of little Jeff at the beginning of the war. You lucky those two survived. But you still mighty frail. What am I goin' to do with you?"

"I know you're right, but I feel driven to do all I can

while I can. And I'll be eternally grateful for the survival of Jeff and Cora. You know Jeff lived because Georgiana had just had little George and she nursed him when I couldn't. I only regret we couldn't save George when he got sick."

"I know. That was so sad."

"Then Nancy was wetnurse for Cora. Thank heaven for her."

"Yes, we thankful."

"I've always felt close to you and Lurany, but now I see Georgiana and Nancy in a new way. Of course, Susan has been present for all my births in her role as midwife. Some kind of bond has been formed with them." Trudy slowed her pace. "Let's stop and sit on this bench a little while and rest. I'm very tired."

"That's a great idea. I'm worn out myself."

Trudy sat quietly for a few minutes. "I've been thinking about some things for a long time. I want to confess to you that I have decided slavery is immoral. I see so many evils in it now that I never saw when I was younger. When I was growing up, Pa had slaves and justified it by saying the Bible condoned it. Then I started reading anti-slavery writers like William Lloyd Garrison and Harriet Beecher Stowe. I had to sneak to do it. Mama especially would have been outraged. Pa probably wouldn't have liked it either. Some of the things they said and described I had seen with my own eyes. Their words made an impression on me and made me think."

"I know. I sneaked and read some of them, too. Surprised those folks knew so much."

"Good. You know what I'm talking about. But what I hate the most is the way white masters take advantage of their slave women. It is horrific. They rape them, and when the women have babies that are fair skinned, they often sell them because they bring more money. It happens on all the plantations, but no one talks about it. The white women know about it and abhor it. I believe they hate it. I even wrote in my journal what I believe:

> *All Southern women are abolitionists, and the institution of slavery degrades the white man more than the Negro and exerts a most dangerous effect upon our children.*

But if I said these things to my family, they would be horrified. I know my husband would not agree. But I want to say these things to you." Trudy put her arm around Amanda.

"Trudy, I don't know how, but somehow I knowed you were changing. I saw little things you said and did. You were different from when you were young. College changed you, too. You were different when you came back."

"Yes, my good friend and roommate Jo Freeman came from a family that didn't believe in slavery. We had many conversations about it."

"That was good. Now on that other subject, I'm fair skinned and so is Mama. We never talk about that either. I don't know who my daddy is, and Mama probably don't know whose hers is either. And we don't care. We got each other. That has always been mighty important to us. Thank God we been able to stay together, 'cause lots of families all broke up. Ain't right, fo' sure."

"Yes, separation of families is another abominable thing about slavery."

"But I've always been glad you and me could share everything. Got to get some things off our chests. We always been honest with each other. You did teach me to read when

I know no one else would, and we had fun together playing as kids. I've always felt like I could say anything to you, and it would be okay. I don't feel like that with any other white folks."

"This world is so complicated. I can't make sense of it. I don't know what's going to happen with this war. I have a foreboding that we're in for more bad things. You and I aren't going to be able to solve all the problems. But if the South loses the war, that will be the end of slavery, and I'll be happy about it." Trudy paused for a moment to catch her breath. "I have something else I want to tell you. It's sad news—I'm with child again."

"Oh, no, don't tell me that. You too weak. You in no condition to have another baby."

"Yes, I know. And I will tell you what I haven't said to another soul. I don't want this baby. I hope it dies and that I die with it."

"No, you can't talk like that. No, no, that's evil. You can't wish that."

"Oh, yes I can, and I do."

Seven months later, Trudy gave birth to a premature boy who did not live. As thin as she had ever been, she refused to eat or drink anything. Amanda held her head up off the pillow. Trudy's eyes glazed over, and she could barely breathe.

"Trudy, I know you feel mighty bad. Ain't nothing I can say to make you feel better. But please take a little bit of water. You got to eat something, too," Amanda pleaded. "You can't give up and die."

"Yes, I can. Having poor baby Charley at the end of the

war was so sad. All we could give him was his name."

"He was too small and came too soon. Not your fault."

"Yes, it was. I prayed God would take him and he did. Now I should die, too."

"No, don't say those awful things. You need to live for your other children."

"But Pa is dead. How could my dear Pa die?" Trudy muttered through sobs.

"Now get those thoughts out of your mind. Don't do no good."

"I can't. I loved him so much. He was so wise and loving. I can't live without him in my life."

"Everyone is sad your Pa died. He was a good man, but it was his time, I guess." Amanda leaned down and gave Trudy a hug.

"We've lost almost everything. Now Sherman's coming, and we don't have Pa here to help us figure out what to do. I do want to die."

"I will not let you talk like that. You just sad and so weak. I have never known you to just give up. I tell you what you goin' to do. You're goin' to rest and I'm goin' to take care of you. I'm goin' to get you through this. The world might be turned upside down, but we are survivors. You and me. We are survivors. Bad suffering just makes you stronger. You wait and see. Now please take a sip of water." Amanda held the cup to Trudy's mouth. "Please, you got to take some water so you can be here for your other children."

Trudy raised her head and managed to take a tiny sip.

"Good. That's the Trudy I know. You goin' to come out of this dark place."

For two months Trudy stayed in bed, not caring whether she lived or died. But then, as she always did, she somehow came back to life. When she got out of bed, she walked slowly to her journal, picked it up, and wrote the truth: *I came nearer the valley and shadow of death than ever before.*

Chapter 16

Atlanta

1899

"Oh, Miss Trudy, that is so sad. You really wanted to die. I'm thankful Amanda was there for you and could help you find the will to live. We always talk about the war—the battles, the men who died, and of course the Lost Cause. But you never hear about what the women suffered. To hear it firsthand from a woman who lived it makes it all very real to me," Lizzie said with tears in her eyes. "Was anyone thinking about what the women endured?"

"I don't know. I certainly didn't think anybody cared. At the end of the war when little Charley and Pa died, I was more depressed than I had ever been. But thank goodness Amanda was there. She saved my life. I wish I could see her again to thank her. She left after the war. She wanted to be free. I didn't understand then, but I do now. I've missed her. I've looked for her high and low. Another casualty of the war. But no, I don't think folks know what the women suffered."

Trudy sat quietly for a few minutes. "That's enough sad talk for today. It's getting late. Catch the streetcar and go home and rest. Come back tomorrow, and I will tell you what happened after the war. I always said it was worse than Sherman. Let's meet at 1:00. I've got important meetings every morning this week."

Lizzie stepped off the streetcar still thinking about the hardships during the war and the babies that died. She wondered how Miss Trudy had grown from that defeated person to such a strong woman. Lost in thought, she hardly noticed how hard the wind was blowing. She wrapped her jacket tightly around herself as her hair whipped around her face. She was almost running when she opened the door to her shop. A man and a woman stood talking to her mother. As Lizzie closed the door, she thought she heard a familiar voice. *Oh no, it's Jonathan Hopkins, the handsome man who came in yesterday.*

"Mother, here's the artist, E. S. Jeter, that I wanted you to meet," Jonathan said as he extended his hand to Lizzie. "May I help you with your jacket? It looks like you were nearly blown away."

"Oh, thank you. I'm a mess." She tried to smooth her hair, thinking she must look awful.

"Well, I don't think so. That brisk walking puts color in your cheeks." He smiled at her.

"You are kind," Lizzie said, flustered again in his presence.

"Mother, please meet Lizzie Jeter. May I call you Lizzie?"

Lizzie nodded to the attractive older woman in a long gray coat and matching hat. "It's a pleasure to meet you, Mrs. Hopkins, and yes, of course, call me Lizzie."

"I'm delighted to meet you. Jonathan has told me about your lovely shop, and I wanted to see it."

"I know you're wondering why I'm back so soon," Jonathan said, looking a bit flustered himself. "But Mother wanted to see Grant Park and your shop right away. The sooner the better. So here we are. I hope it's okay that your mother kept the shop open until you returned."

"I don't mind at all. I'm glad you're here." Lizzie was catching her breath and still fidgeting with her hair.

Mrs. Hopkins gestured around the shop. "My dear, your studio is lovely. I have enjoyed looking at all the art. Your mother has told me how you were brave enough to start it and to continue painting. I like that in a woman very much."

"My mother is progressive," Jonathan said with pride. "You must hear her story sometime. She has spent her life working for women's rights in upstate New York—an active part of the country with a lot of women's history. Remember I told you she has written newspaper articles for years, signing them only with initials: S. M. Hopkins for Sara Manderson Hopkins. When she started years ago, not many women wrote newspaper articles. I'm very proud of what she has done."

"Thank you, dear, you're sweet to brag on me, but I want to hear about this art. I've been admiring these miniature portraits. They are so good. Who painted them?"

"Aren't they beautiful? My friend and teacher, Lucy Stanton, did them. This one is of her sister Willie. Lucy was my instructor at Cox College, and she encouraged me to start this shop. She has gone to New York to continue studying and plans to go to France soon, too. She's good now but is going to get even better. I think she will be well known someday. If you are interested in buying a piece, it would be a wonderful investment for you," Lizzie said excitedly. "I love her work."

"I like your enthusiasm. Your friend Miss Stanton sounds interesting. I believe I will purchase this one," Mrs. Hopkins said, pointing at the portrait of Lucy's sister.

"That's wonderful. You'll enjoy it, I'm sure." Lizzie

glanced briefly at Jonathan and saw his wide grin.

"I love your enthusiasm, too," he said. "Your face lights up when you talk about your friend and her art. Doesn't she have a glow, Mother?"

"She sure does. I love a woman who can get excited about her work. She then transfers her joy and dedication to other people. Brisk walking is also good for that kind of glow. I'm a big believer in a lot of walking for exercise. Miss Jeter does both." Mrs. Hopkins nodded meaningfully at her son. "She has my approval."

Lizzie was moved by their praise. She hadn't heard many compliments since her father's death. No one else seemed to understand her love of art. But now she had met these two new people who understood and even appreciated it. When she looked at Jonathan, his eyes were glued to her. She smiled and said to his mother, "Oh, let me wrap it for you."

Lizzie picked up the miniature and went to wrap it in brown paper and tie it with twine. She could tell Jonathan was still watching her. She felt giddy and happy.

"Do you think we could go to see the portrait you are working on next week?" he asked. "I don't need much more proof, but I would like to see it before I sign a contract for you to paint Mother's portrait."

"Yes, and I'm sure Miss Trudy would love to meet you. You will both enjoy her. She is a strong, talented woman just like you, Mrs. Hopkins. I think you two will be good friends. She is involved in many organizations that work for the betterment of women."

"That is wonderful," Mrs. Hopkins said. "I've wondered how I could meet likeminded women down here in the South."

"There are probably not as many as you know in New

York, but there are some, and Miss Trudy knows them all. I would even say she is the best one for you to meet."

"Perfect. I look forward to meeting a new friend. I know Jonathan will be busy with young people his own age." She raised her eyebrows as she looked from Lizzie to her son.

"I will be going to paint tomorrow, and Miss Trudy and I will set a date. I'm so excited for the two of you to get together. I feel like you have a lot in common."

"Marvelous, my dear. Jonathan will drop by again in a couple days and find out when our meeting will be."

Mrs. Hopkins paid for her purchase, and as they turned to go, Lizzie realized Jonathan's eyes were on her again. Their hands touched briefly as she handed him the package. They kept looking at each other without saying a word.

Finally, he spoke. "When I return in a few days, do you think you could take a late afternoon break and have a coffee with me? I saw a nice shop down the street."

"I'd love to," Lizzie said, maybe too enthusiastically. She felt her heart racing. "Yes, I'd like that."

"I would, too. Say next Monday?" He took her hand again and squeezed it. "Until then."

Lizzie felt lightheaded as the two of them walked out of the shop. She stood and watched as they battled the wind, Jonathan sheltering his mother as well as he could manage. *Is this what it feels like to fall in love?*

The next morning Lizzie walked quickly up to Miss Trudy's door. When Jeff answered in his Confederate uniform with a scowl on his face, she hardly noticed. No one could destroy her good mood.

"Miss Trudy, Miss Trudy, I'm so glad you're already here in the parlor. I can't wait to tell you what happened yesterday evening. You won't believe it. Has anyone ever told you that you were a matchmaker with magical powers? When I got back to my shop, there stood Mr. Hopkins—I should say Jonathan—and his mother. They were so nice. His mother bought one of Lucy Stanton's miniature portraits, and now they want to see you and the painting I'm doing of you."

"My dear, that's wonderful. But slow down. You are talking so fast. And you must breathe. Take a breath or two. I can see you are very excited."

"I don't know what's happening to me, but I'm happy. Both of them were complimentary of me and seemed to like me."

"Well, I'm sure they did. What's not to like? A beautiful, talented young woman like you."

"You know I never think of myself that way. Since Daddy died, all I've done is worry. Now I feel happy. Am I being foolish?"

"No, of course not. I'd say you're falling in love."

"I'm almost afraid to say it, but maybe I am."

"I must meet this young man and his mother. I'll look at my calendar. I'm sure we can find a day soon. We'll get out the fine china cups and have an English tea party with little cucumber sandwiches and sugar cookies. We'll have delightful conversation and get to know each other. How does that sound to you?"

"It sounds splendid."

"Now get that smock on over your pretty white blouse. Let's get busy finishing up this painting. I'll talk a little more about my story. Defeat was hard for the South, especially the men like Jeff. Let's start in 1866, a year after the war ended."

Chapter 17

Augusta

1866–1872

Trudy looked out the train window, watching the world go by. "Since the war ended, I'm encouraged and feeling so much better. And I'm glad you made this trip to the Wesleyan Alumnae meeting. It was wonderful to see Macon again."

"I'm glad I came, too. I've always heard you talk so fondly of Wesleyan, and now I understand," her sister Cora said.

"If the war hadn't started when it did, I believe you would have gone to college, too. I would have loved to see my younger sister at Wesleyan."

"Oh, I would have loved that. But the war changed everything. Pa's death made everything harder. He would have persuaded Mama that it was a good idea for me to go." Cora laughed.

"You're right about that. Pa believed in me, and he would have believed in you, too. He wasn't perfect, but more than anyone, he thought girls were just as smart as boys. I've been thinking about Pa a lot on this trip. I remember how scared I was on my first train ride to Macon. Pa and Anne were with me. A woman would never travel alone on a train back then. Look at us now, Cora. Two women without a male escort. That's a first for me."

"Yes, for me, too. And I was proud of how you stood up in the alumnae meeting and joined in the debate. You were forceful. Got elected second vice president, too. Don't you think?"

"Thank you. I was pleased by that election. I don't know what has come over me. I've changed so much from the somewhat hesitant young girl I was when I first arrived at Wesleyan. Then all the hardships of the war—they make you into something else, or they destroy you. I believe I am becoming what they call a public woman."

"I don't think you were ever hesitant or shy. But I do see you as a stronger woman now."

"I hope so. All the burned buildings in Atlanta, abandoned plantations in the countryside, destroyed roads and bridges disturb me. Scars of war…a skeleton of the state where I grew up. But look at that old farmhouse. People are out there working to rebuild it. That's what we must do—rebuild and reinvent our lives."

"You inspire me. I'm proud to be your sister." Cora patted Trudy's knee.

"I'm proud to be your sister, too."

"I want to be a good example like you have always been for me."

"I hope we can inspire others. I've made up my mind not to wallow in the past. I only wish Jeff could be more positive. Since he returned from fighting, he has been depressed. Losing the war made him worse. He can't come out of whatever is dragging him down. I'm always saying I'm glad the war is over, but he can't see anything good."

"It seems many men who returned from the war are like him. They saw so much horrific fighting with friends dying around them. If they lived, many lost arms and legs. Remember how they thought they would win the war in a day? They were Southern gentlemen who were going to whip the Yankees and come home heroes. Now they don't know who they are or what they should do. Many of them even refuse to accept that they lost the war."

"Jeff says he's worried 'in mind and body.' He can't get excited about planting. He's worried about the price of cotton going down. He says the freedmen, as he refers to the freed slaves—'conspire to annoy him.' But his problem is that he doesn't have the money to hire them. We asked our slaves to stay, saying we would try to find the money to pay them. Some stayed for a while. When we couldn't come up with enough money, they began to leave one by one. Sometimes we were really hurt when they left. I was so sad the night Amanda slipped away. She left me a note. I guess she didn't want to face me. I couldn't blame her. She had done so much for me. I wish her well.

"But money is scarce. Our Confederate money is worthless. Only gold and silver are acceptable. At the end of the war, I remember having only a few coins of silver. Sometimes it's impossible to find just the essentials of food and clothes for the children. We have land but no laborers—or as some say, we're land rich and cash poor. I believe it's all driving Jeff mad."

"I believe most of our men feel that way," Cora affirmed. "The lack of money is a huge problem for everyone. There's no money to pay taxes, make repairs, or hire workers. No one knows what to do."

"I worry as much as Jeff does. He borrowed money from our brothers and sisters who seem to have come out of the war better off than us. He's tried several different things. Last week he started talking about going into business with two men from Columbus. Something about manufacturing and selling ceramics. I don't know much about it. He tells me so little. As he puts it, I'm not supposed to worry my head about such things."

"Well, if he does start this company, I hope it works out."

"It might just be talk." Trudy glanced out the window again as the train pulled into the station. "Speak of the devil. There he is in all his finery to pick me up. He looks almost out of place here. Look, Mama has sent someone to pick you up." She touched her sister's hand. "Cora, I have loved having you with me on this trip. It was fun to spend a couple nights away with my little sister. Makes me feel young, too." She kissed Cora's cheek. "I love you."

The sisters gathered their belongings and stepped off the train. Jeff waved enthusiastically. "Welcome back, ladies. Hope you had a good trip."

After saying goodbye to Cora, Trudy said, "You look energized today. Something must be up."

"Yes, something is up. I've made it official. I'm a businessman now and have set up shop on Broad Street. Come, I'll show you."

"Jeff, what have you done?"

"Remember I told you about these two men from Columbus—Mosher and Schaub? I've been meeting with them for a couple weeks."

"You said something about them, but I didn't take it seriously."

"We are now partners in Mosher, Thomas, and Schaub. It has a ring to it, don't you think?"

"What is it again that you are doing?"

"We are manufacturers, importers, and dealers in china, porcelain, and glassware."

Trudy was shocked and didn't respond. As they walked toward the business section of town and the office on Broad Street, she tried to get her head around what she was hearing. "What do you know about china and porcelain? And why you?"

"I don't have to know anything about them. They wanted someone in town with good connections—you know, a well-known man in the community. Also, as they say, a 'monied man.'"

"Did you have to put up a sum of money to be a partner?"

"Of course, I did. But that's not a problem. My brother Pinckney has loaned it to me. I put up the Burke County property for collateral."

"No, you couldn't have."

"It will be fine. I've also invested in stocks of kaolin—that white clay used in the manufacture of ceramics. Great deposits in South Carolina and Georgia. Everything is coming together quite well."

"What? You mean we have more debts now. We've already borrowed from my brothers and sisters and from your sister Jule. We have a big loan from the National Bank of Augusta. And also that loan from Cousin Polly Walton. Now we have more loans. How could you do this? You know I hate to owe people money, especially family members. What were you thinking?"

"Trudy, calm down. This is how business is done. You never use your own money. You borrow money, make money, and pay the loan back. Simple as that. This was such a great opportunity. I had to move fast."

They walked briskly toward the business section of Augusta. The day was sunny and warm, not a cloud in the sky. Huge bales of cotton were stacked in the wide expanse of Broad Street, cutting off any breeze. People hustled by them as they talked. When they entered the new rented office space, Trudy was breathless. She felt lightheaded and sat in the first chair she saw. She feared she might faint.

"Trudy, are you okay? You look a little peaked."

"No, just let me sit here and gather my thoughts and take a few breaths." Trudy tried to compose herself. She did not want to get into a big argument here in town where so many people would see. At that moment, a tall, heavyset man with a white beard walked into the office.

"Trudy, I'd like you to meet Philip Schaub, my new business partner."

Trudy politely made conversation but was too shaken to say anything significant. She could only think about how to repay all the loans. How could they even pay some of the loans? She felt physically ill.

~

Trudy never felt good about the business. In the early years, she held her tongue. Jeff seemed happy and enthusiastic. But once his mood began to change, she knew she had to speak up. "Jeff, I know you don't want me asking about the business, but I can't help myself. Tell me why anyone would want to buy porcelain and china when they can't pay taxes and feed their children. It was the wrong business from the beginning."

Jeff shook his head. "I've told you to stay out of this."

"How can I? I know things have gone wrong, but you never really tell me anything. I only know from your grumbling and depression that it's not going well. Let me help you if I can."

"There's no way you can help."

"How do you know? You never give me a chance. I believe I might have inherited some of my father's business sense."

As the days passed, they had more conversations. She called them "heated discussions," but they were just plain arguments. Their relationship grew more and more tense. Trudy took to her journal as she always did in tough times:

> *Tears gather, it is only with an effort that I prevent them from rolling down upon your pages.... Jeff is so depressed, "run to death" as he expresses it.*

One day Trudy was straightening Jeff's desk. Stacking papers, she came upon a report made by the R. G. Dun Company, who had done credit ratings for the business. It seemed Jeff had thrown them on the desk. She picked them up and began to read an outline of the business's history.

On 30 July 1866, the representative reported that the *firm is solvent, and all its member are monied men,* and on a later visit he recorded, *Mosher, Thomas and Shaub keep the largest stock of crockery in town and are agents for kaolin works...collectively worth $50,000, good businessmen.* In February 1868, he briefly noted, *credit good and doing a fair business,* and in May 1868, *no change.* But on 30 October 1868, the company was *not worth over $5,000.* And *they are not paying their debts.* The agent recommended the company should be required to *pay cash.* Finally, in May 1869, the representative wrote simply, *Dead broke and the U.S. Marshal is now selling out their stock: dissolved.*

Here was all the information her husband would never tell her. Why couldn't he talk to her about the business? She had known from the start that something like this could happen. She was furious. With trembling hands, she straightened the papers and happened to see the front page of the newspaper, advertising a sale of their remaining merchandise. More embarrassment. How could she bear it? Jeff walked in the room, startling her.

"Oh, Jeff, look at this advertisement in *The Chronicle*. The stock of the store is to be sold at a public auction on May 11th. I'm mortified."

"It's humiliating for me, too. Don't you know that?"

"Yes, but you have dragged me and my good reputation down with yours. I can't dare to go into town. I'm too embarrassed."

"Stop yelling at me. I'm destroyed. Don't you see that?" Jeff stalked out of the room.

Trudy sat at her desk and cried. She picked up her pen and with a shaking hand began to write.

Oh my God! I have been so proud a woman.
What have I done that I should be so punished?
My life, my glory, my honor has been so intimately blended with my husband.
Now I see him broken in fortune, health, and spirit.

If they thought things could not get worse, they were wrong. Instead of being helpful, their family members began calling in their loans.

"Cousin Polly Walton, it's good to see you. Come in." Trudy offered her a seat.

"I can't stay long," Polly said. "I brought you a bag of fresh butterbeans."

"How nice. Thank you very much. The kids love butterbeans."

"My garden has produced well this year. I thought you would enjoy them. But I also wanted to talk to you about the $5,000 I loaned you and Jeff. I know you're having a hard time, but these times are hard for us all."

"Yes, but we seem to have it worse. Everyone in town knows about us. It's mortifying."

"I'm so sorry for all that has happened. And I hate to add to your troubles, but I need my money back right away. I hope you can do it quietly."

"But we don't have the money now to repay you. Can you give us more time?"

"No, I have taxes due, and our cotton crop is bad this year. I must insist you repay before the end of the year."

"It's such a large sum. I don't know what we can do other than sell our home. I will talk to Jeff and see what's possible."

"Thank you. I knew you would understand. Now I must get home before dark. Nice to see you." Cousin Polly turned and walked out the door quickly.

No, Trudy did not understand. How could her family members treat them this way? Polly didn't even blink when Trudy said they would have to sell the house.

After a couple of months, they had a buyer for their charming home. They sold it for $7,500 and gave Cousin Polly what they owed her. When she was successful, other relatives decided to try the same route and came for their loans, too. By the end of 1869, Jeff and Trudy had lost their home and business in Augusta.

"What else can go wrong?" Trudy wondered. She held up the newspaper to Jeff. "Have you seen this advertisement in the paper for the sale of both plantations in Burke County? Did you know about it?"

"Yes, but that's not all. Now your brothers and sisters are suing me for the $4,000 they say I owed your father's estate before he died."

"That's ridiculous. How could they? They don't need the money now. I think it's just mean-spirited." Trudy couldn't help it. She put her face in her hands and wept. "I bet you anything Anne is behind this," she said through her tears. "She has always been jealous of me. I'm disappointed the others went along with her. We certainly won't be going to Mama's for Thanksgiving this year."

Later, she took up her journal, sat down, and began to write.

> *I suffered during the war. I lost a great deal after its close, but it was so general a loss we could sympathize with each other, but this is worse.... Why, this is infinitely worse than Sherman. Then I was one of a crowd; now I am alone.*

As the months rolled by, Trudy did her best to stay busy and keep her mind off their troubles. She worked hard to be attentive to the children. One afternoon she was sitting by the fire reading to them when Jeff came storming into the house and threw some papers on the table. "This is outrageous!"

"Please calm down. I'm reading to the children. What are you talking about?"

"Look at the front page of the newspaper." He picked up the paper and shoved it at her. "Read this."

> *On 21 October 1872 in the case of The National Bank*

of Augusta v. J. Jefferson Thomas, the judgment was rendered for the plaintiff for the sum of $35,185.86 principal and $11,268.22 interest.

"Dear God, this is a staggering amount on top of all the other lawsuits. Nothing can save us. We've lost our home in Augusta, plantations in Burke County, city lots, and all the money in my trust account. What will we do to survive?" As she had so often lately, Trudy bowed her head and sobbed.

"We're bankrupt. I'm the worst broken man in the world. I have none of my cotton out and nothing in the world to go on."

The children looked on in horror and began to cry. Trudy realized she had to try to pull herself together for them.

"Jeff, please stop talking like that in front of the children. Don't you see you're scaring them?" She glared at Jeff and gestured toward her little ones. "Come here, my loves, let me give you a hug. Mama and Daddy will think of something. We will take care of you always."

In the following days, Jeff and Trudy argued constantly. Jeff was at his lowest. "I don't know what to do. I'm losing my mind. If I could turn over the care of you and the children, I think the best thing for me would be to go to a lunatic asylum."

"I don't believe you mean that. We must think of something." But in her heart, Trudy knew Jeff was in serious mental and emotional trouble. She tried a different idea. "We still have the modest farm Pa gave us before he died. We could go live there. I'd like to get out of Augusta where everyone stares at us all the time. Yes, let's go to the farm and figure things out."

What else could she do to help? She knew one thing: it

did no good to moan and groan about all that had gone wrong. She had to let go of the past and find a way to help her family. Maybe she could make money from some of her writing. So far she had received only rejections. Maybe she could teach. She knew teachers were needed. Before the war, a woman of her status would have never worked for a wage. But everything was different now. This was a new reality, and she would do whatever she could to help clothe and feed her children. Jeff seemed lost. Trudy knew her family's survival was up to her.

Chapter 18

Augusta

1870s and 1880s

After much discussion and arguing, Jeff and Trudy moved the family to the farm, about twenty miles out in the country. Their home was indeed a farm and not a plantation, sitting on thirty-plus acres of flat land with a half-acre pond. The farmhouse was a one-story wood frame in need of paint. The plaster peeled off the walls, and the old rugs were so frayed that Trudy rolled them up and threw them away, preferring the hardwood floors instead. There were four bedrooms, a small parlor, a dining room, and a kitchen at the back. The house was run down and needed renovating, but Trudy was determined to make it a home.

Despite the poor condition of the house, Trudy liked two things about it. One was the covered porch at the front that looked out over a large yard where the children could play, with fields of oats and cotton in the distance. The other was her small garden to the left of the porch where she immediately began to plant flowers that she hoped would brighten their dreary home in the spring.

Trudy was now a teacher while Jeff worked their farmland. He and a couple of hired workmen built her a simple, one-room school with windows and two doors. One door faced the public road, and the other opened into one of the bedrooms on the side of their house. Attaching the school to the house made it convenient for Trudy to go back and forth between the two when she needed to care for the smaller children. Teaching a room full of eighteen or twenty students of various ages along with her own was no small task, but somehow the arrangement worked.

She was grateful when spring finally arrived, and another school week ended. Now if she could just get the children safely out of her classroom without them forgetting something.

"Mrs. Thomas, I can't find my hat." Johnny was looking under the table.

"Here it is. You dropped it." Trudy scooped it up.

"Give me a hug. Please, give me a hug." Susie held up her arms.

"You sweet girl. Here's a big hug." Trudy leaned down to the little girl and put her arms around her. "Have a good weekend, and I'll see you Monday."

She waved goodbye to each of her students as they streamed out of the classroom. By the end of each week of teaching, her bones ached, but a feeling of satisfaction spread through her body. She sat on the porch at the front of their farmhouse and propped her feet on a stool. Finally, it was quiet with no children to herd around. Her own were happy to play in the yard. She gazed out at the peaceful scene. April brought green plants to her garden again and promised beautiful flowers. Things were going well here on the farm.

She and Jeff had endured crippling embarrassment and humiliation when they lost their place in town. They knew when it was time to move on. Now they were through the worst of it, and she could see relief on the horizon. Lost in thought, she leaned her head back and closed her eyes. Jeff walked in from the pasture and joined her, startling her from her rest. He was covered in perspiration, clutching his dust-covered hat.

"Isn't it a glorious day?" Trudy asked, gesturing at the

chair next to hers. "I love looking out at the pasture, seeing the new leaves on the trees and the children running around playing. We're both exhausted from the week's work, but isn't it a good feeling? We've accomplished so much."

"No, I don't think it's a glorious day," Jeff said as he slouched in the rocking chair beside her. "Remember, we lost the war and are living on this pitiful land your father gave us. Work on this farm is grueling and never ending."

"Let's try to think about the good things, not the bad things. Look what we've done. Think how far we've come since I took over Mrs. Carmichael's position at this school. Teaching and working this little farm are saving us."

Jeff reached for the pitcher of water on the table and poured himself a big glass. "You've made good use of the schoolhouse. Who would ever have thought I would do carpentry work?" He took a gulp of water.

"Before the war, it was unheard of for a woman of my class to work for wages. You would have just gotten some of your workers to build me a school room. We were the class of folks who had servants to do everything and wait on us hand and foot. But no more," laughed Trudy. "I don't love teaching, but I do love the children, even though they drive me crazy some days. And I'm proud of the thirty dollars I bring in every month. My Wesleyan education is finally paying off. Maybe even Mama will think so now."

"Your salary is a godsend," Jeff admitted, wiping his brow. "Our crops will probably be bad again this year. I work so hard and have so little to show for it. I never dreamed I would try to be a farmer. I was raised to be a gentleman. Even my attempts at business have failed. My porcelain company went bankrupt. In fact, I've been a failure at everything."

"Jeff, don't be negative. It does no good. Try to think

positively. I'm so glad the war is over. We don't have to worry about Sherman and his troops trampling our crops or burning our homes. I'm glad the slaves are free now. Aren't you? No one should own another person."

"I'm not glad the slaves are free. I have no labor force to help me and no money to hire any workers. Those damn Yankees destroyed our way of life. I'll never be glad for any of it. Trudy, you shouldn't be happy about such things either."

"We may never agree, but let's at least try to find something good. We have seven beautiful children. Since the war, we've been blessed with the births of two healthy boys and baby Kathleen. Our sons can make something of themselves in this new world, and our daughters will have opportunities I didn't." Trudy sat quietly and looked out over the fields. "I have an idea. Why don't you take Julian and Clanton out to the cabin on the lake and spend the night? Have a fun outing."

"Anything to get away from this farm for a spell. Yes, that's a good idea."

Trudy got up and went into the kitchen. "Boys, would you like to go fishing with your Pa? You can quit playing with those toy soldiers and get out in the fresh air."

Julian and Clanton began squealing and jumping up and down. "Yes, Mama. We want to go." Julian threw his arms around his younger brother. "Isn't this great?"

"Go in your room and put a clean shirt in a bag. Hurry now."

Trudy packed a basket with biscuits and ham along with some apples. The boys soon jumped onto the wagon with Jeff, and they rode off giggling. As she watched them, she breathed a sigh of relief. It would be nice to get some rest and not have to listen to Jeff. All he did was complain. It irritated her. She had decided to look for the good in life. So many bad things had happened to them, but they must start changing their outlook or life would destroy them.

The next morning, she sat again in her favorite spot on the porch. The older girls laughed and played with little Kathleen in the yard. The day was pleasant with spring in the air. She was thankful for this beautiful day. In the distance, she saw Jeff directing the wagon toward her with Julian sitting at his side.

"Where's Clanton?" she called out, concerned.

"He's laying down in the wagon. He has a bad headache and doesn't feel good. We were going to stay for the day but cut it short. I don't know what's wrong with him."

Trudy felt Clanton's brow as Jeff carried him into the house. "Go get Dr. Eve," she said to Jeff. "Clanton has a high fever."

She put Clanton to bed, but he hardly responded. *Dear God,* Trudy prayed, *please don't let this be a bad disease. He is such a precious child, so sweet natured. Everyone loves him.* She knew too well what a fever could mean. She would not let her mind go there.

On Saturday and Sunday, their son remained unchanged. Dr. Eve advised them to wait and see if the fever would break. He didn't know what was wrong. On Monday morning, Trudy's students began to come into the classroom. She put Clanton in a bed in the adjoining room where she could check on him periodically. Jeff went out into the fields to work, and Cora was assigned to look after Clanton. When the children were at recess, Trudy found that Clanton had labored breathing and did not seem to recognize her. She was anxious when she had to leave him again.

"Cora, come and get me if he gets worse," she said.

Finally, the school day was over, and she rushed in. "Is there any change?"

"No, Mama. He seems to be sleeping peacefully," Cora answered.

Trudy leaned over his bed. Something was wrong. The look on Clanton's face was too peaceful. Horror gripped her chest. No, no. She quickly put two fingers on his neck. There was no pulse. Nothing. Little Clanton was dead. She screamed.

Dear God, Trudy thought. *How can this be?* This blond, blue-eyed, seven-year-old angel was gone. He was such a good boy. Never in trouble. Always happy. He brought joy to all of them. She dropped to her knees beside the bed. Had she missed a warning sign? He had been so healthy. Trudy let out a long, mournful cry. Her son had died without her. She was in another room, teaching other people's children. She was overcome with grief and guilt.

The school year was nearly over, so everyone understood when she ended the session early. All she could do was sit on the porch watching her children play as she cried and grieved. Just when she was beginning to look at life with a positive attitude, this had happened—another lost child.

The days rolled on into months and then into years following Clanton's death. Trudy tried hard to overcome her grief, to push it down into the place where she had kept this sorrow before. The beauty of nature always touched her soul, so she sat for hours looking out into the garden. Of course, the laughter of her children cheered her too.

One day in the spring three years later, Kathleen came and crawled into her lap. She had her brother's blue eyes and blonde hair. It was almost as if Clanton were speaking to her. "Mama, don't be sad. We love you."

That day, Trudy decided to come out of her sad place. She would do it for her other children, for the lives they had yet to live.

Chapter 19

Augusta

1880s

In spite of Trudy's resolve in the years that followed her son's death, teaching became more of a task than a joy. Jeff grew more negative and depressed about farming. They had to figure out how to change their lives. Fortunately or unfortunately, the decision of what to do next was made for them.

On an early March morning in 1884, Trudy was sitting in her favorite rocking chair on the porch, drinking a cup of coffee, when her older sister Anne pulled up in her buggy. They had never gotten along well, and Trudy was surprised to see her. "Sis Anne, welcome to our little farm. I see you so seldom. What brings you out here to visit? Come sit on the porch with me."

Anne climbed down slowly, walked up on the porch, and sat in the chair next to Trudy. "I know we've never been close, but we must put our feelings aside for once. I've come with sad news. It's about Mama."

"I know she has been sick, but is she worse?" Trudy asked anxiously.

"Yes, she is very weak. And she's in that big twenty-four-room house all alone. All the siblings have taken turns staying with her, but we need a more permanent arrangement."

"You know I've wanted to come take my turn but couldn't because of the school. We desperately need the money I make teaching."

"Yes, we know, but we have met and come up with an idea that we would like to present to you. That's why I came today. You could close your school and live in the house with Mama. We know the farm is not producing. Jeff doesn't have enough help to run it, and he hates it anyway."

"That is certainly true, but you're asking a lot. And I don't like my brothers and sisters meeting to decide what my family should do."

"Calm down. Hear me out. You have a big family. Six children. You need more room. You could all move into the mansion, take care of Mama, and stay there after she passes. We have decided you could turn the place into a boarding house. Of course, you would receive some of the proceeds from the rental fees for your salary."

"That's outrageous. Our big, beautiful home that Pa built for Mama—we all love it so much. How could you suggest the idea of strangers living in our home?"

"None of us want this. It hasn't been an easy decision. But to keep the house and pay the taxes, we must make it profitable. The war has changed everything. We would have never dreamed of this before the war, but now it is a necessity. This is a new world, Trudy. We must find a way to live in it."

Trudy sat quietly for a few minutes. "As much as I hate to say it, you're right. I don't love teaching, and Jeff hates farming. I'm sure he will be glad to make the move."

They sat, drank coffee, and visited a bit longer. Then Anne insisted she needed to get back to town. "Please come as soon as you can close your house. Mama doesn't have long."

Within a couple of weeks, Trudy and her family had moved to Augusta. Even if it was a sad occasion, the change was good for the family. Jeff was happy to give up the hard labor on the farm, and the kids were excited about the adventures ahead.

"Mama, I love this big staircase," Julian said as he straddled the railing and started sliding down. His siblings soon followed him.

"Children, please quiet down. You can't be so loud. Remember, your grandmother is sick. Why don't you go in the parlor and read some books while I say hello to her?"

"Sorry, Mama. We'll be quiet." Julian took his little sister's hand and led her away.

When Trudy walked into her mother's room, she could not believe the change. Her mother looked frail propped up on her pillows. She gave Trudy a weak smile.

"My dear, come and sit beside me. It is so good to see you. Tell me all about the children."

"Mama, first I want to know how you are doing. Tell me how you feel."

"Oh, I'm feeling okay. Tired. No energy. That sort of thing. But no pain."

"That's good. I'm here to make sure you're comfortable. I'll be taking care of you now. We can sit and talk all the time. I'll wait on you. Bring you food. I've actually learned to cook a few things."

"I can't believe that." Mary laughed. "You always hated anything to do with the kitchen."

"Well, times have changed. When you don't have a cook and you have six children, you'd better know how to put food on the table."

"I'm happy to hear that you are managing. I know I'm going to love getting to know your children better."

"I don't want them to wear you out. I thought I would let them come in one at a time and talk to you, tell you what they've been doing. The older ones have gone out and gotten jobs, but the younger ones are here every day. It will be nice for them to have one-on-one chats with you. How does that sound?"

"Wonderful."

The next morning, Trudy brought her mother a tray with coffee, toast, a few berries, and an egg. "Mama, here is your breakfast." She put the tray where Mary could reach everything. "I have a cup of coffee for myself, too. I want to sit and visit. I think I need to apologize for driving you mad when I was growing up. Always asking questions, refusing to go to sewing circle, being careless with my clothes. You name it, I did it. I know you were frustrated. Now that I have children, I understand what a naughty child I was." Trudy laughed and took her mother's hand. "I'm sorry."

"You don't need to apologize. All you children gave me something to fret about. None of you were perfect. I'm just glad you're here now. We have some time. Tell me about that school you ran for years. Do you miss the kids now? I've been proud to tell folks my daughter was a teacher."

Trudy smiled. She was happy to hear her mother approved of her—something she had not experienced much when she was young. "I'm so glad to hear that. Yes, I miss the kids but not all the noise and discipline that goes along with teaching."

They sat and talked for hours each day, remembering the parties and lovely dinners they had shared until her mother grew tired and nodded off to sleep. The children paid their visits and made her happy. Each day she seemed less able to talk. But she smiled and laughed softly. They both enjoyed their memories. In later years, Trudy would always be grateful for those long conversations.

One day in May, Trudy brought in the meal tray as she always did. Her mother was weak and barely spoke most days, but she looked different this morning. Distant, as if she were slipping away. She was seventy-two years old but worn down by the war and all its hardships. The doctor said she had heart failure.

Trudy knew this could be the end. She took her hand. "Mama, I'm here. I love you."

Her mother said in a low, weak voice, "Love you, too." She struggled for some minutes. Her breathing was labored and slow. She squeezed Trudy's hand, gently let go, and then breathed her last breath. It was May 11, 1884.

Trudy sat by the bed with tears running down her cheeks. She had not thought her mother's death would affect her this way. She had not been close to her mother the way she had been with her father. She had always thought Mama was distant and didn't care about her the way Pa did. But now Trudy was devastated and realized she had never understood her mother. She had assumed things and taken her for granted. At that moment, she resolved to try to be more understanding of people. Life was precious. Each day should be treasured. And each person was an individual trying their best to get through the difficulties.

Trudy left the room to notify her siblings of their mother's passing. Immediately friends and neighbors began to call, expressing their condolences. Mrs. Phinizy from next door appeared. "Trudy, I'll handle everything. I'll keep a list of who brings what. Don't worry your head." The callers brought hams, casseroles, pies, and cakes. There was more food than they could ever eat. But they appreciated each expression.

Trudy and her siblings had already planned the funeral. "We have no new decisions to make," she assured them as she looked around the room. "The service will be at the

Methodist church, and Mama will be buried beside Pa in Magnolia Cemetery. I assume we are all agreed." All heads nodded yes.

In light of the hard feelings after the war, Trudy was anxious about being with her brothers and sisters. But everyone was polite and on their best behavior. The family came together to greet well-wishers and get through the church service and the burial. It was afterwards, when everyone came back to the house, that Trudy saw a change. Each sibling and their spouse began to talk about what they wanted. The grandfather clock was a favorite item.

Thankfully, Anne stepped in. "Hold on, everyone. I must insist that the furniture remains for the boarding house."

For once, Trudy appreciated her older sister's assertiveness. She was determined not to get into the squabbles that erupted, but she was sure about one thing. "The big portraits of Mama and Pa should stay in the dining room. Somehow those portraits make it feel like home." She was grateful when all the siblings agreed.

The long day finally came to an end, and Trudy and Jeff stood at the front door and told everyone goodbye. They were relieved to be left alone. The house was eerily quiet. It was their first night in the home without a sick patient or a funeral to plan. They were in charge now.

"It's almost as if Pa could walk into the room the way he always did. I can hear and see him. And I can see Mama, too, always busy organizing something, inspecting the room, and giving instructions to us kids. Their spirits are still here."

Jeff nodded, but Trudy frowned. "I have so much guilt. I was never close to my mother, and I realize now how busy she was, trying to take care of this big house and giving Pa eleven children, with four of them dying. It's so hard for women. Now I know she was doing the best she could to survive."

"Your mother was a good Christian woman trying to do her duty."

"Yes, she worked all her life to be the epitome of a good wife and mother. I'm afraid I didn't understand her at all."

"You're always telling me not to beat myself up, and now I'm telling you the same thing. Let go of it." Jeff put an arm around his wife.

"You're right. There's no time to hang our heads. Even though this is embarrassing, we must do what we have to do." Trudy began to walk around the large entryway.

"Look at this big, beautiful house. Remember that debut party Pa gave me when you met him for the first time?"

"I remember it well. I was terrified."

"Everything was so lovely, with flowers everywhere, music, men and women in gorgeous clothes, and the dining room table piled high with food. It was a fantasy world." Trudy laughed and shook her head. "We never dreamed it would come to this. Now we must divide the house up and rent out the rooms. We have moved into a different world."

"I told you the Yankees ruined everything."

"Don't go there. The war is over. Now let's just figure out how to divide the rooms. How about this bedroom downstairs with the parlor for one apartment? The rest of the downstairs we will use for our family. Now let's go upstairs and divide the bedrooms. No matter how embarrassing or demeaning this is, we can do it." Trudy walked up the stairs, and Jeff followed.

"By the way," she said as she neared the landing, "one positive thing I can do is go back to church. When we were out on the farm, it was hard to get to town and attend church regularly. I look forward to seeing more people, and I want to get involved in some women's groups I've heard about. There is so much work to do. I think those things will help me. It's time I got out more and looked for some strong women who have also suffered. We've all come through the war stronger, and that's a good thing. No matter what happens to us, we must look for the positive things in life. That's my new mantra."

Over the next few weeks, the family quickly adjusted. Trudy actually enjoyed being back in her childhood home, which provided many positive memories. She loved the old house and wished she and Jeff could buy it, but that was out of the question. They couldn't afford it. The family agreed that Trudy's family could rent it for $500.00 a year, and they would get the money back when the home was sold. As soon as they put an ad in the *Augusta Chronicle*, renters began showing up. The Greek Revival Clanton mansion on Greene Street, with its massive columns and stately rooms, was often referred to as the most beautiful house in town.

Trudy spent much of her days helping the renters get settled.

"Mr. and Mrs. Brown, it is so good to see you. I am putting you down for three rooms upstairs for three months at eighteen dollars a month. Welcome."

"Dr. and Mrs. Patrick, I think these two rooms will be comfortable for you at only sixteen dollars a month."

"Mrs. Allen, you will enjoy that room with a nice parlor for a whole year at eighteen dollars a month."

Trudy went to the Irish section of town and hired a

cheerful young woman named Nora who could help with cooking and cleaning. They had decided to provide an evening meal each day in the big dining room. Nora specialized in simple, delicious comfort food.

"Heaven knows I'm not a good cook," Trudy said as she showed her around the mansion. "I need help with this crowd of folks. Thank goodness you could come."

Nora was delighted with her new job, especially the children. "Miss Trudy, it is a joy to work in this big, beautiful house. And I love your children. Hope to have a bunch myself. I've got a good man I'm courting." Nora chattered away, but Trudy enjoyed her company and couldn't help being amused.

They all worked hard every day. Trudy grieved her loss of privacy, but the plan was working, and the people were coming. She tried to get rid of her feelings of shame, though it wasn't easy.

The best part about the move to town was seeing friends again. In a matter of weeks, Trudy began to feel better and have more energy than she had experienced in a long time. One day in the fall, she was bustling around straightening up the front parlor when someone knocked on the front door.

"Cousin Jane Sibley, it's so good to see you," Trudy said, throwing her arms around her friend. "I'm glad you came by to pay a visit. Let's sit in this little parlor. I guess you've heard that we're renting out rooms and turning this big mansion into a boarding house. I've been embarrassed, but we must do it."

"Trudy, the war caused havoc for everybody. We are all doing what we must to make money to pay taxes and feed our children. Be glad you still have this house to rent out to boarders. There is no shame in it. Anyway, that's not what

I'm here to talk about." Jane sat in an old straight-back chair opposite Trudy.

"You're right," Trudy agreed. "I'm trying to see it that way. I must admit that sometimes it's hard. But what do you want to talk about today?"

"I want you to join a group that has grown enormously popular with women in Augusta—in fact, throughout the state. It's called the Women's Christian Temperance Union. Our main objective is to fight demon rum. The use of alcohol by our men who came back from the war is destroying lives. There's no regulation. We must do everything we can to fight it, but our focus is on the damage done to families when alcohol is abused. We're doing so many things to help all the women and children left in need after the war."

"I've heard about the group. You call it the WCTU, I believe. I know what the women are suffering. Jeff has taken to drinking so much now that it really annoys me. I try to talk to him about it, but he gets angry. He is your cousin, and I know you love him. But he has a problem."

"I've thought that might be so. Jeff was always the life of the party and enjoyed taking his sips of whiskey. I'm not surprised. But I think you will like this group and can help us. You're a smart woman with her own mind. We need that now more than ever."

"I've already made up my mind that I want to find ways to help others, especially women and children. You don't have to say another word. I'll be happy to join your work. I'm tired of thinking only about my problems. Everybody has problems. We need to help each other."

Jane gave Trudy a wide smile. "I knew you would feel this way. Our next meeting is this week on Friday at the Methodist church. I'm so happy you'll be joining us. Now

I've got to get going. I must go recruit some of your neighbors."

Trudy stood in front of the mirror. She wore an old dress, but it still looked decent. After having all her babies, she had remained slim. The years on the farm had provided few reasons to get dressed up. Now she rummaged through her old clothes every Sunday to find something for church. Even if she didn't have any new frocks, the old ones looked presentable. Looking in the mirror, she liked what she saw.

As Trudy put on her hat, Kathleen came into the bedroom. "Mama, you look nice. Where're you going?"

"I'm going to the WCTU meeting where we talk about how to help women and children who have suffered since the war. Sometimes their daddies drink too much alcohol. We're trying to do something about that."

"Like my Daddy."

Trudy had not expected that response from her daughter but was amazed at her perception. "I wasn't talking about any particular person—just men in general. Hand me those gloves. Must always wear gloves to be a proper lady."

As Trudy walked out the door with her head held high, Kathleen said, "Mama, you look really pretty. Have a good time at your meeting."

"I will, dear. Thank you." Trudy felt she was setting a good example of service for her daughter. She was confident that she still had a lot she could do for others. She was pleased that Cousin Jane had invited her to join this important group. It would give her life more meaning.

Trudy liked the energetic women she met at the

meetings and enjoyed conversations with them. She threw herself into all the activities, eagerly volunteering for every job they asked her to do. She was elected treasurer the first year. Then the next year, she was chosen as president of the Augusta chapter, and Cousin Jane Sibley was president of the state organization. Three years into Trudy's membership, she was writing articles for the local newspaper reporting on the group's activities.

Trudy was thrilled in the fall of 1887 when Jane extended a special invitation to her: "I want to invite you to go to South Carolina and hear Frances Willard, the woman who started our organization. We will be representing Georgia at the fifth annual convention in Columbia, South Carolina. Don't worry. We can leave early one morning and come back in the evening. She is speaking in the middle of the day. We can take the train."

"I can take one day from running the house. And Nora can watch the kids. Thank you for inviting me." Trudy stood and hugged her old friend. "This is such an honor."

"One more thing. I want you to write an article for the *Augusta Chronicle* describing our trip." Jane smiled. "I think you'll do a great job."

Trudy had always loved to write and easily described the charming Frances Willard, who was such a gifted speaker. *Since I have attended the convention, I have found a consciousness of enlarged views. Of greater love for humanity.* She realized that it was women who suffered at the hands of drunken fathers and husbands, and it was women who must bring change to society. This was work worthy of women. Women might not have the vote yet, but they had the power of example. Trudy had found her passion—something that helped her forget her personal problems.

For the next few years, she was convinced that her work was important. It not only brought her fulfillment but also helped other women. She found something she had needed for years, and she would never look back on the past. She would look to the future.

While Trudy found gratification in her volunteer work, the boarding house began to lose clients. It had never been ideal for her family, but it provided income. Her brothers and sisters felt it was time to sell the house, and Jeff and Trudy agreed. They had grown tired of living with so many strangers and trying to please their every desire. But what were they to do? Where could they go?

She and Jeff sat by the fire in the parlor one evening in the new year of 1893. "Our children have grown up," Trudy said, watching the flames. "Turner and Jeff are in business, and Julian has gone to medical school."

"Yes, he's doing what I decided I didn't want to do." Jeff shrugged and sighed. "Maybe I should have stayed with medicine."

"No, it wasn't for you. But I think Julian will be a great doctor. I'm proud of him. His move to Atlanta to start a practice will probably work out well."

"Yes, and Mary Belle and Cora have married and moved there, too. Kathleen may not be far behind. She's eighteen."

"Jeff, I've been thinking. Maybe we should go to Atlanta. There is nothing for us here in Augusta anymore. You might try another business. There's a lot going on there."

"What the heck. I'll probably fail again, but let's do it."

Trudy shook her head at her husband. "Will you ever learn to be positive?"

"I'll try. I promise."

"Okay, the decision is made. I'll begin cleaning up here

and make arrangements. Cora has already said we could live with her and Patrick. I'm excited. It will be a new beginning."

Trudy and Nora sat talking in the old basement washroom where Lurany had lived for years.

"Nora, you've been such a help to me. I wish I could take you to Atlanta." Trudy hugged her friend.

"I'd like that. But you know with Bobbie Lee and our kids, I've got to stay here."

"Of course, you must stay here. It was just wishful thinking. We've been together every day for years now. I've told you about Lurany and Amanda many times. This was Lurany's workroom and bedroom. When I was a child, I never thought to come down here. I didn't think of it—had no idea the way she lived in this tiny room and worked day and night."

"Yes ma'am, you've told me lots of stories about her and what a seamstress she was."

"Amanda was upstairs with me taking care of my every need. She was my constant companion. So talented, too. They were both slaves and left us after the war. I never found out what happened to them. Oh, I hope they made it. I would love to see them. Lurany may not be alive still, but Amanda could be."

"I'm sure that would be nice." Nora smiled and stood up. "I better get going. Thank you again for all you've done for me."

"I'm the one thanking you. I never could have managed this house without you."

Trudy waved as Nora walked out the door. "Don't forget

to have Bobbie Lee come get the black wrought-iron wash-pot outside the door. I remember seeing Lurany boil clothes in it. I'd like you to have it. If you don't use it for washing, it would be a great outside flowerpot."

After Nora left, Trudy sat again on a stool in the tiny room, thinking about Lurany and Amanda. She could see them both so clearly. It was as if she could feel their spirits. They had been such a big part of her life. Amanda had saved her life more than once. *I know it was hard for them, but dear God, I hope they have had a good life.*

Part Two

Chapter 20

Augusta, Georgia

1866

I'd always wanted to be free, and now that it was here I couldn't hardly believe it. But it was here fo' sure. And I was glad of it. I didn't sleep a wink all night. Uncle Sykes supposed to be there at 2:00 a.m. with his wagon out by the entrance to the plantation. I only took two dresses Mama made for me, wrapped up around a book Trudy gave me—*Uncle Tom's Cabin*. She always had to hide it, so she gifted it to me.

I felt bad not telling Trudy I was leaving. But I knew she would try to talk me out of it. Didn't want to get in that conversation. So I left her a note on the bed.

> *Trudy,*
>
> *I am going tonight. Uncle Sykes picking me up to go get Mama.*
>
> *I am another mouth for you to feed. You got no money.*
>
> *You doin fine now. You know I always wanted to be free. Now I am.*
>
> *You stay strong and take care of your kids. Maybe we see each other again someday.*
>
> *Amanda*

It was a cool night with a full moon. Almost seemed like daylight. I threw an old shawl around my shoulders. I held my head high with my bundle under my arm and just strolled out the door. I breathed in the air, and it felt so good. I'd always dreamed of walking out real casual, and now I was doing it. Yep, felt mighty good.

"Here I am. Ain't this a beautiful night? Magical. And we are riding off into freedom. Hallelujah." I climbed up on the seat by Uncle Sykes.

"Yes, hallelujah."

We rode along in silence through that night, listening to the night sounds. It was real peaceful.

"Uncle Sykes," I said after a while, "I been meaning to ask how you come by having a mule and a wagon."

"When Sherman was coming, Massa Thomas had us take all the livestock into the woods so soldiers wouldn't get 'em. Everybody was doing that. The Union men found 'em anyway. Took horses and cows. Later I found this mule. Real poorly. Wasn't Massa Thomas's. Guess no one wanted him, so I took him. Got him healthy again. Saw this wagon all broken up by the road and mended it. Mighty proud of both. Never thought I'd have a wagon and mule."

"I'm sure thankful you do. We'd be walking tonight otherwise, and it's so nice riding along, not worrying about no one coming up chasing us or anything."

As the sun rose up, it was so beautiful, all orange and pink. Made tears come to my eyes. Real quiet like we rode into town and up to the back of the big house. When I went in Mama's room down in the basement, she was sitting on one of her chairs holding her sewing bag.

"Mama, we here. You ready to go?"

"I'm just sittin' here thinkin' about all the years I've spent in this room. It's been home to me. Hate to leave it in a way. But I know home is where you is." Lurany smiled. "Thinking maybe I should say goodbye to Miss Mary, but it seems easier to just leave."

"That's what our folks are doing. You know Daniel, who's been Mr. Thomas's companion for years. A couple nights ago, he took off his uniform and left it on the bed. Then he walked out the door. I think Mr. Thomas was shocked, but he didn't let on. Acted like it didn't bother him. Daniel figured he was free, and he could do it that way."

"Guess I'll do the same."

Uncle Sykes walked into the room. "What can I carry out for you? Mighty fine chairs you got here."

"These two chairs and this table my pride and joy. Ole Ben made 'em for me with his own hands. You remember Ole Ben."

"Sure do. Had club foot. Fine carpenter for Massa Clanton. Always did the hard detail stuff."

"He had some leftover heart pine. Good hardwood and so pretty." Lurany rubbed the smooth arm of her ladder-back chair. "He carved the legs and arms. Look at these. He called these things here on top acorn finials. I didn't know things like that. He taught me. Said these are woven oak splint seats. So strong. Pretty and never wear out. Me and Amanda done set in 'em a long time. He was right. They ain't changed a bit. This little table heart pine, too. He waxed it all and rubbed 'em down. I've always loved 'em."

"I'll be real careful loading 'em in the wagon."

"Here, take these two old quilts I made and wrap 'em up. Don't want nothing to happen to my table and chairs. Here's an old oil lamp, too. Miss Mary gave this to me once so I could see what I was sewing."

"You know, I think Ole Ben was sweet on you. That's why he made these for you." Uncle Sykes picked up one of the chairs to take it to the wagon.

"Maybe. I don't know. But he made me so happy I made

him a quilt from old scraps of cloth I had around. I remember he cried when I gave it to him. He said it would always be a treasure to him. Other than a few carved things he made from scraps of wood, the quilt was his only personal possession."

"I never heard that story about Ben," I said. "Sweet. But we need to get goin'." I picked up the lamp and wrapped it in an old cloth. "Let's go."

I made Mama sit up by Uncle Sykes. I stretched out in the back of the wagon, put my bundle under my head, and before I knew it, I was sound asleep, exhausted but happy about our adventures ahead.

After riding all day, we arrived at Mr. Graham's plantation, somewhere out in Burke County south of Augusta. Uncle Sykes had got word that Mr. Graham was hiring workers. After the war, some plantation owners seemed to end up with money and others didn't. Graham must have been a saver or a good manager. For whatever reason, we was happy to hear someone had money and was hiring. Lots of folks working in the fields of cotton. We rode in real slow with everyone staring at us. Pulling up to the back door, we asked who was hiring. We waited and then a man rode up on his horse.

"Hello, I'm Mr. Thornton. I hear you looking for work. Where you come from? What can you do?"

"We from Augusta," Uncle Sykes said. "Miss Lurany belonged to Massa Turner Clanton. Her daughter Amanda belonged to his daughter Miss Trudy Thomas, and I belonged to her husband Mr. Jeff Thomas. Miss Lurany and Miss Amanda good seamstresses, and I was a driver. Took care of animals and such."

At about that moment, Mr. Graham came out the back

door. "Hello, welcome to my plantation. Thornton, you taking care of these folks?"

"I don't think these folks can help us, Mr. Graham. This man was a driver, and the women are seamstresses. We need field hands."

I decided to chime in. "Pleased to meet you, Mr. Graham. We hard workers. We can do whatever you need. Mama can help in the house—clean or cook. I can do field work. I'm sure Uncle Sykes can, too. Whatever you need."

"I don't know about that," Thornton said immediately. "You are not what we need."

"Hold on, Thornton. These folks have come a long way. I'm sure we can work something out. I'm sorry, but my wife has passed away and I don't need any sewing done. However, maybe Miss Lurany could help Rebecca with the house. She's my housekeeper. My kids have moved to Savannah. Maybe she could help with cooking, too."

I jumped into the pause, relieved to keep Mama out of the fields. "That sounds great. She can do whatever you need in the house. What you paying?"

"I intend to pay ten dollars a month. That includes lodging with some food, not all. How does that sound to you?"

"I'd like more, to be honest. But if that's what you paying now, we'll take it," I rushed to say.

"Whatever you say, Mr. Graham. It's your money." Mr. Thornton motioned and we followed him.

He took us to some little buildings out behind the big house that had obviously been former slave quarters. A few old women sat out front on some of the porches, tending small children. Strange there was no laughter.

"I'm the manager on this plantation," Mr. Thornton told us. "I don't always agree with Mr. Graham on how to run this place. I like to run a tight ship. We chopping cotton now. Field hands report at 7:00 a.m. Miss Lurany, I'd say you go up to the big house early in the morning and talk to Rebecca. Do you want to stay or not?"

I spoke up quickly. "We staying."

He took us to a row of small shacks. "This little cabin is empty. You and your mama take it. Sykes, go to that men's cabin down the way." Thornton went back to his horse and rode off.

The cabins needed repair and looked run-down. "Not too impressive," Uncle Sykes said. "This plantation not nearly as nice as Massa Clanton's." He started unloading Mama's chairs.

When we entered the dark room, it was depressing. Mama picked up an old broom by the door and started sweeping. "Look at all this dust. This place is filthy. How they expect us to live here? My room at Massa Clanton's never like this. No windows here. Even small ones."

"Mama, we'll clean it up." I unwrapped our oil lamp and used the old rag to dust off two cots. "We'll clean these and then put those pretty quilts of yours on 'em. Won't be so bad."

After a brief cleanup, Mama started opening a cloth bag. "Let's sit here and eat some biscuits and ham I packed this morning. I'm mighty tired."

"Yes, let's rest. We got to think." I tried to encourage her. For a day that had started so happy, it was having a sad ending. But we were here and would have to make the best of it.

Chapter 21

Burke County, Georgia, a day's journey south of Augusta

1866

We were all up at the crack of dawn the next morning. When I opened my eyes, Mama was already going out the door. "Imagine breakfast got to be cooked and cleaned up. I'll get on up to the big house. Be careful today."

"You too, Mama." I threw on my dress and some boots. I wanted to be one of the first out in the fields. Saw Uncle Sykes and we walked out together. He was right by my side. I was so thankful I had him, 'cause I was nervous. Never chopped cotton in my life. Had no idea how to do it.

"Do you know how to chop cotton?" I whispered to him.

"Sure. I did it when I was a boy. You just separate the plants that too close together. Want 'em about a shovel width apart. Then you dig up the weeds—Johnson grass, coffee weed, and thorns. Stuff like that."

"That sounds hard. I know Johnson grass tough to dig up in the garden. Guess you don't want the thorns to scratch you either."

"You right about that. After you get the weeds out, break up the soil a little bit around the plant. Nothing is too hard, but be careful the way you bend over. Your back can start hurting real bad."

At that moment, Thornton came up and gave us old metal hoes. Handles had some splinters. Uncle Sykes took a pair of gloves out of his pocket. "Here, I brought these for you."

"Thank the Lord. Didn't think about needing gloves."

"You'll need 'em. Fo' sure." Uncle Sykes grinned. "But I'll be watchin' out for you."

We were each assigned a long row of plants. I started doing what Uncle Sykes had told me to do. I kept glancing over at him to see if I was doing it right. We worked along real steady for about an hour. I knew pretty soon what he meant about my back hurting. I was in trouble. Mine was already killing me.

"What you do when your back starts hurtin'?"

"Try to stretch it a little. Squat a different way."

About that time, Thornton rode up again on his horse. "No talking. Wasting time. You're behind the other workers. Look how far down their rows they are."

I wanted to yell back at him, but for once I held my tongue. I didn't like him one bit. I was doing the best I could. Wouldn't dare tell him it was the first time in my life I had chopped cotton. And I had already decided I didn't like it one bit either.

We had a brief break for lunch. Uncle Sykes and I had not brought anything with us. A nice man named Rufus gave us each an apple. Best apple I ever had. There was a creek by the field, so we ran down and splashed water on our faces and gulped as much as we could from our hands. It was May, but the sun was beating down on our heads by now. I had not thought to bring a hat. Didn't have one even if I had thought of it. I couldn't imagine how in the world I was going to make it until the end of the day. I just knew I had to do it.

It was almost sundown when we stumbled back to our cabin. I had never been so tired in my life. My back hurt so bad. In fact, I was tired to my bones. I knew I would wake up with stiff, sore muscles in the morning. Thankfully, Mama was already there. When I saw her, I thanked God she didn't have to work in the fields. It really might kill her.

"I know you two exhausted. Sit down here. I got a few things Rebecca gave me from the kitchen. She's mighty nice, by the way. Got a pitcher of tea. Also, I got some big baked sweet potatoes. That's all I got, but they goin' to taste so good."

The three of us sat in silence, gobbling our sweet potatoes and drinking that delicious tea. "Mama, it's a good thing you workin' in the kitchen. I don't know what we would do for food. Ain't nowhere else to get anything."

"Rebecca knew that. She says she'll try to slip things to us, but we got to be careful. She loves to talk. I learned a lot from her today. She says Mr. Graham is a nice old man grieving his wife's death and his kids moving away. She also says Mr. Thornton is mean as a snake."

"We done learned that today. He treats us like we still slaves. Driving us all the time to work harder in that hot sun. There was a poor lady out there today expecting a child, and he treats her awful. No mercy for her. I don't know how long I can stand it here."

Mama agreed. "Rebecca said Mr. Graham don't have as much money as folks think he has. Seems he's trying to sell some of his land to get money to pay us."

"That ain't good. Remember yesterday he said, 'I intend to pay you ten dollars a month.' I bet he can't pay until that land sells. Who knows when that will be. Ain't nobody got any money to buy land around here."

Uncle Sykes spoke up. "Remember we is free. We don't have to stay here and do this work. I agree that Thornton is a devil. We ain't gonna work this hard and not get paid. Let's talk about what we can do. I got my mule and my wagon. We can take off anytime we want to."

"You're right. We got to learn to remember we free. Takes some getting used to."

"Lurany, you mentioned Mr. Graham's kids went to Savanah. That's a big city. Sherman didn't burn it like he did the rest of Georgia. It might be doing better than the rest of the state. Bet there's lots of work there." Uncle Sykes seemed lost in thought. "Yes, I bet good things goin' on down there."

"How far is it to Savannah from here?" I asked, real excited.

"I'm not sure. But we about a day's journey south of Augusta here. I'd say Savannah is about one hundred miles away."

Mama looked concerned. "That's an awful long way. How we do that?"

"How far can your mule take us in a day?" I asked. "By the way, does your mule have a name?"

Uncle Sykes looked at us and grinned. "I call him Gus. Don't know where that came from. But I call him Gus. And I'd say Gus can go about twenty miles a day."

"We can work along the way. Mama, we could stop and ask folks if they need something picked. We can carry it where they need in the wagon. If they don't have money to pay us, we can work for food. What do you two think of that?"

"Sounds mighty good to me. When do you two want to go?" Uncle Sykes was laughing now. "We free. We can go when we want to go."

"I don't think I can stand another day of Thornton. I say we go tomorrow. Maybe Rebecca could slip Mama a few more potatoes."

"I'll go wherever you two say to go. It might be nice to ride along and see some more of the state. We've never been nowhere. I'd sure like to see Savannah," Mama said with a smile on her face.

"It's decided, then. We'll set off tomorrow. Mr. Graham can just pay us for one day's work with sweet potatoes."

Chapter 22

From Burke County to Savannah, Georgia

1866

Just like I thought, I woke up sore all over my body the next morning. But I was so thankful I didn't have to get back out in that field with Thornton glaring at me. All excited, Mama and I dressed quickly and headed to the big house. Uncle Sykes went to get the wagon and Gus ready to go.

"Mr. Graham, we sorry we can't stay here. But we got to go somewhere we can find jobs as seamstresses." I stood in front of him in the yard while Mama went in to see Rebecca.

"I understand. Field work is hard. I'm sorry there's no need for seamstresses here. My wife would have had work for you, I'm sure. She loved pretty clothes."

Bless Mr. Graham. He seemed to miss his wife. Looked sad. But in his heart, he was probably also glad he wouldn't have to pay us.

"Where you planning on going? Nothing much different around here."

"We goin' to Savannah. We figure it's 'bout a hundred miles away."

"That's a good idea. My son's there. I'll go write a note to him for you. He's in the construction business. He might be able to help Sykes get a job. Be right back."

Uncle Sykes pulled up the wagon with Mama's stuff already wrapped and packed. Soon after, Mama and Rebecca came out and quickly put a big bag in the wagon.

"I figure you need some food. I'd go with you if I didn't have kids in this area. Ain't much here for you." Rebecca dusted off her apron from baking a batch of biscuits.

"We thank you. Mighty nice of you."

"I figure Mr. Graham owes you for one day's work."

Mr. Graham came out the door with a letter. "Here, Sykes. This is a note to my son, Cyrus Graham. Address is on there, too. You go see him when you get to Savannah. He can steer you in the right direction."

"We don't know a soul there. We'll go see him right away. Thank you."

It did seem like Mr. Graham was trying to help us the only way he could.

"You get on that main road out there and stay on it. Goes more or less southeast right to Savannah. I've ridden it in a buggy before. Not bad. Good luck to you."

We climbed in the wagon and waved goodbye to those two nice folks. As we passed the fields we waved to Thornton, too. He wasn't the same kind of human as Graham and Rebecca. I smiled real big when we passed him, happy to make the escape. I said a little prayer for those poor souls out in that field, especially the woman carrying a baby in her belly.

It was a nice day in mid-May and didn't seem nearly as hot as yesterday. Of course, riding along in the wagon enjoying the scenery was different from chopping cotton. Mama was up on the seat by Sykes, and I was in the back of the wagon looking up at the blue sky, imagining what Savannah would be like. The movement of the wagon on the smooth road rocked me into a mellow state. Didn't take me long to fall asleep again. By the time I woke up, it was lunchtime. When we opened the bag from Rebecca, we couldn't believe it.

"I saw her put the potatoes and apples in the bag. But my goodness, looks like she had some leftover fried chicken from yesterday. She was also making a big batch of biscuits this morning. I'd say we lucky folks with all this food." Mama spread one of her quilts on the ground for us to sit on and eat.

We enjoyed eating quietly. Sykes had pulled over into a clump of trees for shade. Not a soul in sight. "I'd say we got this food now, but we got to be careful," Mama warned. "Got to make it last as long as we can. I don't see much of anything goin' on along this road. Don't know where we goin' get any more food."

"You right about that. Never seen such a quiet road. We ain't seen nobody today. Got to look out for creeks to get water, too. For us and Gus."

I thought it was so quiet it felt spooky.

We found a nice campsite that night by a little stream. Mama and I slept in the wagon with Sykes on the ground. "Did you ever dream we would be doing something like this?" Mama put her arm around me.

"No, I didn't. But I'm proud of us. Taking off into freedom. So far, so good. Say a prayer that it'll continue."

The next day was about the same. We saw a couple farmers in wagons who waved and rolled past us. Strange, but I still got a little afraid when I saw white folks. Got to remember we free.

On the third day, we were beginning to run low on food. "Keep your eyes out for berries on bushes or anything we can eat," Sykes hollered to me in the back of the wagon. Later that day, we did come on some wild blueberries. We picked as many as we could that looked ripe. Tasted fine. That afternoon we began to see rows and rows of big red strawberries.

"Never seen strawberries growing so big. I bet they mighty good." I looked around. No one in sight. "I figure we can pick a few." We jumped out of the wagon. Mama and I were loading our aprons when we heard gunshots. We fell on the ground, terrified. My heart was beating out of my chest. *Dear God, don't let us get shot.* I grabbed Mama's hand. She was shaking all over. "Stay calm, Mama. And pray."

Up rode a man, hollering for us to get out of his strawberries.

"Mister, we sorry," I said. "Meant no harm. Don't hurt us." We stood up with our arms in the air, strawberries falling all over.

"This is my farm. Private property. You're stealing. I can have you arrested for that." The man looked mad and meant what he was saying.

"We didn't mean to be stealing. We on our way to Savannah and just got hungry. We been picking wild blueberries and eating 'em."

"These berries aren't wild. Don't you see they been planted in rows? This is a strawberry farm. We harvest these berries and sell 'em in the market. You are stealing our livelihood."

"Sir, please don't report us. We weren't thinking. Just hungry. There's so many berries. Maybe you could spare a few."

"What do you mean? I can't just give them away. I'm having a hard enough time getting 'em picked before they rot. I got to get as many as I can to market so I can feed my family."

"We sure understand that. We all trying to feed ourselves. Looks like you have a lot of strawberries to pick. What do you think about hiring us to pick for you so you can get 'em before they go bad? We got a wagon here and can even take 'em to market for you. We honest folks and hard working." I was talking fast and hoping he would put his gun down.

The man sat there on his horse, thinking. I figured he must really need help if he was thinking to hire us. Before long, he lowered his gun and said, "When can you start?"

"How 'bout right now? We'll work hard for you."

"Follow me up to the house. I might be crazy, but I got to get these berries picked now. If I put you to work, don't let me down. I'll be watching you."

"We won't. Thank you, sir. Thank you." I was breathing a sigh of relief. I didn't look, but I knew Mama and Uncle Sykes were, too. *Thank you, God, for saving us this time.*

The man was named Jason Stanley, and his farm was called Stanley's Strawberry Farm. When we pulled up to his home, we saw several buildings and a barn out back.

"You can stay in this bunkhouse with the other workers who're coming in from picking now. You'll start first thing in the morning. All my slaves have left, and I'm desperate for help."

"We appreciate it. Looks fine to us."

"If you'll stay for a couple weeks to help get this harvest in, I'll pay you fair and square. Then you can take off for Savannah."

"We glad to do that for you."

"Get settled, then. My wife will send out a big pot of stew and cornbread in a few minutes."

"Yes, sir. Thanks again." Hallelujah. We had gone from fearing we'd be shot to having a nice, hot meal. God was good. It was a miracle.

Picking strawberries was a lot easier than chopping cotton. It wasn't quite as hot, and we usually got a nice breeze. Some of the folks would sing while they picked. All told, the days were not bad at all.

I don't think Mr. Stanley ever trusted us. He watched us with a close eye. But who could blame him? We made a bad first impression trying to steal from him.

"I appreciate that you stayed here a few weeks to get the strawberries in," Mr. Stanley said as he gave us our pay. "Eight dollars each for two weeks, and food and lodging. Not bad. And my wife is packing some food for the rest of your journey."

"That is good of her. She's served us good meals. Tell her how much we appreciate it."

"Not much between here and Savannah. Be careful of wild critters. Make fires at night to keep 'em away. They don't want to have anything to do with you except food."

Why did he have to say that? I worried all the way to Savannah. But thankfully, we didn't have any more excitement on our trip. We pulled into Savannah a few days later, anxious to see the beautiful city and joyful our journey was over.

Chapter 23

Savannah, Georgia

1866

Riding into Savannah for the first time was a magical experience. We had been riding in the hot sun and got there in the early afternoon. "I think we here, Mama. Hallelujah."

"Augusta got some big trees but nothing like these huge oaks with moss hanging from their long limbs. Ain't they pretty."

"Yes, beautiful. It's like they make a roof over us and everything gets cooler. Feels good. Look at all these fine houses. We got a few in Augusta, but not this many. We in another world now. We'll find work fo' sure."

Mama and I were awestruck. We loved Savannah instantly.

Uncle Sykes pulled up at a park where some folks were gathered. "Goin' straight to Mr. Cyrus Graham's business. Goin' to stop and ask for directions."

"Okay, we'll wait here." I took Mama's hand and squeezed it. "Mama, this city's going to be our home now. I have a good feelin'."

"There're still a few azaleas and dogwoods blooming. It's late but you can imagine what they like in full bloom. Sorry we missed 'em."

"You'll get to see 'em for many years. We here now, and we ain't goin' nowhere else."

Uncle Sykes stepped back in the wagon. "We got to go to the business part of town by the river. See some of the city. Won't take long."

After riding for a while, we came out to the wide Savannah River. "This here called River Street. Bumpy ride 'cause them old cobblestones." Uncle Sykes laughed. "Business somewhere near here."

We soon pulled up to Graham Construction. "I'll run in." He was back in no time. "Cyrus sure ain't as nice as Mr. Graham, but he did read the letter. He say they don't have nothing for me. Say I should check with the livery stable tomorrow. He handed me this newspaper. You got to read it, Amanda."

I took the newspaper, always grateful I could read. "This here is the *Daily News and Herald.* It's got a section of ads where people tell what they lookin' for. That's good. We can start checking these out."

"Thank goodness you can read. What we do if you can't?" Mama said.

"Don't know. Sure glad I can. Now let's think about where we goin' to put the wagon tonight and then start reading this paper."

We found a nice spot down by the river where we could get water for Gus. It was out of the way and quiet. Real nice place for our first night in Savannah. Mama was getting out our food and I started looking for folks needing seamstresses.

"Here's a Women's Dress Shop. They need help. Don't say what kind, but we'll see." I circled the ad. "And here's a list of folks needing cleaning help. I'll circle those, too. We don't want to do that but will if we have to. Here's one asking for help with sewing. Looks promising—Mrs. Bridges. Says she has living space. We'll definitely check that one out. Uncle Sykes, here's something about a livery stable. We can go there, too. Now let's eat and get started early tomorrow. I don't know 'bout y'all, but I say this is a pretty good first day in Savannah."

We were up early the next morning. "This sure is a busy city. Lots of folks goin' somewhere. Dressed pretty nice, too. Mama, that's good if they care 'bout their appearance and clothes, don't you think?"

Our first stop was the Women's Dress Shop. A woman with a stern face opened the door. "This is a respectable dress shop," she said. "We need sales ladies." Looked at us like we crazy for asking. She was snippy. I knew we didn't want to work there anyway.

Next, we stopped by the livery stable that was nearby. The man seemed impressed with Uncle Sykes's knowledge of horses and mules. Told him to come back tomorrow when the bossman was there. We were all excited 'bout that.

We had to keep asking directions how to get to places, but we soon became familiar with some of the streets. Truth was, we enjoyed riding around watching the folks and looking at the houses.

"Here's that house where they needed help with cleaning," I pointed out. "I'll go in."

I jumped out of the wagon and went to the front door of the big brick mansion. A woman in a uniform answered my knock. "I'm here about the ad in the newspaper. You need help with cleaning."

She looked at me real hard. "That position has been filled." She slammed the door.

I went back to the wagon. "Ain't nothing here. I hate to say it, but I'm getting a little discouraged. I won't stop, though."

We pulled up to one of those big houses that had one porch all the way around the downstairs and another all the way around the second floor. It was yellow with white porch railings. "I sure like this house. Wish me luck." I walked to the front door, thinking maybe I should have gone around to the back. I waited and then knocked again. Finally, the door opened, and a middle-aged lady with a cane answered.

"I'm here about the ad you put in the *Daily News and Herald.* My Mama and I are seamstresses. My Mama is great, and I'm getting better all the time."

"Come in. Yes, I'm looking for help."

She motioned me inside a beautiful, big foyer area, reminded me of the Clanton mansion. "Come into the parlor. Sit down. Tell me your name."

"I'm Amanda. My Mama and I also can clean for you. Mama can even cook some. I ain't much of a cook. Still learnin'."

"That sounds wonderful. My husband died during the war. We had one son who went to Princeton and stayed in New York after he graduated. This house has been in my husband's family for years. He loved it. I try to take care of it in his memory. I had some slaves to help with that before the war, but of course they're all gone now. I don't have anyone at the moment. I had an old woman who stayed on after the war, but she recently passed away. Bless her, she did the best she could. I try to do as much as I can for myself, but I have some medical issues. Having you and your mother would be a godsend to me."

"We be happy to help you any way we can. Your ad mentioned living space, too."

"Yes, I have a cottage out behind my house. It is small, but I think you and your mother could manage there. Would you like to see it? Where's your mother?"

"She outside. We in a wagon. We can pull around back. Thank you, ma'am." My heart was beating fast. I couldn't believe it. I was so excited when I ran to the wagon.

"Uncle Sykes, pull around the back of this house. This Mrs. Bridges wants us to see her little cottage. Mama, she wants to meet you, too. This could be what we lookin' for. Come on." I ran to the back.

That was the first time I saw that tiny cottage. It was yellow, too. Trimmed in white and nestled among some green bushes. It was pretty as a picture.

Mrs. Bridges came out the back door of her house and got there about the same time Mama and Uncle Sykes pulled up. I noticed she moved slow. Seemed to have a problem with one leg.

"Here is my Mama. Lurany is her name. She is the great seamstress I told you about. Can sew anything—jackets, coats, gorgeous women's dresses. I help her. And we both can help you in the house." I knew I was talking too fast but couldn't slow down.

"I'm pleased to meet you. And who is this man?" Mrs. Bridges held out her hand.

"This is Uncle Sykes. He lookin' for work too. Goin' to the livery stable tomorrow. Looks promising for him. I'm sure he could help you with animals and such too."

"I don't have any animals, but maybe some things in the yard occasionally. Let's go in the cottage now."

She took us up onto a little porch that already had two rocking chairs. Then she opened the door. "This room is a combination kitchen and living area. Back here is a little bedroom with two small beds. Would these work for you?"

I didn't hesitate. "Yes, ma'am. These rooms perfect. Don't you agree, Mama?"

"Yes, I do. They mighty nice."

"Well, in that case, you two are hired. I try to pay a good wage. I have a little money. Would twelve dollars a month be good for each of you? I'll allow you to take in sewing from other folks to help you earn more."

"Yes, that will be fine." I didn't even ask Mama. I knew she would be happy.

"If you want to start today, have Mr. Sykes unload your things. I am pleased you are here. Get settled, then come into the house and I'll show you around."

When Mrs. Bridges walked out the door, I grabbed Mama and squeezed her. Lifted her off the floor. We were both so happy we started to cry. Couldn't believe our good fortune. We had found our home in Savannah.

Uncle Sykes got work in that livery stable the next day and found boarding with some other menfolk.

Mama and I loved that little house. Kept it clean as a whistle. Real proud. Mrs. Bridges was nice, too. We learned folks called her Miss Mitsy. So that's what we called her, too. Most nights Mama and I'd lay in our beds and talk.

"Amanda, I know how hard it is out there in the world to find food and a place to work. Most of our folks not as lucky as us. I give thanks to God."

"Amen to that. Amen and thanks. We blessed."

Chapter 24

Savannah, Georgia

1866–1879

Mama and I got real busy. Miss Mitsy had a big, neglected house. There was dust everywhere, so cleaning took up most of our time in the beginning. Miss Mitsy had a lot of things to be dusted, fine things—little pieces of glass and porcelain. Artwork all over the walls. She would sit mostly and tell us about things, where she got 'em and who gave 'em to her. I think she really liked our company. She had been alone so much during the war and after.

When we got a little extra time, we put an ad in the *Daily News and Herald.* We said we could do alterations and repairs. Of course, we advertised that Mama could make coats and fancy dresses. Work started coming. We got so busy we didn't have time to do anything else much. Except we did start going to the First African Baptist Church on Sunday, which was mighty nice. Met some folks but mostly we cleaned and sewed.

Months then years passed by. We were content. We always did what Miss Mitsy needed first before we did other folks' work. Then we sat at Mama's little table and sewed. We started having a regular stream of customers coming in to get something made or repaired. After we been there about five years, something really important happened.

A man knocked on our cottage door late one afternoon. "Hello, anybody there?"

"Yes, we here. Come on in." I was sitting at the table and didn't look up. "You here to pick something up?"

"No, ma'am. I'm here to get my jacket repaired. I hear y'all do good work."

I looked up and there stood a tall, handsome man. He took his jacket off, and I saw strong muscular arms and a powerful chest. When he smiled, he was as good-lookin' a man as I had ever seen. My heart started pounding. All I could mutter was, "Let me see your jacket."

"This sure is a nice cottage. Bet you enjoy living here. Do you live alone?"

Why he asking me that, I wondered. "No, my mother lives here. We work together." I examined his jacket. "Sure, we can fix your sleeve here. We'll have to reweave the fabric some. How you tear it like this?"

"I work down at the docks on the river. Hard work. We load and unload ships coming in and going out. Big hook caught my sleeve and ripped it. I was mighty lucky it got my sleeve and not my arm."

"You sure were. That hook would've ripped up your arm bad. Now what's your name?"

"Joseph Peterson's my name. I can sign my name but that's about all. Not a good reader."

"I can help you with that, too."

"You don't mean it. That's nice. Where you learn to read?"

I told him about Trudy teaching me. Then I told him about how Mama and I had gotten to Savannah. We had been talking for quite a while when Mama came in from Miss Mitsy's.

"Pleased to meet you, Miss Lurany," Joseph said when I introduced them. "Me and Amanda been having the nicest conversation. Didn't realize it was getting to be so late. Better get going. When should I pick up my jacket?"

"I'd say three days. We'll fix it like new." Mama smiled.

"See you ladies in three days. Might bring my fiddle. I'll come late afternoon after work. I'd like to sit out on that porch and play for you."

As soon as he was out the door, Mama looked at me. "He was a nice young man. I think he might be smitten with you. You need to get out more. You hang around here too much with me."

"Mama, what you talkin' about. I'm getting up there in years. In my thirties already. I'm happy here working with you. Don't need to meet no man."

"You do, too."

"He'll pick up his jacket and we'll never see him again. That'll be fine with me."

But that didn't happen. He brought his fiddle and played one evening, just like he said. It was beautiful. Then he started coming regularly. I couldn't believe it, but I could tell he liked me.

"Amanda, let's go walk on the river tomorrow night. The sunsets are so pretty. You'll love 'em. But tonight, I want you to keep teaching me to read. Now I can read some stuff in the newspaper. Feeling smarter every day." He let out a big, joyful laugh. "You good for me, Amanda. Want to marry me?"

I laughed. Thought he was kidding. "You so funny."

"No, I'm serious as I can be."

"I'm in my thirties. All those young girls like you. Why you interested in me?"

"'Cause I enjoy being with you. We have great conversations. You smart, teaching me to read. I think you're beautiful. You make my heart pound. I think those things will tell you." He put his arms around me and kissed me. "Now, how you feel 'bout me?"

"I feel the same way. I might even love you," I admitted.

"I love you, too. When you want to get married?"

"I'd say the sooner the better. Time's a-wasting. I ain't getting any younger."

True to our word, we decided to get married in one month. We gave ourselves just long enough to find a place for the party after the ceremony at the church and, of course, for Mama to make me a wedding dress. I knew she would create something beautiful for me.

When the day finally arrived, I couldn't help myself. I stood and admired my reflection in the mirror. I couldn't believe it was me. I looked prettier than I had ever looked.

"This is the most gorgeous dress. Mama, did you ever dream you'd make me a wedding dress? This fabric is so fine and all this lace so delicate. Can't believe it."

"I did dream 'bout it sometimes. But I never thought your wedding would be in Savannah, here in this great old church."

"Well, it's true. Let's go enjoy it."

Mama walked me down the aisle. We had music in the church by a spirited choir and a glorious soloist, sounded like an angel. Then one of Joseph's friends played a melody on a guitar, so sweet it made you cry.

I'll never forget the party afterwards that Joseph had arranged at some hall. He had all his music friends playing fiddles and horns. Folks danced and celebrated with us. It was the most fun I had ever had in my life. The dancing went on into the early morning hours. Afterward, Joseph and I spent our first night of married life in a romantic little room down by the river. I never dreamed I could be so happy.

ல

"Miss Mitsy, come look at the new room on the back of the cottage." I took her hand and helped her down the stairs of her porch. "You gonna like it. I sure do."

Miss Mitsy had hired a carpenter to add another bedroom for us. Joseph had helped him, and Uncles Sykes had delivered lumber. It was a joint effort that turned out great.

"I didn't want you to leave your Mama alone," Miss Mitsy said, clinging to my hand. "Also, I thought it would be nice to have a man around the house for heavy-duty stuff. Joseph is a good man, and I enjoy his fiddle playing."

"We mighty happy you feel that way."

I led her through the main room of the cottage and out a back door to a little stoop below the new bedroom door. "I love the way the carpenter attached the room to the house but gave it a private entrance. We never far away."

"I'm glad we had enough land back here in front of the alley. Now I won't think of it as a tiny cottage anymore. It's a good size now."

"We love it. Room for a bed big enough for two and a chest of drawers. Cozy. Never dreamed of a better room."

"My dear, I'm glad you like it."

Joseph and I spent a lot of time in that room talking, laughing, and snuggling—stuff married folks do. Before I knew it, I got the surprise of my life.

One evening when Joseph came in from work, I got him and Mama together. "I got something to tell you. I'm expecting a baby. I'm already three months along. Can you believe it? I'm thirty-nine years old. I didn't know if I could have a baby. But I can."

Joseph picked me up and swirled me around the room. Mama started crying, saying, "Thank you, Jesus. Thank you, Jesus. It's a miracle."

Six months later our baby was born. And a cuter, happier, more agreeable baby boy never came into this world. We were all elated. Named him Thomas after Joseph's father who had died. Joseph was so proud. I loved seeing that big man cradle his tiny baby, so gentle-like. He was a wonderful daddy. Of course, Mama was proud too. Started sewing up a storm for our little fella, making cute outfits. All I could do was watch and tear up. They were both so sweet. Talk about blessings. God was smiling on us for sure.

The years flew by. We stayed busy and watched as Thomas got bigger and bigger. He started talking early. First calling me "Mama Mae." He must have heard the M sound in Amanda. But I liked it. I soon became Mae to everyone. Figured Mae was my new free name and Amanda was my old slave name. But Mama said I always be Amanda to her.

Soon enough, our boy was asking questions about everything. "How birds fly?" "Why it get dark at night?" We could tell he was smart. When he was four, I started teaching him to read. He caught on real fast.

"Joseph, Thomas so smart. I want him to be educated. How I gonna do that? No good schools for black kids."

"You doin' a good job teachin' him. And I think there's some little church schools."

"I ain't educated enough to teach him all he needs to know."

"Keep doin' what you doin'. Knowin' you, something good will happen." Joseph gave me a hug.

I taught Thomas regular in his early years, and he did go to some church schools that were not the best. But then, low and behold, the first public school for black kids opened in Savannah. I determined to get him in. Thomas took tests, and they talked to him; you name it, we did it. Miss Mitsy got into it, too. Praise the Lord, Thomas got in that school. It was in a beautiful old building downtown—Scarborough House. Mama made Thomas shirts and a jacket that were as nice as anybody had. He looked so handsome when he went off to school. He loved it, too. He did great there. One of the best students.

But that's when I started worrying big-time about his safety. Thomas was too smart and too good-lookin'. And he had a way about him. He would talk to anybody. Ask questions. Saw a lot things wasn't right in the world. Lord, I knew he was gonna get in trouble.

"Thomas, you got to be careful. There's lots of folks making trouble these days. Violence out there. We live in this cocoon, away from the world. Me and your grandma just always stay here and sew. I worry about your Daddy, too. You and Joseph got to watch out. There's the KKK, what they call it? They lookin' for men like you and your Daddy."

"Mama Mae, this world's not fair. Folks shouldn't treat us wrong. We free and equal just like them."

"I know it ain't right, but that's just how it is. Promise me that you be careful. That's all I'm askin'."

"Okay, I'll be careful."

But I didn't feel no better. Started worrying all the time about what could happen to Thomas and Joseph.

Chapter 25

Savannah and Philadelphia

1890

It was a gorgeous spring evening. Miss Mitsy's huge pink azaleas were blooming. Mama went to bed early, and Thomas left to visit his friends. Joseph was playing his fiddle at a party for some white folks down on Monterey Square. He said it was at Jerold McGee's house. I only knew the man as an officer at the bank downtown. I had finished cleaning the dishes and sat out on the porch for a few minutes to relax, thinking how blessed I was to have found Joseph and given birth to Thomas. With Joseph working down on the docks and playing his fiddle for parties at night, along with Mama and me sewing, our life was comfortable. I felt peaceful listening to the night sounds of tree frogs and cicadas. For once, I wasn't worried about Joseph or Thomas. I had no idea hell was about to break loose.

I went inside and sat by the old oil lamp Mama and I always used at night and picked up some handwork I needed to finish on a dress for Miss Mitsy. Suddenly, I heard loud footsteps on the porch and the door flew open. Joseph came storming into the house. "Mae, get some biscuits and ham. Throw 'em in a bag. I got to get out of town right now," he said as he opened the closet and started cramming another shirt and pants in a canvas bag.

"What happened, Joseph? My God, you're scaring me!"

"I'm scared, too. This good-looking blonde lady—you know that Sadie McGee, wife of the banker downtown? Party was at their house. She was tipsy, drinking way too much. She kept hanging around me while I'm playing my fiddle, grinning and swaying to the music. I was afraid she was about to pass out. When I took a break to have a smoke and sip of whiskey out behind their house, here she came. Leaning sideways, giggling, and saying, 'Give me a sip, too.' I said, 'No, Miss Sadie, you can't be here with me. Go back inside.' She keeps reaching, I'm thinking she's about to fall, I grab her arm, and 'bout that minute here comes her husband, Mr. Jerold McGee, screaming, 'What you doing out here, Sadie? Get back in the house.' Then he points at me, accusing me of fooling around with her. Now I know I got to get out of there immediately. As he's dragging her off, I grab my fiddle and start running as fast as I can."

Joseph paused and looked around the room. "Give me some of the money in the kitchen jar. You keep half."

I emptied the jar on the table and said, "Where you goin'?"

"To the river. Big ship loaded to take off for Philadelphia at 2:00 a.m. I helped load it today. Got to get on it. Stow away."

"How will I know you made it?" I poked the money in a little pouch, trying to calm my racing nerves.

"After a while, I'll write you and sign it, say…Aunt Peggy. I'll invite you to a family reunion. You can visit. Got to go. Love you," he said as he gave her a kiss. "Tell Thomas his Daddy loves him, too." With that, Joseph tore out the back door and ran up the alley.

I knew as soon as Mr. McGee found out where we lived, he'd be here. My hands shook so bad. I prayed, "Dear God, let Joseph get to that boat." I was saying to myself *breathe, calm down*. I sat there with my eyes closed for a few minutes, and then there's a pounding on the door. I took a deep breath and slowly walked to the door. "Why, Mr. McGee, how you? What you doin' here tonight?"

"Where's that sorry-ass husband of yours? He was fooling with my Sadie tonight. You know we don't allow that from no nigger."

I looked him in the eye. "Mr. McGee, my husband don't do that with no white woman. You must have the wrong man." My hands shook so bad that I wrapped the dress I was mending around them. I saw there were several men with him. One had a big, heavy rope. *Oh, dear God, they goin' to try to lynch him. I got to think fast.*

Calmly, I said, "My Joseph has not returned home. He still playin' at that party."

"No, he left. It was at my house. I assumed he came home."

"No, he ain't been here. Now I'm gettin' upset, too. That rascal, he hasn't come home."

It wasn't hard for me to look agitated. Then I acted like something had dawned on me. "I bet I know where he went. He's probably at that juke joint down on the river where they play music, dance, and drink whiskey all night. You tell him his wife is mad at him, too. The nerve of him. Tell him to get home. I goin' to give him hell when he gets here."

At that, Mr. McGee and his posse charged out of the house and immediately started running in the opposite direction from the way Joseph went. I breathed a sigh of relief, thinking I had thrown them off and given Joseph time to escape. At least that's what I hoped. But I didn't sleep a wink. I prayed all night long that Joseph would make it out of town. I guess my prayers were answered because he got away. I didn't hear a word for a month, and then I got a letter from Aunt Peggy.

Mae and Thomas,
Hello. Hope you fine. I am.
Come to family reunion in Philly. It on July 4th Freedom Day. Bring Miss Lurany too if can.

Love to all,
Aunt Peggy

I cried and cried, so relieved to know Joseph was safe.

Thomas and I would not miss that reunion with Aunt Peggy. Mama didn't feel up to it, though. We took the train. It was the first trip for both Thomas and me. What an adventure. Thomas kept his eyes on the window the whole way. Fascinated by everything he saw, asking one question after another.

Joesph met us at the station. "You growed even since I left. You gonna be taller 'an me soon." He gave Thomas a bear hug and lifted him off the ground. "Not goin' to be able to do that much longer." Then he turned to me. "Mae, how in the world you get prettier every day?" He gave me a big hug and kiss and picked me up, too. "You gonna love this city. And you here the best day of the year. It's the Fourth of July. Picnics, parades, fireworks, all celebrating our freedom. That's just right for us, I figure."

"Joseph, you look mighty good yourself. We so happy to be here, too. Can't wait to see everything."

"Come on to a picnic I got planned. I want you to meet lots of nice folks. I been to this church—a Quaker church. People so helpful. They worked to help free us before the war. You gonna love 'em."

We met some of his friends, and they were as nice as he said. Mr. and Mrs. Elijah Jenkins, an older Quaker couple, had done so much to help him find a good place to live. They made sure he had a similar job at the docks in Philly. Things had worked out so well.

Joseph entertained us with his story. "I got to tell you all how I stowed away that night. I had been loadin' cotton bales all day in the ship I knew was headed to this city. We stack 'em right up against the wall. But I know this one in the corner has a space behind it. I figuring as I'm runnin' where I'm goin' when I get there. It's not long before it's about to leave. Mostly cargo but a few passengers gettin' on. I picked up a bag belonging to one of 'em, said I'd be happy to put it on deck. I walked up ramp like I was supposed to be there. No one said a word. Then I went to where those bales were. I squeezed in behind 'em, so relieved. Wasn't long before I was sound asleep."

"That was a miracle. My friend, God was watching over you." Mr. Jenkins patted Joseph on the shoulder.

"Yes, I thank God every day that you made it to freedom," I said, "but we miss you." Tears began to roll down my cheeks. "Yes, we miss you, and it's so good to be with you now."

The next day, we went to see all the sights—the Liberty Bell, Independence Hall, and the business district downtown. Thomas loved everything about Philadelphia. "Look at all these folks walking around. Black folks all dressed up. Don't see this much in Savannah," he said. "I believe there's more freedom in Philadelphia. Mama, maybe we need to come here like Daddy."

"We can't leave your grandma. But we can come to visit. I really like it here, too."

Our time with Joseph flew by. When we got home, all Thomas could talk about was going back. But we had to get back to our lives in Savannah.

"Mama, did you have any problems while we were away? I know your arthritis bothers you a lot. You so bent over. Do you hurt much?"

"Child, I fine. I was just happy sitting here sewing, knowing you and Thomas having so much fun. I don't have much energy. Probably heart slowing after all these years, but I can still sew, thank the Lord."

"Mama, you still strong in spirit, but always tell me the truth. Do you need anything? I worry when we away."

"Don't you worry about me. Now tell me about Thomas. I know you worry about him all the time now."

"He's seventeen and handsome just like his daddy. With that great smile, all the girls—black and white—love him. Thomas not shy either. Outspoken and opinionated. Guess he takes after me too much. Today I saw for myself what's happening. Thomas was trimming a hedge for the family next door. A pretty white girl visiting from somewhere up north. I heard the conversation. 'Thomas, you sure are strong. How did you get those big muscles?' She grinning at Thomas. Of course, he's likes what she's saying. 'Just runs in the family. My daddy's got muscles, too.'

"I started worrying when I see this white guy coming up. 'This fella bothering you, Mary Jane,' he says. 'He should know his place.' *Oh no,* I say to myself. *Don't you answer him, Thomas.* But Thomas can't keep his mouth shut. 'What do you mean know my place? I live in this neighborhood. Doing an honest day's work.'

"The man says, 'You think you so smart. You go to that fancy school for black folks downtown.' I see Thomas making a fist. I know he about to lunge at that white guy. 'Thomas, come here right now,' I holler out. 'I need you. It's important.'

I yelled at the top of my lungs. 'Get over here this instant.' I wanted to stop whatever was about to happen.

"All three of them looked at me. There was tension. But thank heaven, Thomas came. I knew at that moment I'm gonna have to take Thomas back to Philadelphia. If I don't, something bad will happen. The Ku Klux Klan is out looking for an excuse to go after a kid like Thomas. And folks are clamping down on us with Jim Crow laws. Mama, I've decided to go back to Philadelphia and leave Thomas with his daddy. I want him to have a great education, too. He is so smart. It's really hard. It breaks my heart."

"I know it's awful," Mama said. "But I agree. You got to let him go to save him."

"It wasn't long ago we thought we had everything here. I had a husband and a beautiful son. You had a grandson you never thought you'd have. Miss Mitsy been good to us with this house. Now look at us. It's fallin' apart." I began to sob. Never felt so sad in my life. But I knew what I had to do.

∽

Thomas was excited when I told him we were going back to Philadelphia. He was ecstatic when I told him he could stay.

"Mama, I can't believe I'm goin' to school there. That'll be great. Only bad thing is you're not goin' to stay."

"You know I can't stay because of Mama. I'll visit. But you'll be so busy in no time. You won't miss me." Sweet child hugged me. I knew he was overjoyed.

"Now let's get your clothes packed. Go tell your friends goodbye. Tell 'em you're goin' north to Philly. They'll be excited, too."

I told him to skedaddle so he wouldn't see the tears in my eyes. I had to stay strong.

❧

I went on the trip with Thomas. He probably could have gone by himself, but I wanted that time with him. We laughed and talked, enjoying every minute, looking at the cities glide by. All the time, I was drinking in this beautiful child God had blessed me with. I had to keep reminding myself I'd see him again, but he'd be different. Not this naïve, happy young man.

When we got there, Joseph pleaded with me. "Mae, I want you to stay here with us. I love you. We need you, especially Thomas. I know you like it up here, too."

"I love it here. And you know I love you and Thomas. I'm so pleased Mr. and Mrs. Jenkins are interested in Thomas and want to help with him. But Mama is not well. Don't know how old she is. Maybe late seventies or early eighties. I can't leave her. Her heart's bad, and she has terrible arthritis, stiff. Don't really know all that's wrong with her. She never complains. But she can't manage alone. Mama and I'll both be happy knowing Thomas is in a good school. We won't have to worry about something horrible happening to one of you. Then later, I can come up here."

Chapter 26

Savannah

1891

About a year after I took Thomas north, I came in from delivering a dress to a customer. Mama was sitting bent over her sewing.

"Amanda, you know all I ever wanted was to be with you and sew pretty things. Never dreamed I'd be free, too—and have a beautiful grandson. I know we don't get to see him, but he's safe. Knowing that calms my heart. Thank you, Jesus."

I went over and knelt next to her. "Why don't you come and go to Philadelphia with me? Thomas would love to see you, and so would Joseph."

"Child, you know this old woman too old to travel. I have enough trouble getting around this house. But I don't mind if you go."

"We'll talk about it some more, Mama. I believe you could go. I'd like you to have a ride on the train. Great adventure for you."

"It would be. But no. I believe my days are numbered."

"Don't talk about that. You still spry—sewing all the time. We'll keep thinkin' on it."

"I know you love me, but remember, child, I'm a blessed woman. I'm free, and I ain't ever been separated from you. We get to sit and sew together in this nice house. Yes, I have everything I ever wanted. I'm happy."

"I'm glad you feel that way. You tired now. Come on, I'll help you to your bed." I took Mama by the arm. She was so thin and fragile. "I'm goin' to tuck you in." She sat on the side of the bed. "Let me fluff your pillow. There now. Lay back. I'm goin' to tuck this extra blanket around you. How's that? I'm tuckin' you in like a baby."

Mama smiled. "That's perfect. Feels so good."

I gave her a hug and a kiss. "I love you. You sleep tight. See you in the morning."

Mama died that night, at peace with the world. I couldn't believe it. She went to sleep smiling at me, and the next morning she was gone. I cried and cried, felt so alone. But I kept remembering Mama saying she was happy. She had everything she ever wanted. She knew she was loved, and she was a blessing to us all. I guess you can't die any better than that.

I arranged for a nice service at the First African Baptist Church, the oldest black church in America. Mama and I went every week for years and made a lot of friends. It was a beautiful church, and folks sent lots of pretty flowers.

"Miss Mitsy, it's nice you're here with me crying, too," I said as she patted my arm in the church pew.

"I loved your Mama. We spent a lot of time together. She was a good woman. Helped me in so many ways. More than just cleaning and sewing, I mean cheering me when I was down."

"Mama would be amazed at the crowd today—members of the church, almost everyone we did sewing for, and quite a few white folks, too."

"She had more friends than we knew about, I guess."

"She always loved Savannah from the moment she saw it, and I'm happy she'll be buried in the cemetery here."

After the service, I visited with all the well-wishers at the burial.

"Thank you, Mrs. Stovall, for sending those flowers."

"Miss Jamison, Mama loved sewing for you. Glad you like all she made."

"Mr. Brown, yes, Mama could make a fine man's jacket."

"Thank you for coming, Mrs. Tanner. Thanks for the note."

Finally, I clasped the last hand and said goodbye and thanked them all.

When it was over, I felt exhausted. With Joseph and Thomas so far away, and now with Mama gone, I got depressed. I didn't want to go back to the house. I decided to sit on a bench outside the cemetery. I had gotten a letter from Thomas. I had put it in my pocket, and now I got it out and read it again.

Mama Mae,
I'm so sorry I can't make it back for the funeral. I loved Grandma Lurany so much. I think she would be proud that I have gotten into Howard University. Mr. and Mrs. Jenkins knew about this Quaker scholarship. I applied and got it. Isn't that great. I might go to medical school. I have also met this wonderful girl. You'd like her. She is strong like you. She plans to go to nursing school. We will make a good couple.
I know you know my daddy is not in good health. Not sure what is wrong. Might be his heart. He has a new woman who takes care of him. You know how the women have always liked him. But I'm sure you are still first.
Again, I am so sorry about Grandma. I loved her so much. And I love you so much. Take good care of yourself and stay in touch. Now you can come see me in Washington.

Your loving son,
Thomas

I folded the letter and put it back in my pocket. I was sitting there lost in thought when a friend of Joseph's walked up. We called him Big Jim because of his height and build—a muscular six feet, five inches tall. But he was a gentle giant. I was happy to see him.

"Mae, I'm so sorry for your loss. Ain't goin' to be the same without seeing Miss Lurany's face. She was a mighty sweet, fine woman."

"Yes, she was. I'm proud she was my mama. Thank you for comin'. I'm goin' to miss her so much. Thomas and Joseph, too. Somehow, I'm feeling like I want to do something new—something that might help me get over this sadness."

"Well, let's you and me sit on this bench and talk a spell. Want to?"

"I'd like that. I'm so tired. Haven't taken a breath since Mama died."

"You a smart woman. Got lots goin' for you. You'll come up with an idea, I'm sure."

"I'll keep thinkin'. What you doin' these days, Jim?"

"I got this transport business. I take a caravan of wagons from Savannah to Atlanta about once a month or so. You know railroads don't go through all the little towns. I carry shipments of equipment, produce, furniture—whatever folks want to send to Atlanta. Atlanta is a busy, growing town. I like it. Maybe you should go there."

"Don't know anybody there. But I don't want to go to Philadelphia. Thomas has grown up now and is going to Howard University in Washington. I'm so happy for him. Joseph has taken up with another woman. I don't blame him. I stayed down here with Mama, and Joseph needed someone to take care of him. You know men and their needs. Thomas has told me that Joseph is not in good health either."

"I'm sorry to hear that. But you keep thinking about Atlanta. I'll introduce you around. I know lots of good folks up there. Good opportunities for business. With your sewing ability and hard work habits, you could start something for sure."

"I don't know. Sounds exciting. But how would I get there with my furniture? Wouldn't be easy and probably expensive, too."

"Tell you what. You could come with my caravan. We usually have three or four wagons with drivers. You could help with the cooking. Traveling through that back country, us black folks have a hard time finding food."

"Must be frightening. Not an easy trip."

"No, it ain't. We try to travel twenty miles a day. Takes us twelve days or so. My drivers are all black men. But we have an armed guard that goes with us to fight off thieves and wild animals—not to mention the Klan. Our guard is a white man. That helps." Jim laughed. "Folks think he's guarding us instead of the shipment. But it works. You think about it. It would be an adventure."

"I don't know, but yes, I'll think about it. I appreciate the thought. And thanks for coming to Mama's service."

In the following days, I grew more and more depressed. This cottage that had been such a happy place was now so sad to me. Everywhere I turned, I saw Mama sitting at her table, Joseph playing his fiddle, and Thomas bouncing around as a little boy. Memories haunted me. The violence and hatred in our world robbed us of our peaceful family life. How could I have thought our joy could last? Now what was I goin' to do? Maybe gettin' away from here would help me. I had some money Mama and I had saved. I decided I would go to Atlanta.

The next day, I changed my mind. I didn't know a soul in Atlanta. Why would I think I could start a business by myself? I needed to play it safe. I told myself I would grow out of this depression. I would not go. I was sure.

Then I changed my mind again. This kept happening. Was I going crazy? I tried to work, but my heart wasn't in it. I was turning customers down. Something had to give.

One day Big Jim stopped by to visit. "Thought I'd see if you were thinking anymore about goin' to Atlanta."

"I think about it all the time. One day I decide to go, and the next day I decide to stay. I feel like I'm losing my mind. Some nights I dream about a man standing on this porch with a rope wanting to lynch Joseph. Back to the most frightening night of my life."

"You are not goin' crazy. You're just grieving the loss of what you had. It's sad. I'm still grieving my wife's death. It takes time and prayer. And there is a lot of evil in the world."

"You're right about the grief and the evil. Can't cure 'em overnight, I guess."

"I have an idea. Talk to Miss Mitsy. Ask her to give you some time. Go to Atlanta and see if you like it. If it doesn't work out, come back. How about that?"

"I hadn't thought of that. She would probably be all right with it. We've been here so long. I'll ask her. If she says it's okay, I'll go. I'm tired of indecision."

"Great. Let me know. We leave in a couple weeks."

"Miss Mitsy, we always loved living in that little house. It became a real home to us. I'll miss it."

"I'll miss you all, too, Mae. You and your mama did so

much for me. I still think of Joseph playing his fiddle when Thomas was a baby, trying to get him to sleep. I'd sit on the porch and listen to those old ballads. But I do wish you good luck with your new adventure. Have safe travels," Miss Mitsy said as she gave me a hug. "Keep in touch. If it doesn't work, come back here."

"I'll write and let you know we got there safe."

We drove away in Big Jim's caravan with all my earthly belongings—beds, chairs, dishes, boxes of clothes, linens, and my canvas bag with money in it. Best of all were the wonderful old table, two chairs, and oil lamp that Mama always treasured.

Chapter 27

Savannah and Atlanta

1892

We left in the spring. It was late March, not too cool or too hot. Pleasant weather.

"I sure am glad I decided to make this trip," I said to Jim as we made our way. "It's so exciting. Riding up here on this seat with you, watching these pretty houses glide by. I've always loved the Spanish moss hanging from the big oaks. Don't you?"

"Sure. I think it's pretty, too. But don't ever get it on you. Can have red bugs in it. Makes you itch."

I laughed. "Never thought of that. Thankfully, never had any on me." I found out right away that Jim had a wonderful sense of humor. I didn't know then how important that would be on our trip.

In no time, we were out of Savannah and in a vast, flat land with nothing to see except scrubby trees. "Don't see nothing hardly," I remarked, my eyes hungry for any other sight. "Not many towns around here."

"That's right. Try to get comfortable. Be a while before we stop."

"How am I supposed to get comfortable on this hard old seat? I know I got some natural padding, but it ain't enough."

Jim laughed. "I think what you got is just right."

Is he sweet on me, I wondered. *Well, he's sure goin' to see me as my natural ornery self. This is goin' to be harder than I thought it would be.*

Finally, after several hours, Jim hollered, "Hold up, guys.

We gonna pull in here and stretch our legs. There's a creek over there where we can get water for the mules. Get plenty of water cause we're not goin' to stop again for about five hours."

I thought to myself, *Only five more hours on just the first day. I'll never make it to Atlanta.* Finally, after a twelve-hour day, Jim gave the word for us to stop for the night.

"Hallelujah, we stoppin'. I don't know about you guys, but I'm hungry." We had four drivers—Toby, Carl, Jason, and Bill. Our white guard was Stewart.

The guys started gathering wood for a campfire while I got out the food. "I have some beef stew here in these big jars. Also got some cornbread wrapped in this cloth. Sound good?"

"Yes, ma'am, it sure does," Toby said. "I've made this trip with Jim several times, and we mostly live on dried meat. I hate that sorry stuff. Mighty glad you on this trip."

"Well, I aim to please. I'm not much of a cook, but this is my Mama's stew recipe and it's pretty good."

The men devoured it. One thing they all had in common was a ravenous appetite.

"Thank you, Miss Mae. That was delicious. We so glad you on this trip." All the men said thanks over and over. I was beginning to like them. And I was thinking they liked me. At least, they liked the food I brought.

Carl got out his harmonica and started to play some fun songs. The men laughed and sang, and I joined in. It was a good ending to our first day.

The other days of riding were much the same. Not many communities or folks along the way. Riding on that hard seat was tough. I finally figured out I could fold an old blanket and sit on it. That helped some.

The men loosened up at night. They always built a fire, and I got out whatever I had for dinner—more stew or biscuits with cured ham. Some nights I'd have nice peaches and tomatoes. Whatever I presented, they were always thankful.

Come to find out Big Jim had a great singing voice. He loved the old hymns.

"Sing 'Swing Low, Sweet Chariot.' I love the way you do that." Carl didn't have to ask more than once. Jim belted it out in a great bass voice.

"How about 'Go Down Moses'?" Jim was into the Spirit.

"Now let's do 'Kumbaya.' Everybody join in." Jason was our song leader, singing at the top of his voice. We were all having a time. These evenings were great.

After our singing, we would get out our blankets and sleep around the fire. I'd put my canvas bag under my head for a pillow. But I had a hard time sleeping on the ground. It wasn't comfortable, and there were the night sounds—screeching, chirping, and rustling in the bushes.

"Do you see those eyes peering into the fire from over there?" I pointed to some bushes.

"Miss Mae, there's just raccoons, wild boars, deer, and bobcats. They not gonna bother us," Bill said.

"I'm not so sure. All of them frighten me except the deer."

"Don't worry, Miss Mae," Toby added. "We take turns watching at night. Nothing goin' bother us."

That helped until one night when we had a scare.

"Do y'all hear that?" I realized everyone was listening.

"That yapping and howling don't sound good," Jason said. "Get your rifle, Stewart. Sounds like trouble."

"Oh no, what's that?" I cried.

"Don't know. Might be a wounded or sick animal. He

probably hungry."

"Sounds like it gettin' closer." I was shaking like a leaf.

"Yep, I think so."

It was dark. I didn't know how they could see anything.

"Could be rabies. Dangerous," Jim said. "Mae, you get over by the wagon. Men, make a circle around the wagon." I didn't know how that was goin' to help. All the men had was sticks. Stewart was the one with a gun.

At about that minute, Stewart said, "I see him over there. I'll be right back."

"Be careful," Jim said.

I held my breath, thinking Stewart must have better eyes than me. I couldn't see nothing out there. 'Bout that minute we heard a shot.

Stewart came walking back into the circle. "I got him. I think it was rabies. Bobcat. He was dangerous but no more. Relax, everybody."

That was easier said than done. My heart kept pounding all night. I laid awake, waiting to see if there was anything else out there to hurt us.

The next few nights went along fine without incident. One of the men said singing helped keep the animals away. So I sang as loud as I could. Lord knew I didn't want any more animals with rabies coming around.

But that wasn't my biggest scare. One day I was so happy we were finally stopping that I jumped off the wagon. "Guys, let me help you gather some firewood. I need to move, stiff from that hard seat. So good to finally stop."

My big old boots Jim told me to wear hit the ground hard. I went running, feeling good. "I'll get these limbs off this old tree stump." I leaned over, picked 'em up, and heard a rattling sound. I let out a deadly scream and started runnin' toward Jim. "Snake. Huge snake!"

"Calm down. Where you see a snake?"

I fell into Jim's arms tremblin'. "Over there curled up in that old tree stump. Big and making that rattling sound."

Jim picked up the shotgun, walked over and shot that diamondback rattlesnake, and held it up. "Y'all look at this rattler. It's six feet long. Biggest I've ever seen."

"Biggest I've ever seen, too," Carl said, fascinated by the design of its skin. "Look at those huge fangs."

All the men gathered round, looking at that snake. "Come see this big snake, Mae."

"I don't want nothin' to do with that snake. Give me nightmares. Don't want to see it." I couldn't quit shaking that night. Never been so scared. I always hated snakes. From that day forward, I was so careful, always on the lookout for snakes.

We had rain a few days but no bad showers. We had some big tarps we could fashion into primitive tents with sticks. Thank goodness we didn't need 'em much, 'cause they didn't work too well. We would catch any water we could for sponging off and drinking.

After stopping in little communities along the way, we finally made it to Macon. Jim turned onto a little dirt road. "I have some good friends here. They own a farm. Always invite us to a meal and a night on real beds."

"That's music to my ears. Nothing ever sounded so good to me."

We pulled around to their barn and out came this couple, Jerimiah and Ruth Jones. They were the nicest folks.

"Meet my friend, Mae Peterson. She been helping us with food on this trip."

"Please to meet you. I was planning on frying some

chicken. You better kill another chicken, Jerimiah. We got lots of company tonight." Ruth motioned for me to come in and wash up.

Later, with a full belly, I said, "That was the best meal I think I've ever had. Fried chicken, biscuits, and all those fresh vegetables—peas, corn, and tomatoes. Delicious. I figure you two a gift from God. With your Bible names—Jerimiah and Ruth—I'm sure of it." I kept saying how much I appreciated that meal.

"I agree," Jason said. "Now we gonna sing for our supper. Y'all know what a voice Jim has."

After apple pie, Jim sang his favorite songs, and we had a blessed time. Then I slept on a real bed with nice clean sheets and a soft mattress. I knew for sure I was in heaven.

When we left the next morning, I gave Ruth a hug. "You a true angel. I slept like a baby. Never appreciated a soft bed more in my life. Now you sendin' us off with leftover fried chicken and biscuits. I believe I'll be able to make it to Atlanta."

After we left Macon, there was more hilly terrain that slowed us down some. But somehow it got easier. I enjoyed talking to Jim. "Tell me more about your wife that died."

"She was a good woman. Rose was her name. Loved to sing the same way I do. And play the piano. You should have heard her. We laughed a lot, had fun. Only twenty-nine when she died. Childbirth was hard for her. She gave birth to our first baby, a girl named Jean, and didn't have much trouble. But the birth of our second, a boy called Ozzie, killed her. I been grieving since. If it hadn't been for my Mama helping me raise 'em, I don't know what I would have done."

"I guess we never stop grieving our losses. Mama's death nearly killed me, too. But losing Thomas and Joseph has been a loss of a different kind. The life we had in Savannah was a dream that vanished. Seems like everything important in my life is gone."

"The grief never goes away, but it gets bearable. I think that's the way I'd say it."

"I hope so. I will say this trip has been a help to me. Everything so new and different. The challenges—the rabid bobcat and rattlesnake—somehow helped. I don't know why."

"'Cause you survived 'em. Goin' on with your life. That's what we do. There's good stuff in your future. I can just feel it."

"I love hearing you say that. One good thing that has come from this trip is our friendship. Can't tell you how much it means to me."

"I can say the same. You the first woman since my wife died that I have really talked to. I love to talk to you. But I like everything about you—your sass, your honesty, and your fun spirit." Jim looked at me and grinned.

"Why, that's mighty nice, Big Jim. I say I'm a lucky woman to have you in my life." From that moment on, I knew I had a true friend. Might even be more than a friend someday.

Those last few days were pleasant, and then we came over a rise and Jim stopped the wagon. "Look, there's Atlanta. We here."

"Can't believe it! Looks grand to me. We made it all the way, and I'm still sane. At least, I hope I am." I laughed and almost cried. I was so happy.

Everywhere we looked we saw construction going on. New buildings goin' up and big warehouses. Crossed several railroad tracks as we came into a business section of town.

Jim pulled up and drove the wagons inside one of the biggest warehouses.

"This is a mighty pretty building inside for a barn." I was gawking and pointing. "Look at all the bricks and big beams overhead."

"Yes, it's a pretty building. Has an interesting history, too. Folks say when Sherman was in Atlanta, he used it as a stable for horses and equipment. Might be the reason it's still standing and not burned down like everything else in the area."

"I'll say, that sure is interesting. Sherman left here and marched to Savannah. We just did the reverse. We left Savannah and came to Atlanta. Only difference, we didn't burn buildings, steal horses and cows, and trample crops on the way."

Jim laughed. "I never thought of that before. You clever, Mae. Mighty clever."

"Well, thank you. Never know what's goin' to pop into my mind."

"I sure don't, but it's fun to hang around with you and wait to see what pops. Now we got to get these things unloaded, then I'm goin' to take you to another friend's house. It's over in Grant Park. New, growing area. I think that'll be a good place for you to live and start your business."

In the end, I was happy that I could survive a trek like the one we had. The trip helped push me through my grief and depression. I'm glad I did it. But I'm sure of one thing now: I'll never do it again.

Chapter 29

Atlanta

1892–1896

"Men, unload these wagons and store our deliveries," Jim said to the crew. "We'll get on 'em tomorrow. I'm goin' to take Mae to a friend's house."

"Miss Mae, we sure glad you came on this trip with us. Loved your good food. Come go with us again." Carl was smiling, knowing what I would say.

"I'm glad y'all liked the food, and I'm glad I made the trip. But there ain't nothing make me do that again." We all laughed, and I hugged each one of 'em.

Jim and I rode off a few miles. He said it was southeast of Atlanta. I didn't have my bearings yet. But we rode into this area where new houses were being built. There were buildings along the border with folks walking around, looking in shop windows.

"See those folks out and about? That row of buildings are shops with things for sale. People running 'em live upstairs. Nice, ain't it?"

"I'll say. Everything so new. This looks like a happening place."

"That's why I think it be a good place for you. It's called Grant Park. This rich man—named Grant, of course—gave all the land to the city of Atlanta a few years back for a park and a neighborhood out here. Big area. White folks building big mansions. But black folks providing services like sewing and tailoring. You fit right in."

"Here I go again gettin' cold feet. There's so much

tension out there. You know, between the races. We all divided. You sure black folks starting businesses in Atlanta?"

"Yes, I see 'em. I go to a barber shop run by a black man named Herndon. He has lots of white customers, prominent ones, too. There's a tailor downtown doing well. Like I said, providing services they need and are accustomed to seeing black folks do."

"That's good to hear."

"Here we are. I got someone living here I want you to meet."

We pulled up to one of those shops and Jim walked in. "Jasmine, you here? It's Jim come to see you."

Out walked an attractive woman. Jim started hugging her. "Mae, I want you to meet Jasmine. She's my Rose's sister. Jasmine, this is my friend Mae from Savannah. She just rode up here with me in my wagon. She's a brave soul."

"Glad to meet you. You sure are brave to ride that long way in an old wagon."

"Brave or crazy, one or the other. Don't know which. I'm just glad to be here safe and sound. Happy to meet you, too."

"Have a seat here at this table." Jasmine picked up a pitcher. "Let me pour you some iced tea. Know you tired from that trip."

"Jasmine here to start a little restaurant. She gettin' goin'. Her other sister Daisy is goin' to join her soon. I guess you see their mama named all her girls for flowers." Jim laughed.

"We might have sweet-sounding names, but we tough, hard-working women." Jasmine gave Jim a shove. "Don't forget that."

"Oh, I'll never forget. My Rose was cut out of that same mold."

"You mighty brave startin' your own business," I said.

"That's what I want to do. I'm a seamstress. Want to have a shop for alterations and design."

"That's wonderful. Nothing like that here yet. I believe folks will come to you."

"Tell me 'bout what you startin'."

"My sister and I are goin' to start a restaurant with good home cooking. Everybody likes Southern cooking. We want to make a nice atmosphere with little tables and tablecloths with flowers on the table. We got this fireplace in the back. Can be real cozy, especially in the winter. Cheerful setting. We working on gathering everything now. My sister is young. She's excited to join in. One thing Mama taught both of us was how to cook good food. We enjoy it, too."

"That sounds wonderful."

"Jim, I had an idea yesterday. I heard about some women in Atlanta starting restaurants called tea rooms. Of course, ain't no teapots anywhere. Just use the name to sound lady-like. I'm thinking Jasmine's Tea Room sounds real good."

"Good idea. Makes folks want to come see what you all about in your tea room." Jim chuckled.

"I think that's a great idea," I said. "Folks used to black women cooking good food, too. Like Jim just told me, you providing a service."

"Glad y'all like it, 'cause that's what I'm goin' to call it."

"Agreed. We all like the name. Now since Daisy is not here yet, do you think Mae can stay with you? I bet she'll help you out any way she can. You two can work something out."

"I would love the company. Got an empty room upstairs for a few months. Daisy got to finish school first."

Jim looked toward me with his eyebrows raised. "Would you like that, Mae?"

"Of course I would. I didn't have any idea where I was goin' to go when I got here. Thank goodness, you thinkin' ahead for me, Jim. Thank you so much."

"Let me start unloading your stuff. I'll help you get set up."

Jim unloaded the heavy things. Jasmine and I carried the smaller things up the stairs. We spent the day getting it all organized.

"Now I believe you two need a good meal," Jasmine said. "You came to the right place. Fixing a meat loaf with good vegetables—beans and squash. Would y'all like that?"

"Sounds mighty good to me," Jim said immediately. "I've always got a good appetite."

We enjoyed that meal, talked and laughed. By the end, I felt like I had known Jasmine forever. Before it was over we were making plans for her tea room.

"You goin' to need a lot of tablecloths. How about a set of white ones and then red and white checked for more casual? I can whip those up in no time."

"Sounds great. Then we can start looking for a good location for your shop. There's one right down the street under construction now, going to be ready in a few months. You could rent. Assume you got some money. If so, that might work out just right."

"Yes, Mama and I worked for years in Savannah. Except for a train ticket every now and then, we saved every cent. Of course, I need to be very careful."

"Same for us. We have some money but got to be cautious, too. Need to get our businesses going as soon as we can."

Jim got up from the table and laid his napkin across his plate. "Ladics, I hate to leave this good company, but I got to get back to work. I'll be in touch regularly. I can see y'all goin' to be fine."

"Yes, you skedaddle. We women help each other. That's what we do. We goin' to be okay." Jasmine and I both gave Jim a hug and sent him on his way.

I slept better that night than I had slept in months. I felt like this experiment was goin' to work after all.

One year later, I was squared away in my nice new shop down the street from Jasmine. I remembered how I read those ads in the newspaper in Savannah, so I put ads in *The Atlanta Constitution.* Folks started coming to me right away. There was no seamstress anywhere nearby. I encouraged Jasmine to put out ads, too. They helped get her noticed. Jasmine and I saw each other every day. I got along with Daisy just like I did with Jasmine. Daisy young enough to be my daughter. I liked her. We had a great trio goin'. I'd send folks to their café, and they'd send folks to my alteration shop.

I worked so hard, time flew by. A couple of years later, I was happy to have Thomas come for a visit.

"Mama, you so busy. I'm proud. Wanted you to get to know my wife, Melanie. We just had a small wedding in a chapel. It would have been hard for you to get there. We couldn't wait any longer for her to meet you. So here we are."

"I'm so happy to see you to get to know this beautiful woman. You finishin' medical school and Melanie already a nurse is great."

"Mama, we want you to know we are expecting a baby. Waited to surprise you."

"Really? That's wonderful." I started crying right away,

so happy. I hugged both of them.

"Mama Mae, I'm sorry Daddy died and didn't get to hear about the baby. But he had a hard time in the end. I think his heart just gave out."

"I'm sorry, too. But I'm grateful I had him in my life for a while. If it hadn't been for him coming along, you wouldn't be here."

Thomas and I hugged, remembering Joseph.

A few days later, I waved goodbye to them at the train station. "Y'all come back now. You got to bring that new baby to see me."

"We'll be back. I promise."

⁂

Another year passed, and Jim went with me to the train station. "I'm so glad you here to meet Thomas and Melanie," I told him. "They bringin' the new baby. I have never been so excited."

"I'm excited for you. Nothin' like a new baby. I remember what it was like when I first saw my grandbabies. It's one of the greatest joys in life."

When they stepped off the train, I went running to them. "So glad to see you and this baby. Oh, how precious." I tried to hug all three of them at once.

Melanie had the baby wrapped in a pink blanket and held her out to me. I took her in my arms and looked down at the sweetest face I had ever seen. Lo and behold, that baby—only a few months old—looked up at me with her big brown eyes and smiled. At least, I thought it was a smile. It was love at first sight. I was so happy.

At that moment, Thomas said, "Mama, want you to meet Amanda."

"You named her for me." I started crying. "That's the most beautiful baby I've ever seen, since you, of course. She so precious and you named her for me."

"Melanie liked the name Amanda, too. I told her you didn't use it anymore. I hope you don't mind."

"Are you crazy? Of course, I don't mind. You the one who started calling me Mae. Mama never called me anything but Amanda. I'm honored. Oh, this is my friend Jim. Forgive me for forgetting you."

"You excited about this baby. I don't mind that. But glad to meet you, Thomas. Your Mama brags about you all the time. You too, Melanie."

"I've heard a lot about you, Jim. I know how much you've helped Mama, and we appreciate it."

"It's a joy to help your mother. She's a good woman." Jim put his arm around me as I held baby Amanda with tears rolling down my face.

"I tell you what I am today. I'm a grateful woman. I am so blessed. Now let's go home and celebrate this baby girl's arrival."

There was a time when I didn't think I could be happy again. But I had a new kind of happiness. I might have lost my Savannah life forever, but I had my new Atlanta life. I had new friends, Jasmine and Daisy and especially Jim. And I had a family—Thomas, Melanie, and Amanda. What more could I ask for in life? I prayed nothing would happen to none of 'em.

One thing that was a mystery to me: how could time go by so fast? I worked around the clock and years passed quickly. I got into tailoring. Mama had taught me well, but it was her specialty. She usually did that work and now I was doing it. I was good at it. There was quite a demand for my services. And it paid well, too. As they say, I was gaining a reputation.

I had to hire a young assistant to help with answering the door and taking orders. I hired a young white girl named Bridget. She was Irish with the prettiest red hair and a joy to have around. She told me her name meant strength and power. I said that means you are perfect for this job. I remembered Jim telling me the story of hiring Stewart, the white man, to guard the wagon train. I figured white folks might be more likely to come in and place an order with Bridget there. I was always conscious of white folks being a little uneasy sometimes when they came in and saw I was black.

One day a woman walked into my shop and Bridget came to get me.

"Miss Mae, there's a young lady here that would like to talk to the owner of the shop. I told her it wasn't me."

When I walked into the front room, I saw an attractive young white woman.

"Hello, I'm Lizzie Jeter. I'd like to visit with you if you can spare some time."

"Happy to talk to you. How can I help?"

"I'm looking to rent that shop down the street. How has Woodward Avenue been for your business?"

"It's been fine. I work hard. Got to work hard. Nice folks around here. It's a mix—black, white, all working class in this area. White folks building those big houses around the park. What kind of business you want to start?"

"An art gallery where I sell other people's art. I'm an artist myself. I do portraits, watercolors, and things like that. Do you think it will sell here?"

"I don't know nothing about art, but I know this is a growing place. Lots of folks in and out. If you work hard and have something folks need, you can make a livin'."

"That sounds good. I'm really nervous about it. My daddy died not too long ago and I'm trying to support my mother and my sister, who has a baby. Mama sold their house, and we've got a little money but not a lot. I've got to be careful."

"Dear girl, you got a lot on you. I know how you feel. When I came here, I was scared and nervous, too. But things are going okay for me. Tell you what. Would you like to have lunch? There is a wonderful tea room down the street. I'd like you to meet the women who run it. They doing the same thing. We all in the same boat. All of us nervous but helping one another. That's what women do, help each other. We'll help you, too.

"That sounds great. I'd love to have lunch."

Jasmine, Daisy, and I all liked this young woman—Lizzie. She was wringing her hands and seemed so anxious. We did everything we could until she was finally smiling a little. We told her we thought she could do it and encouraged her to advertise in the newspaper. Of course, we'd be here to help her. By the time lunch was over, she had decided to rent the shop. We were all happy.

"By the way, Mae, I've been thinking I need a nice new white blouse," she said to me. "I want it to be pretty but also professional looking, something a real artist would wear."

"I don't know what a real artist would wear, but I can sure make a blouse you will like. It'll be comfortable and fit just right. Come by my shop when we leave, and I'll take your measurements."

That day was the beginning of another friendship with a woman who was just as scared as I had been. But it was great to have one another. Woodward Avenue was becoming a wonderful little community of caring women, working hard and helping each other.

Only a few months later after Lizzie rented her shop, we had a visit we took to be a good omen. A nice woman came by and wanted to talk to the three of us. "I've seen your ads in the *Atlanta Constitution.* I think you three women would be perfect for the women's pavilion at the state fair. We're going to have a big entrance room where we will have displays of things women are doing. Lizzie, we could put some of your art up for display, maybe a portrait and a watercolor. Amanda, you could display a couple of your tailored suits on mannequins. Jasmine, you could serve some tea biscuits with jam and tea on trays with your cards. It would be good advertisement for all of you. Would you like to participate?"

We immediately answered yes. We were honored. We couldn't think of anything better to help us get the word out. Good things were finally happening. We would quit worrying—at least for a while.

Part Three

Chapter 29

Atlanta

1899

At the end of three weeks, Lizzie was finishing up Miss Trudy's portrait and reflecting on the older woman's story.

"Miss Trudy, losing a seven-year-old child must have been devastating. Then your mother died, you lost your home and business, and you had to make your childhood home into a boarding house. Not to mention the war. You are amazing. How in the world did you survive?"

"I'm not sure, but I think I know some of the reasons. I know my Christian faith helped, even though I sometimes questioned God. I didn't understand how he would let these awful things keep happening. But then the realization came to me that bad things always happen. It's the way of the world. It isn't always God; sometimes it's man's doing. But in the end, it always comes down to how we respond. Somehow, over time I began to find peace.

"This may sound unusual, but my journal was a huge help. You know I kept it faithfully for forty-one years. I would write more when something awful happened, like the death of a child. I didn't have anyone who understood and would listen to me, especially when I lost track of Amanda after the war. I personified the journal, addressing it 'Dear Friend.' I wrote to it as if it were a person. Somehow that helped me. I recommend introspection and writing to my friends who are suffering.

"Finally, I made a conscious decision to think about other people more than I thought about myself. I started turning outward. I didn't want to talk about my trials and tribulations anymore. I met so many strong women who had also suffered. They helped me, too. We helped each other. I believe in that very much. That's what women do for one another."

Lizzie took Miss Trudy's hand. "I can't begin to tell you how much you have helped me. I think of what I was like when I first came through your front door—fearful, worried, afraid. I began to change the first day, and the longer you told your story the stronger I became. I realized I didn't have it so bad. Of course, then I met Jonathan, and he made me happier. It's all a miracle."

"If I've been able to help you, that makes me happy. Thank you for your kind words. Now, where are we on our painting?" Miss Trudy said as she stood.

"Almost finished. It's taken me a little longer than usual because we talked so often. But I would like to come this Friday and do a few touchups. Then we'll be ready to show it."

"Great. We will have our little tea party the next Thursday. I'm looking forward to meeting Jonathan and his mother. And, of course, seeing the portrait."

"Okay, let's say we'll finish this Friday. And one more thing. I always give my clients a gift, and I've been thinking about what I could give you. You have admired my blouse so often. I'd like to have my friend make one for you. She will come by and take measurements. She has some errands in this area and will stop by Friday when I'm here."

"My dear, that is so generous. I do love your blouse. It would be much more comfortable than this high, stiff collar. That will be perfect. Thank you. Friday we will finish the painting, and then we will have our tea party next Thursday.

Does that sound good to you?"

"Yes, it does. We have a plan."

Lizzie arrived at Trudy's home Friday at 1:00, just as Jeff was going out the door. Before she could speak, he tipped his hat, "Hello, Miss Jeter."

Startled that he knew her name and sounded polite, Lizzie responded, "Mr. Thomas, hello to you, too. Where you off to today?"

"Off to a meeting of Sons of Confederate Veterans. Important meeting. We're planning a parade down Peachtree Street. You'll have to come."

"I'll try to do that. Have a good meeting." Lizzie glided past him.

She found her subject already settled and looking out the window. "Hello, Miss Trudy. I just saw Mr. Thomas going out. He seemed in a better mood today."

"It happens occasionally."

"Well, that's good to hear. Have you sneaked a peek at the painting? Remember, peeking is no fair." Lizzie laughed.

"Honestly, I've been so busy I haven't been tempted. I trust you to do a good job. Although I don't know how you can make a sixty-five-year-old woman look attractive."

"Now, Miss Trudy, you have beautiful brown eyes, lovely white hair, and a strong face. Don't talk negatively about yourself. Aren't you always telling others that?"

"You have me there," Trudy said with a smile. "I guess we never outgrow a little vanity."

At that moment came a gentle knock on the front door. "Stay where you are," Lizzie said, getting up to open it. "That must be my friend here to get measurements. I'll let her in."

Mae walked into the parlor with a sewing satchel and stopped suddenly in front of Miss Trudy's chair. When Trudy looked up and saw her, she let out a gasp. "Dear God, Amanda, it's you," she said as she jumped up and threw her arms around her long-lost friend. "I can't believe it. Is it really you? Stand back and let me look at you. You look wonderful. I'm so glad to see you."

Trudy held Amanda at arm's length. "Yes, it's you. I've looked for you. Didn't know if you were dead or alive. And now here you are in my home."

"It's me alright, fit as a fiddle. I didn't know what had happened to you either. Then Lizzie started telling me about this woman she wanted me to come get measurements for. I asked her name, and when she told me, I was flabbergasted. Didn't let on to her. Wanted to surprise you both. I was afraid she would let the cat out of the bag." The two women cried and laughed together.

"This is wonderful. We have a lot of catching up to do. Come sit on this settee. Tell me what happened to you and Lurany when you left after the war."

As the two women sat down, holding each other's hands, Lizzie stood frozen. She had heard so much about their relationship. Was this really Amanda? And Lizzie was part of making this reunion happen. It was truly a miracle. She didn't understand how this was possible. She sat down, wanting to hear the story, too.

Trudy and Lizzie were mesmerized as Amanda began to tell them her long, twisting story. Like many former slaves, she and her mother Lurany had struggled after the war, unsure where to go or what to do. Then Amanda shared the story of Mr. Graham's plantation, the trip to Savannah in

Uncle Sykes's wagon, Miss Mitsy's little cottage, meeting Joseph, and then her son Thomas's birth. She had them on pins and needles when she told them about Mr. McGee coming after Joseph with his posse, trying to lynch him. Then she explained how she took Thomas to Philadelphia because she was so worried about him. Finally, she shared about starting her business in Grant Park and meeting Lizzie. By the time she finished, it was late afternoon. Trudy and Lizzie had not moved, stunned by what they heard.

"Well, I've got to say that is one of the most amazing adventures I've ever heard," Lizzie exclaimed. "And you say Thomas gave you the name Mae. That's the reason I never had any idea you were Miss Trudy's friend Amanda."

"Yes, Mama never called me anything but Amanda, but everyone else has called me Mae. Now that I have a granddaughter named Amanda, I might take my old name back."

"That's just unbelievable. I can't believe you made that wagon journey. You've never mentioned it to me before."

"I don't talk about it much unless I'm with Jim. As I said, I'm glad I did it but wouldn't do it again. I sure wouldn't recommend it to any other woman."

"I'm sitting here dumbfounded," Trudy said, shaking her head in awe. "You've had such an unbelievable life story. You should be very proud. I'm certainly proud of you." She leaned over and gave Amanda another hug.

"I thank you. When I think back on some of it, it's hard to believe. But I'm here now in a good place, and I'm thankful."

"I'm glad to hear Lurany died happy. She was a good woman," Trudy noted. "What a gift she had. She could create beautiful dresses from a plain piece of cloth. It was true art. And she was able to pass that gift on to you. I love hearing how close you two were. I can see you sitting by that old oil lamp, sewing, talking, and laughing. Yes, she lived a good life and died a free woman with a sense of satisfaction.

"As for your trek through the wilderness, it makes me think of rites of passage that young men must endure in some cultures to prove their manhood. In our world, most folks would say a woman is too weak to do what you did. But you could prove them wrong. I have benefitted from talking to women who have suffered and grown strong. There were so many women—black and white—who suffered during the war years and after. You started with the burden of grief and depression. But somehow your journey made you stronger. I hope you know that."

"I do. I was a changed woman afterwards. It helped me know I could start my business. It gave me confidence. I believe I'm a different woman from who I was before that trip. I take more chances now."

"Mae," Lizzie said, "I've told Miss Trudy this week that I've changed since listening to her story, and now I've heard your story too. Both of you make me believe I can do what I have to do. Thank you. I'm honored to be here for these revelations."

"If I can be a help to you, that is wonderful. Never thought much about helping other women when they hear my story. That is mighty nice. Thank you, Lizzie."

"What about your friend Jim?" Trudy asked with a smile. "He sounds like he is more than a friend. Do you think you two will ever get married?"

"We don't ever talk about marriage. I think we're both enjoying where we are right now. No strings attached, but you never know," Amanda said with a sheepish grin. After sitting quietly for a minute, she acted like she didn't know how to start what she wanted to say next. "I have another revelation for you," she finally said. "This one may be surprising, too. Before Mama died, she said there was one thing she wanted to tell me. She wanted me to know who my daddy was. Of course, we all knew it was a white man because I was so light skinned. Many of the white men preyed on the slave girls, so I didn't know if she even knew who it was."

"I know and that was one of the things I detested about slavery," Trudy said with conviction. "I even wrote about it in my journal. I didn't care who knew how I felt. What they did was a sin. And to think some of the white men would sell those light-skinned babies because they brought a good price. It was deplorable."

"Mama knew that about the fair-skinned babies," Amanda said. "That's the reason she was so worried." She paused briefly and then continued, "Trudy, you wouldn't know this man because you weren't born yet. But there was a man named Carlton living on your Pa's plantation. He was no good, Mama said. He was always getting in trouble. He especially liked the slave girls, Mama in particular. She was always trying to hide from him, but he would find her and have his way with her. She knew he was my father because that was the only man she had relations with." Mae looked away.

"I'm sorry Lurany had to endure that," Trudy said. "I hope Pa got rid of him."

"He did. Mama went and told your Pa, and he was furious. He said he didn't put up with that on his plantations. He asked Carlton for the truth, and he didn't deny it. Your Pa sent him off immediately. Sent him out west and no one ever saw him again. After that your Pa arranged for us to live in the big house where no man could get to Mama. I had that little cot in your room, and Mama had her sewing room and her own cot. She was always grateful that she didn't have to worry about that happening again."

"I'm glad to hear what Pa did for you and Lurany. But he might have had more to answer for. You weren't the only fair-skinned woman on his plantations. There were lots. I'd ask Pa about them, and he'd tell me I shouldn't be concerned. Of course, now we'll never know."

"But Trudy, you got to hear something else. Carlton was your Pa's cousin. They were related, and that means we're related."

"Oh, my goodness. You don't mean it! This is truly a surprise. I never dreamed it. How could I have never thought to ask if you knew who your father was? I remember folks always talking about the mulattos on other plantations but never our own. The subject was ignored, I guess because folks were afraid of who the stalkers were. Was it the father, brother, husband, overseer, or, in this case, a relative?"

"You right about that. No one ever brought it up. Folks were afraid to talk about it. I didn't even bug Mama to tell me who my daddy was. I never asked her. I don't know why she told me. Maybe she thought this day might come."

"Lurany was wise. Maybe she did hope for this day. We'll never know, but I'm glad she told you. I'm happy knowing we're kin. Maybe this explains why we always had some kind of bond. I remember how we talked about everything. And you were honest with me. Always told me the truth. You were never afraid to tell me what you thought. And of course, you saved my life when I wanted to die. That was my darkest moment, and more than anyone, you pulled me through it."

"I remember that well. By God, I wasn't goin' to let you die. Scared me half to death. But I was so happy when you came out of that dark place."

"Amanda—I just can't call you Mae—we've been through so much. I think you could tell that I cared. Couldn't you?"

"Yes, I knew you cared. I told Mama one time that I thought you loved me, but she said we could never know how white folks felt about us. But I felt that from you."

"When I was young, I was so self-centered and thoughtless. All I could think about was myself and my next new dress. I know there were many times when I should have been more aware. Please forgive me. I had great affection for you and wanted to protect you and help you. I might not have called it love then, but it was affection for sure. I see life differently now. Hopefully you can understand that. But I know I love you now. I am so happy to see you." Trudy gave her friend and newfound relative a smile.

"I always felt there was some connection between us. We grew up together in the same room, laughing and talking. You taught me to read when it was against the law. That meant everything to me through the years. Wouldn't be able to do my business without knowing how to read. All that other stuff is in the past. And now we've found each other. It's meant to be, an outright miracle. I'm sure we'll never understand it." Amanda laughed as she pulled a measuring tape from her satchel. "Enough talking about the past. Didn't I come here to take some measurements? I'm going to make you the most beautiful blouse you've ever had."

"I'm sure I've not had anything as beautiful as those dresses your mother made me for my wedding," Trudy said as she stood up for Amanda to measure. "I'm going to be sending you a lot of business. I'll make sure everyone knows about the great seamstress in town. Oh, I forgot to ask the name of your shop."

"It's L. and A. Alterations and Design. It stands for Lurany and Amanda Alterations. I thought that was too long, but I wanted to honor Mama in the name," Amanda said with pride. "I started liking the name 'Amanda' after Thomas got married and named his daughter after me. So the Amanda in the name also honors my granddaughter."

"I like that. What a day of surprises this has been." Trudy turned for Amanda to measure from her neck to her waist.

Lizzie sat in awe of these two women who had suffered so much but survived. In fact, they were both prospering. Somehow, they had come into her life at just the right moment to show her how to do the same.

Chapter 30

Atlanta

1899

On Sunday afternoon, Lizzie sat on a park bench with her sketch pad and pencils. It was a beautiful, sunny day with a little chill in the air. She couldn't stop thinking about Friday's visit with Miss Trudy and Amanda. These two women had found each other again after so many years apart, and Lizzie had been the one to bring them together. Their stories had changed her life. She was a different person after listening to them.

Lost in thought, she watched some children play in the falling leaves. One group tried to catch the leaves before they reached the ground, and the other played in a big pile, throwing leaves in the air and laughing. They played with the great abandonment and joy that only children seem to have. But one little girl stood to the side and watched them. She didn't seem to share their joy. Lizzie had started sketching the scene. She was busy with her work when she suddenly realized the lone little girl had moved to stand next to her.

"That's pretty. How do you do that?" the little girl asked.

"You just start drawing with these pencils, sketching an outline, filling it in," Lizzie explained. "It's fun. I used to do it with my daddy at a park like this when I was a little girl. You can learn to do it, too."

"My daddy's dead. I can't do that," the child said sadly.

"I'm so sorry. My daddy's dead, too. I didn't mean you had to have a daddy to draw."

At that moment, a woman walked up. "I hope my

daughter isn't bothering you."

"No, she seems interested, and we were just chatting."

"I've tried to get her to play with the other children and get interested in some activity. But since her father's death, it's been hard."

"I'm sure it has been. I'm sorry I brought up my own father. That might have made her sad."

"No, she's just sad no matter what."

At that moment, the little girl pointed at Lizzie's pad, smiled, and said, "I want to learn to do that."

"That's wonderful," Lizzie responded. "Why don't you and your mother meet me here next Sunday afternoon at this time? I'll bring you a pad and some pencils and give you lessons."

"You're kind to offer to teach her," the mother said, "but I'm afraid our budget is tight since my husband died. Susie, we can't afford to take lessons from this nice lady."

Susie looked disappointed but Lizzie immediately said, "Oh, you don't have to pay. It will be my pleasure. There will be no charge. Let's meet next Sunday, say 3:00 p.m., and get started. How about that?"

"Mama, please, let's do it. I want to learn to draw and paint."

The woman gave Lizzie a small smile. "That is so generous of you. Are you sure?"

"Yes, I'm sure. My name is Lizzie Jeter. I have an art shop right over on Woodward Avenue. If the weather is bad, come there. Is that okay?"

"That's perfect. Sunday afternoon is the saddest time. It's family time, so it's when we miss John the most. Thank you, thank you. My name is Janet Johnson. We will see you next Sunday afternoon." The young mother and her daughter walked off holding hands. Lizzie could hear Susie say, "I'm excited, Mama. I like that nice lady, and she makes me feel better."

Lizzie was glad she had made the offer, but what had gotten into her? She would never have done such a thing a couple of weeks ago, when she was too worried and wrapped up in her problems. No more. She would no longer live that way. She picked up her pad and pencils and began to walk back to the shop, feeling like a new person.

On Monday morning, Lizzie gave her mother the day off and kept the shop herself. She always enjoyed these days. She admired the shop's bright, cheerful atmosphere, its walls painted white to show off the art. More artists were bringing their art in for display. She had recently picked up folk pottery from North Georgia. A man named John Meader had produced beautiful jugs and pitchers—a few called "face jugs," a rich, dark brown with whimsical faces. The beauty of these jugs made everyone love the artist's work. That Monday, she enjoyed talking to a young mother whose child was fascinated with one of them. The day passed quickly, and she was beginning to look out the window for Jonathan when her sister Nellie walked in the room.

"Mama's watching little George," Nellie said with a grin. "I wanted to be downstairs to meet this handsome man."

"Oh, he's just a friend. Don't make more out of it than it is."

"He's more than a friend, that's for sure."

The bell rang, indicating someone coming in the door.

"Sorry I'm late. Got tied up in a meeting. Thought I'd be

here before now." Jonathan smiled at the two of them as he took off his hat, revealing a full head of beautiful, wavy brown hair.

"No problem." Lizzie's heart had started beating faster. *Gosh, calm down.* "Jonathan, this is my sister Nellie."

"I'm so happy to meet another lovely lady in this family," he said as he took Nellie's hand in his.

"I'm glad to meet you, too." Nellie grinned again and looked at Lizzie.

She's a goner, too. Lizzie grabbed her jacket. "Nellie, keep the shop open until six and then close. I appreciate your help," she said, following Jonathan to the door.

They walked to the tea room together, with Lizzie willing her heart to slow a bit. "This restaurant belongs to my friend, Jasmine. I love the small tables with white tablecloths and fresh flowers. Oh, and a fireplace."

"My goodness, I had no idea this place would be so charming. With the smell of fresh bread, no less." Jonathan asked the waitress for a table in the back by the fire. "Instead of just coffee, how about we have an early dinner? I skipped lunch and I'm hungry. What do you think?"

"Sure. I'm hungry, too. I didn't have lunch either." Lizzie took off her coat and sat down. "The food is delicious here."

"I love this part of Atlanta. I'm excited about some lots I've found on the other side of the park. They're on a rise with a nice view of the forest beyond the development. I'm actually thinking about buying two of them so I can build a nice Victorian cottage, or whatever they call it, with some trees in the yard. Forgive me for rattling on so. I'm just excited." Jonathan gave her a smile.

"No, don't apologize. I like your excitement. Remember, you said that to me the first time we met, when I got excited about describing art."

"I do remember, but that's not all that excites me about you. You are a truly lovely woman. I'm sure you know that." He took her hand and looked into her eyes.

"Thank you for the compliment. You're very sweet, but I'm not sure I know that."

"You should. May I be so bold to ask if you have a beau or someone who is courting you? Is that the way you say it?" He laughed. "I'm sure there are many other men who think you're beautiful, too."

Lizzie blushed and pulled her hand back. "If there are any others, I've been so worried and frantic for the last few years that I haven't noticed them."

The waitress came over and took their orders.

While they waited for their food, Lizzie told Jonathan about her father's sudden death, her gamble of starting the shop, and the struggle of being the sole breadwinner for her mother, sister Nellie, and baby George. "Frankly, until the last couple of weeks, I've worried myself sick. But miraculously, I've changed. It is quite amazing. While I've painted Miss Trudy, the one you're going to meet this week, she's told her life story. Her family was very wealthy before the Civil War. Her father had thousands of acres of land and hundreds of slaves, and growing up she wanted for nothing. When the war came, they lost everything. They went from wealth to poverty. Then she gave birth to ten children and saw four of them die. After the war, her husband couldn't recover from the trauma, but somehow, she has. She grew up in a slave culture but eventually decided it was immoral. After the war, she was glad the slaves were freed. She reinvented her life. Now she lives a meaningful life helping women in so many ways. When I heard her story, I decided I didn't have it so bad. How could I feel sorry for myself anymore?"

"I do think people can change," Jonathan commented. "Not all people, but some. Obviously, you can."

"But there's more to this story. There's another woman who was a long-lost friend of Miss Trudy. Her name is Amanda, and she was a slave on the plantation Trudy's father owned. They were close, and Miss Trudy had been looking for her since the end of the war with no success. It's a long story, but suffice it to say, I brought them together Friday. Amanda is a seamstress, and I took her to Miss Trudy's to get measurements for a blouse I plan to give her. You should have seen their reunion. We were all stunned. I can't get it off my mind."

"I'd say that fits the category of miracle," Jonathan said with a nod.

"The first day I walked into Miss Trudy's house about three weeks ago, I was a mess—worried, fearful, unhappy. When we got to talking, I told Miss Trudy I didn't have time for men. I had decided I would never marry. I was too old. Had too much to worry over. I was having a real 'pity party,' and she scolded me. She told me I was wrong about everything, that I didn't know what might be right around the corner. And guess what? The next day I met you."

"Hallelujah! This woman has magical powers. I can't wait to meet her and thank her."

"We're set for next Thursday afternoon at four for an English tea party—you, your mother, Trudy and her friend Amanda, and me. I'm sure Trudy's daughter Cora will be there, too."

"I can't wait. Mother will be on cloud nine. All these strong women are just her type."

They sat and talked as they ate their dinner—Georgia

mountain trout, mashed potatoes, green beans, and fresh baked biscuits, topped off with pecan pie. Lizzie told Jonathan how she had been inspired to start giving art lessons to troubled children. He thought it was a great idea and wanted to help her. They laughed and told stories, and before they knew it, they had been at Jasmine's Tea Room for almost two hours.

"I'm glad we came early," Jonathan said as he took the check from the waitress. "We could talk all night and close this place down, but I have one more request. I'd like you to go look at the lots with me. I'd like your approval."

"Sure. I'll be glad to look at them. They sound ideal."

"It's important to me that you like them," Jonathan said as he took her hands again and squeezed them. "I want to build a house there that you would love to live in someday."

Lizzie lost her breath.

Jonathan noticed and hurried on. "Lizzie, I know this is awful fast. But I was taken with you the first time I saw you. I've heard of love at first sight but didn't think it would happen to me. And then it did. I don't want to make you feel rushed. But I feel something I've never felt for another woman. I believe it's love. Do you understand what I'm saying? I hope it makes you happy."

Tears came into Lizzie's eyes as she looked at Jonathan. All she could say was, "Yes, I'm happy, too."

They held hands as they walked back to the shop. To think that only a couple of weeks earlier, she had felt so alone and unlovable. Now this wonderful man said he loved her. She had not believed she could have such joy. They stood and looked into each other's eyes and then kissed for the first time. Lizzie thought just maybe she knew what real love felt like. She was happier than she had imagined she could be.

How could her life change so quickly? She didn't know, but she would take this joy over her former life, no questions asked.

Chapter 31

Atlanta

1899

After continual rain all night, the day arrived cloudy and damp. A mist of fog fell over everything, making it hard to see very far. Normally Lizzie would have felt depressed on such a day, but not today. She was still giddy. She and Amanda got off the streetcar and saw Jonathan and his mother rounding the corner. The four of them quickly met up and exchanged greetings.

Jonathan put his arm around Lizzie's shoulder and pulled her toward him. "I hope you've had a good week. I know I have, just thinking about our dinner Monday night."

"Me too. I've had a wonderful week."

Lizzie smiled as Cora opened the door at Miss Trudy's.

"Welcome, please come in. We're so glad you all could be here this afternoon."

Jonathan's mother Sara went in first. "We are, too, I assure you. Thank you for having us."

At that moment, Miss Trudy walked out of the parlor and began going around the circle, hugging everyone and taking jackets. "Please come in and get out of the damp. Cora has outdone herself with our lovely refreshments. She knows how to do these things so much better than I do."

When they entered the parlor, they saw a beautiful, antique silver tea service on a small table surrounded by lovely china cups and saucers. Silver trays featured little cucumber sandwiches, tea biscuits with ham, and an assortment of sweet treats.

"My goodness, this really is a genuine English tea party," Sara said as she took her seat. "How lovely. This will certainly brighten this dreary afternoon." The others gathered round, finding their places and admiring the sumptuous repast.

"My mother would be happy today," Miss Trudy said. "She was always disappointed that I didn't show enough interest in her tea parties with friends. You remember, don't you, Amanda? She thought I was an utter failure with social graces. However, somehow Mama's skills skipped a generation and went to Cora."

"Mama, you exaggerate. I'm sure you weren't that bad, but I must say I enjoyed preparing these things. Now let me begin to pour coffee or tea." Cora began passing cups around the circle. When she came to Amanda, she leaned down. "I've heard Mama talk about you all my life. I know what you meant to her. I'm glad you're here. I hope you're comfortable."

"Haven't set at any white folks' table before. Feels nice. I thank you."

"I'm sure Jonathan and his mother are accustomed to it in New York, but this is a first for me, too. It's a good beginning." Cora smiled.

Trudy sat down with her cup of tea and surveyed the group. "I must share a wonderful story about this old tea service. It was my Mama's prized possession, and she had a servant bury it in the backyard when she thought Sherman and his men were coming to burn the big house. After the war, no one seemed to remember it, and it stayed buried. Then one day some years later, we went out in the backyard to have a burial ceremony for a favorite family pet—a cat named Pearl. My husband jammed the shovel in the soil and hit metal. To the delight of everyone, it was the old tea service.

Here it is, all cleaned and polished and restored to its former glory."

"What an honor for us to use the prized tea service and to be here for this special occasion—the unveiling of the portrait. You have made the occasion unforgettable," Sara said.

"I haven't seen the portrait yet. Lizzie asked me the other day if I had peeked. I promised her I had not. But first, let's have some refreshments and get to know each other. Jonathan, Lizzie has told me you are from Auburn, New York, in the beautiful Finger Lake region upstate."

"Yes, Auburn's a lovely little town on Lake Owasco about sixty miles from Rochester. You might know it as the home of William H. Seward, Lincoln's Secretary of State. His home was part of the Underground Railroad. He helped Harriet Tubman purchase a seven-acre farm nearby. I've always been proud of the history associated with our town. I loved growing up there and going to the University of Rochester."

"What a fascinating history. I'd love to visit sometime. I've only read about it. Now you've come to live in Atlanta and work for one of the railroad companies. Quite a change for you."

"This is a huge change for me and my mother," Jonathan acknowledged. "But I'm excited about all that's going on. I'm here working for the Seaboard Air Line Railroad."

"What a coincidence. I have plans to go to Washington DC in February on the new Seaboard Air Line. A friend has told me the cars are elegant."

"You're in for a treat. I'm very proud of our service. I'm sure you will enjoy your trip."

"I look forward to it. I'm excited to be going to the National American Suffrage Association convention where

Susan B. Anthony, at the age of eighty, will pass the torch of leadership on to a younger leader, probably Carrie Chapman Catt, who is only forty-one. It will be even nicer for me knowing you are associated with that line. Now, Sara, Jonathan is happy with his work. What about you? How do you like Atlanta?"

"I have enjoyed everything about it so far," Sara said, smiling at Lizzie and then at Trudy. "And I love that you're busy with women's activities. I was hoping to find some like-minded women down here."

"You've come to the right place. I will tell you about what I'm doing later, but I want to hear how you got involved. Upstate New York has a wonderful history. I met Susan B. Anthony, who you know is from Rochester, when she came down for the convention in '95. What a dynamo. She has given us lots of good advice."

"You were fortunate to have input from Anthony. She goes like a house afire. I've heard her speak but she wasn't one of the first I met. I'm sure you've heard of the Quaker Lucretia Mott, who was one of the early warriors for women's rights. She lived in Philadelphia, and her sister, Martha Coffin Wright, lived in Auburn. Lucretia would come to visit Martha occasionally. My mother was a friend of Martha and took me on some of those visits. Elizabeth Cady Stanton lived only fifteen miles away in Seneca Falls, and she would come to see her old friend Lucretia. They met at an anti-slavery event in London in 1840. When they refused to seat the women, Elizabeth and Lucretia walked the streets of London talking about how someday they would do something about women's rights in America."

"I seem to remember something about that protest the women made," Trudy said. "I believe it was fortunate for history that those two visionaries were booted out of the meeting in London."

"Yes, but it took them eight years to do something about it. Elizabeth's private life took so much of her time and energy. Did you know she had seven children?" Sara looked incredulous at the idea. "I spent time with them while the women talked. Let me tell you, those kids were a rowdy bunch. I had fun with them for a while, but I was older and would tire of them. Then I just sat and listened to the women. While they were visiting, they began to plan a meeting to be held in the Wesley Chapel over in Seneca Falls in July. Of course, that was the first women's rights meeting in 1848. Those women even started writing the Declaration of Sentiments, listing all 'injuries and usurpations against women by men.' You can say I was present at the very beginning of the movement. It was great to be a fly on the wall with these smart, courageous women."

"How wonderful. I can't imagine being present at the birth of the women's movement in this country. What a privilege for you. I'm sorry to tell you that we've been about fifty years behind down here. I never heard any talk of women's rights growing up. I only read about it secretly in books. You were fortunate."

"Yes, I was lucky. My mother was asked to write reports to be published in the newspapers of what the women were doing. They wanted to advertise their meetings, too. I loved to write, so naturally Mother enlisted me to help. It didn't take long before I was writing all the time and going to meetings. I got a wonderful education on the status of women at a young age."

"I hope you won't be disappointed about how far behind we are," Trudy said. "Most folks down here don't believe women need any rights. The old states of the Confederacy are still conservative. You'll hear folks say women don't need rights because their husbands and fathers will take care of them. That women don't want rights. That women aren't smart enough to vote. That we're too emotional. When we had the national convention down here in 1895, we hoped that would change things some. But the clergy came out against us. Warren Candler of the Methodist Church wrote my friend, Jane Sibley, that suffrage for women was not scriptural and was sinful. The pastor of First Baptist, Dr. Hawthorne, said any man who let his wife participate in suffrage must be feeble-minded. That gives you an idea of what we've been up against. But in spite of the opposition, a strong group of us is determined to fight on."

"We've got some of that opposition in the North. But you are correct; I sense it's different here. That's the reason I'm happy to be here. I want to help any way I can."

"I'm sure your advice will be priceless. We'll put you right to work. And your timing is perfect. I've been working hard on our first state convention, which will be held on the twenty-ninth of November. That's what I've done every morning while you've been painting, Lizzie."

"You said you were busy, but you didn't say what you were doing. That's great. The first state convention. That must be progress."

"I think it is. We have women coming from all over the state. We are particularly excited to meet in the House of Representatives. You know the amendment has to be passed in each state legislature. It is a hard 'row to hoe.' At this point, only four western states have voted to give the vote to women—Wyoming, Utah, Colorado, and Idaho. We've been trying to get the legislators' attention and persuade them to change their thinking. We've had a hard time getting to them. But they can't help but see all these women down in the capital making a ruckus." Trudy laughed. "We tell our women to be Southern ladies but do whatever they must to get the legislators' attention."

Everyone laughed and Jonathan said, "I can see those men wondering what hit 'em."

"And I'll tell you a secret. I've been nominated to be president."

"That's great. What an honor, Miss Trudy," Lizzie exclaimed.

"Yes, it is an honor but a huge responsibility at the same time. I've been working on an important speech for the opening. I'm inviting you all to come. It will mean so much to me to have you in the audience. Can you be there?"

Everyone nodded and said, "Of course," but Amanda was silent.

"Trudy, I'll be with you in spirit, but you know I can't come. I'm a 'colored' woman. I know you're different, but those other white women don't want us there."

"Unfortunately, you are correct. Most of the white women don't want you there. They are consumed with hatred. But I do. And it's the right thing to do. You put on one of your tailored suits with one of those lovely blouses, and you'll be the best-dressed woman there. Hold your head high and walk right in. Some may look at you funny. But if a single person says a word to you, tell them you are my guest. Send them to me."

"I don't know. Are you sure I should come? I don't know much about the vote for women."

"Yes, you should come," Trudy assured her friend. "And the fact that you don't know much is the very reason you should be there. You need to know what we're working on. Anyway, I happen to know another woman who has come to some of our meetings, and she is just like you. Her name is Adella Hunt Logan. She grew up in Sparta, Georgia, in Hancock County where Pa did a lot of business. Everyone in town knew the white Hunt men favored Negro women, some of whom were free and had Cherokee blood. Some couples lived openly together, but Georgia law did not allow them to marry. Adella is a child of Henry Hunt and Cherokee Mariah, daughter of Judge Nathan Sayre. Most Spartans knew about these arrangements, but no one talked about them. Adella is lovely and fair-skinned—proud of her Negro-Cherokee heritage. Well educated, she teaches at Tuskegee Institute in Alabama, and her husband is the treasurer.

"Adella was interested in the vote for women, heard about our '95 convention, and decided to come. If she needed to, she could pass as white, referred to as 'wearing the veil.' I happened upon her when she was meeting Susan B. Anthony. When we walked up, she was telling Miss Anthony that she looked forward to her speaking at Atlanta University, which was her alma mater. She went on to tell Miss Anthony that she wished colored women, other than those who could pass for white, were welcome to sessions there in the hotel. Miss Anthony, probably wise to what was happening, looked past her and did not respond. No one else had anything to say either."

"That is certainly something I never thought about," Amanda said. "Didn't know anything like that went on at your convention."

"Please come. It is important that you carry our message to your community. Your churches are so important, and some church women have already started organizing. You can join them."

"Well, if you put it that way, I guess I don't have a choice. You always been so pushy, telling me what to do." Amanda laughed. "But I'll be there. We might cause a brouhaha. Just like when we were growing up. Always getting in trouble."

"That's right. Cause some trouble, some good trouble. And Lizzie and Jonathan, you'll be important to communicate with the younger folks out there. Young people are so busy working and raising their kids, we have to find new ways of getting the message to them. Many women working in the movement are older. And of course, the men who understand and support the movement are essential."

"You know you can count on me," Jonathan affirmed. "Mother has raised me to be an advocate for women. I would have been in trouble long ago if I had not toed the line! Now can we see the famous portrait?"

"No, wait one minute. I have a gift for Miss Trudy that Amanda made. I want her to open it first," Lizzie said as she handed Miss Trudy a tissue-wrapped package.

Trudy opened the package and showed everyone the exquisite blouse with beautiful handwork. "Have you ever seen a prettier blouse? It is beautiful, yet serviceable and comfortable. I am so pleased to have one. Thank you, Lizzie and Amanda. What a special gift that I will treasure."

"Yes, it is gorgeous. May I order one immediately?" Sara asked.

"Of course, you can. I told Amanda we'll be working to get her new business, and here we have it already. Maybe you would like more than one." Trudy laughed. "Well, I guess I've delayed as long as I can. I'm not really anxious to see a painting of myself, but I can't avoid it any longer. Lizzie, you do the honors and unveil it."

Lizzie rose and walked to the easel by the window. "Before I take the cover off the portrait, I want to say what an honor it has been to paint this woman's likeness, but even more to hear her life story that she told me while I painted. It is an amazing story of survival. In the short time I have been with Miss Trudy, she has changed my life. I have no doubt she will change many more. Thank you again, Miss Trudy," Lizzie said as she looked at the older woman. "Now I will show you the painting."

When she dropped the cloth, a round of applause filled the room. "How lovely! Lizzie, you captured her character and strength," Sara exclaimed.

"You got her brown eyes! Trudy could always stare you down with those eyes. You know, hold your attention until she got her way. Yes, you got her eyes just right." Amanda nodded her head in approval.

While everyone was making favorable comments, Trudy just sat and stared at the painting. "How can I be that silver-haired woman? Sixty-five years, no less. Where did the time go? I still think of myself as young. I think I look like that eighteen-year-old girl in my wedding portrait that hangs in our dining room. This proves me wrong. But Lizzie, you have done an admirable job, and I appreciate it very much. Thank you."

At that minute, the front door opened and a man began hollering. "Where's everyone? I can't get this mud off my boots, but I'm coming in anyway. Hello, hello?"

"We're in the parlor with guests, Mr. Thomas," Trudy calmly responded as the man stomped into the house.

A gray-haired old man dressed in a Confederate uniform, wearing knee-high leather boots and a big cape, filled the doorway. His floppy hat was drenched and hung limp to one side. He had a rifle over his shoulder.

"What's going on here? A fancy tea party while I was in a parade? I thought you and Cora were coming."

"My dear, I told you we had guests this afternoon. Please meet Jonathan and Sara Hopkins, who just moved to Atlanta from New York."

"Well, welcome to Atlanta. Know you're glad to get out of New York and into God's country down here."

Trudy ignored his comment. "You may remember our Amanda from years back. I'm happy to say she just showed up in our life again."

"Oh yeah, Amanda. Trudy's been concerned about you, wondering what happened to you. Me, not so much. But I'm sure you're happy, Trudy. Got to say times sure have changed, everybody sitting down together."

Again, Trudy ignored him. "You met the artist Lizzie Jeter the other day. Remember? Would you care to join us?"

"No. Just came by for supplies. Attendance was low today because of the weather. We have to start planning another parade. Meeting some men down in the tent I keep at the park. Love to be outside in all kinds of weather. Cora, could you come help me find that bottle of good whiskey and put some food in a bag? I'll be spending the night. Well, you folks have a nice tea party. I prefer more manly pastimes myself." He walked out of the room, followed by Cora.

Miss Trudy was not fazed. "That was my husband, J. Jefferson Thomas. Sometimes I refer to him as Mr. Thomas, but mostly I just say Jeff now. I apologize for his bad manners, but he has never recovered from the war all those years ago. I didn't think he would be here this afternoon, or I would've prepared you. It's sad, but he had some kind of trauma in the war. I've never known what exactly. He just keeps refighting the war and talking about the Lost Cause. I must share with you that he only fought for nine months and then bought a substitute. You would never know it now. He's always preparing for the next battle. I've tried to get help, but there isn't much available."

"You don't have to apologize to us," Sara responded. "So many men came out of that war maimed, physically and mentally. Something like seven hundred thousand killed, but so many more permanently wounded. The tragedy of our time."

"Thank you for understanding. I do not believe in divorce. My Methodist faith prohibits it, and I also believe I should take care of him. We had a love once that has changed into something else. We've worked it out."

"That is admirable. I know it hasn't been easy," Sara commented.

"Yes, we have gone through so much. After the war he endured one disappointment after another. Children dying, bankruptcies, lawsuits, fights with relatives over property. Finally, he just lost control. Once he told me to send him to an insane asylum. But I don't think he meant it. At any rate, this is what we have worked out. He lives his life, and I live my life. He chose to live in the past, and I have chosen to live in the present and plan for the future. I want to help other people, especially women. That has saved me."

"You didn't tell me these things when we were talking," Lizzie said. "I admire you even more for the way you have chosen to handle Jeff's situation."

"You're kind. But I don't see it as admirable. I just see it as a necessity. There are so many men out there like Jeff. He has no interest whatsoever in what I'm doing. He doesn't understand my work for women. That's part of what we're up against in the South. I've decided to ignore him and work on. I never abandon hope that he will come around."

Trudy paused for a minute and straightened her dress. "Well, now you know all the family secrets. We are friends for life," she said, laughing. "Would anyone care for another cup of tea?"

Chapter 32

Atlanta

1899

Trudy's entourage—Lizzie, Jonathan, Sara, Amanda, and Cora—arrived early and took center seats in the front row of the balcony. They had a bird's-eye view of everything happening below on the floor of the House of Representatives. The wood-paneled room was beautiful, with an elevated, carved podium and seats arranged in a large semicircle. The seats were packed with women in their Sunday best, including hats and gloves. Some of them successfully cornered elected legislators and peppered them with bullet points from their wish list on women's rights.

"I'd say things are going well, wouldn't you?" Lizzie whispered to Jonathan.

"Seems so to me. Attendance is certainly good. I'm sure Trudy and her friends are happy about that." He looked around the room.

"Quite a lovely chamber," Sara remarked. "I'm sure it's intimidating to know you're about to stand and speak in front of this audience."

"I would be terrified. How many do you think are in the hall? Two hundred fifty or three hundred? I can't stand up in front of a handful of people and make a speech, much less to a crowd like this," Lizzie admitted. "I'm really nervous for Miss Trudy. I know how much it means to her."

"Oh, she'll do fine," Amanda assured her. "She has some kind of confidence she was born with. I'm not worried about her speech. I'm more worried about somebody pointing at me and asking me to leave. I just saw some woman staring at me from over there on the left. Did you see her, Lizzie?"

"No, but I'm sure she was just looking at your lovely outfit. I must say you look like a dignitary in your elegant navy-blue suit and that little hat cocked to one side. Yes, a foreign dignitary, perhaps visiting from Spain."

"You're getting carried away. But I do appreciate the compliment. I am right proud of this tailoring job. Mama was so good at it. It's taken me a long time to approach her talent. Maybe I should just must mutter a few words in Spanish to convince these folks." Amanda laughed.

At that moment three women approached the steps and walked up to their places on the dais. Earlier in the morning, new officers were elected to the Georgia Woman Suffrage Association during a business meeting. Along with the outgoing president, Mary Latimer McLendon, came the secretary, Mrs. Claudia Howell Maxwell, and the newly elected president. The three women took their seats, and the room grew quiet. Mary Latimer McLendon rose and walked to the podium.

"It has been a joy to be your president for the past year," she said. "We have worked hard and have made progress, but there is so much more that must be done. One of our best accomplishments has been to organize this convention—our very first statewide meeting. As we approach the new twentieth century, we will need strong, intelligent leadership more than ever. I can think of no woman more suited for this important task than my friend and colleague who has been elected our new president. Ladies and gentlemen, may I present our new president, Ella Gertrude Clanton Thomas."

The entire room rose to their feet to give Trudy a standing ovation. She stood quietly for a few moments before she began to speak. "Thank you. This is the greatest honor of my life. Being elected to lead our organization into the new century has caused me to think long and hard about what I want to say to you today. I've decided to go back fifty years to when I was a young girl in Augusta, Georgia. I remember well when a woman rose to speak in our Methodist church. I don't remember her name or what she said, but I recall the outrage. People were horrified that a woman would dare to stand and speak in our church. You all remember the strict interpretation of 1 Corinthians 14:34, 'Let the women keep silent in the churches, for they are not permitted to speak.... And if they want to learn something, let them ask their husbands at home; for it is shameful for women to speak in church.'"

Trudy paused and noticed folks nodding.

"After the war, women wanted to organize prayer groups and try to help the widows and orphans left behind. They were told they could not have a prayer group or any kind of meeting without a man to lead them. Yes, that is true.

"My friend Sara Hopkins from Auburn, New York, who is here today, reminded me only yesterday that when those pioneers of our movement—Elizabeth Cady Stanton and Lucretia Mott—met in Seneca Falls to kick off the first women's rights meeting in 1848, they asked a man, Lucretia Mott's husband James, to lead them. Even these courageous women did not feel comfortable being leaders and conducting the meeting. Fifty years later, in the heart of the Old South, here I stand to tell you, 'No more.' Women will stand and speak. And we will not be afraid to lead."

Applause rippled through the room. Every eye was glued on her. Trudy had captured the minds and hearts of everyone present.

"When I went off to college at Wesleyan in that same

year, 1848, my own mother was horrified that I learned to stand and state my opinions. For whatever reason, I do not know why, it just seemed to come natural to my pushy nature." Laughter rang out through the hall. "I and others like me were called 'strong-minded' women. It was meant as an insult, but I always liked it. Strong-minded is better than weak-minded.

"After that first meeting in Seneca Falls, other women began to organize women's rights meetings all over the country. Those groups were often closely associated with the antislavery movement, something—unfortunately—we did not have down here in the South. Therefore, we have gotten a late start. We are fifty years behind the North. Our first organization in Georgia did not happen until 1890 in Columbus. So we have a lot of catching up to do.

"Let me remind you of some of the things we will be fighting for in the next century. I say 'century' because it will take a long time. At present, women have almost no legal rights in our country. A single woman can inherit property, but as soon as she marries, she becomes 'one' with her husband. That means everything she has becomes her husband's—her property, her clothes, and her jewelry. She does not even have guardianship rights of her own children, who can be willed away from her. She cannot sue, be sued, or make a contract. She does not have full access to education. We must have equal education, admission to the University of Georgia and all other universities. We demand prison reform where women are housed separately from men. Wife beating must be made illegal. If a woman is fortunate enough to have a way to earn money, she should own her wages, not give them to her husband. And when a woman works, she should have equal pay for equal work. She should be allowed to serve on juries and run for political office. Of course, at the top of this list is the all-important vote. Women should be guaranteed a voice in their government. We must keep working until we reach all these goals."

Again, there was enthusiastic applause.

Trudy lifted a brochure from the podium and held it up to the audience. "This was put out by the Georgia Anti-Suffrage Association. It says if women get the vote, it will destroy the home, wreck our federal government, and unleash the demons of the lower world." Trudy waved the brochure as people laughed. "But the opposite will be true. Homes will be happier, the government will be stronger, and certainly fewer demons will be running around amongst us."

Trudy paused as the laughter died down. "Now let me be serious a moment. I am a God-fearing Methodist woman. I try to live a good Christian life. I believe God gave us all minds that we are supposed to use wisely. I remind you that our Bible in the first book of Genesis teaches us, 'God created man in his own image…male and female he created them.' This implies equality of the sexes. In another part of Genesis, God gave us the rib narrative. He said woman was not taken from the head of man; she is not his superior. Woman was not taken from the foot of man; she is not his inferior. But woman was taken from the side of man, and there she should stand his equal in the work of the world. I am telling you today that I believe God meant for men and women to work side by side for the betterment of mankind. We don't just want the vote; we want equality.

"Some will say we are asking for too much. These rights will take too long to achieve. No, we are not asking for too much. We make up one half of the population and are entitled to these rights. But I do agree that it will take a long time. I may not be living when these rights come. But I am convinced they will come. I want to do all I can to make sure we reach our goals. Join me. Let's work together. As my friend Susan B. Anthony has said, 'Failure is impossible.' So, on that happy note, let us begin. We do not have a moment to lose. Let's get busy working to change the world. Thank you very much, and God bless you all."

The attendees immediately jumped to their feet and began clapping enthusiastically. Trudy stood and waved around to the audience, saying, "Thank you, thank you." There were tears in her eyes but a smile on her face. It was as if she had awakened from a dream. She had found the courage to speak what she knew was the truth. She also knew that her life had made a difference. At that moment, she was happier than she had ever been.

After being congratulated by most of the people in the room, she watched as her little entourage made their way to her.

"That was a great speech. Amazing. I'm so honored to be here. I'll never forget it." Lizzie hugged Miss Trudy tightly.

"I feel exactly the same. What an honor to be here," Jonathan agreed.

"You did it. I never doubted you a minute. You've always had that fight in you," Amanda said with a chuckle. "And thank goodness, no brouhaha over me."

Sara stepped up to have her say. "I've heard all the great speakers in the movement—Elizabeth Cady Stanton, Susan B. Anthony, Anna Howard Shaw, and others. I must say you are right up there on that pedestal. It was a magnificent speech and a great way to kick off your term."

Trudy hugged each one of them and said thank you.

"Now, that is enough bragging on me. How about we head home for dinner? I don't know about you, but I'm starving."

Cora had left the dining room table set with china, silver, flowers, and candles ready to light. Her husband Patrick arrived home from work and planned to join them for dinner.

"My, my, how lovely," Trudy said when the table was ready. "It looks like one of Mama's grand dinners with family and friends gathered around. Let's get seated. Cora got her friend to prepare everything. It will be a feast—roasted chicken, green beans, squash casserole, sweet potatoes, biscuits, and gravy, topped off with pumpkin pie for dessert. Please, everyone take a seat." Trudy sat at the head of the table with her guests on either side. "I am so happy to have you here with me tonight. Cora, would you please pour everyone a glass of tea?"

As Cora went around the table pouring tea, Jonathan spoke. "We're honored to be here in your lovely home to celebrate this grand occasion. And such a sumptuous dinner. Mother and I feel so welcome here. Thank you." He took Lizzie's hand and squeezed it.

Everyone was soon talking and laughing about the afternoon, telling stories.

"I was introduced to this legislator as a guest from New York," Sara recounted. "He was a big, heavy-set man with a long white beard. He was absolutely terrified of me. This Yankee woman telling him how to vote. I don't know what he thought I was going to do to him. I almost laughed. I sort of felt sorry for him."

"Well, talk about somebody being afraid," Amanda said,

her eyebrows raised. "I was so nervous one of those women was going to ask me to leave. I pointed out someone looking at me and Lizzie told me to relax. Said I looked like a Spanish dignitary. I think that was taking it a little too far. That idea made me nervous, too."

"Miss Trudy, you were so calm. I don't know how you were able to speak to that big crowd of folks," Lizzie said.

They were all so engrossed in conversation that they did not notice the side door opening. Suddenly they all grew quiet, not knowing what to expect. There stood Jeff in a pressed black suit, clean shaven, his hair neatly combed. "Would you all mind if I joined you?" he asked shyly.

"My dear, we will be honored," Trudy said as Jonathan got up and pulled out the chair at the end of the table. "We always leave a place set for you, hoping you might join us. Remember how Pa and Mama sat at opposite ends of the big table for those wonderful dinners we used to have?"

"Daddy, let me help fix your plate," Cora said as she jumped up and started serving Jeff.

No one else spoke, as if Jeff's past actions made them wonder what he would do next. Finally, he said very softly, "I seem to remember dinners like this long ago."

"Yes, Jeff," Trudy affirmed. "We had meals at Mama's and sometimes at our house, mostly before the war. Some after the war, too. It's nice, isn't it, to be together with family and friends?"

"Yes, it is. All these pretty candles and good food. But you can't bring back yesterday, can you?" Jeff frowned as if trying to remember how to act and what to say.

"No, dear, we can't bring back yesterday. We must live today and look to the future," Trudy said with understanding.

Jeff looked around the room. "Cora told me about today.

I should have been there."

"That would have been nice. But we know you had things to do." Trudy smiled.

"No, I should have been there. What I was doing was not as important as you are. Family is more important. I love you and all my family. Trudy, I can do better."

The guests glanced at one another, unsure about this interaction. Finally, Trudy said, "I love you, too. Yes, we can all do better. Thank you for joining us this evening. I suggest we have a toast to Mr. Thomas, my husband, who has joined us this evening and suggested that we can all do better. And family is important."

A slight smile appeared on Jeff's face. "Don't you have something better to toast me with than tea?"

They all laughed. Trudy knew in her heart that Jeff had probably not come back completely. But it was a beginning. A good beginning. She knew that if a person is to come to new realizations about life, they must take the first step. Jeff had taken that first step.

A curtain was lifted. They could all see better. Trudy looked around the table with a sense of gratitude. She smiled, raised her glass, and said, "To my husband, Jeff, who has joined us this evening. To new friends, Lizzie, Jonathan, and Sara. To my daughter, Cora, and her husband, Patrick. To my oldest and dearest friend, Amanda. We are all at a new beginning. Yes, we can all do better. I pray that is what the future will hold for all of us: a better world."

—THE END—

Gertrude "Trudy" Thomas.

Painting by Lizzie Jeter, ca. 1899.
Courtesy of Carolyn Newton Curry.

Sources and Acknowledgments

As soon as I finished my biography of Ella Gertrude Clanton Thomas in 2015, I started thinking about writing a historical novel with her as a main character. I realized that my history book with footnotes and more advanced topics would not appeal to my granddaughters, who were in middle school at the time. I first thought this book would be a young adult novel. Then, when I started writing, I changed my mind. I believed this book would be interesting to young and old alike.

I used my book, *Suffer and Grow Strong: The Life of Ella Gertrude Clanton Thomas 1834–1907*, as a source for her life. Gertrude had a wonderful way of expressing her emotions, and I used her direct quotes occasionally in this book. When I did, the page number is listed in "Notes."

I also reference Adele Logan Alexander's book about her grandmother, Adella Hunt Logan, titled *Princess of the Hither Isles: A Black Suffragist's Story from the Jim Crow South.* I refer to a conversation Adella had with Susan B. Anthony at the 1895 National American Women's Suffrage Convention in Atlanta. That quote is included in "Notes" as well.

I wandered through various online repositories for dates and occasional references, but much of this book came from my knowledge of my hometown—Atlanta, Georgia—and my years of living on Peachtree Street. Also, I grew up in College Park, Georgia, and went to high school in the original Cox College building. My husband's grandmother, Mary Lou Farrar Barnes Rosser, who is now deceased, attended Cox College and studied art. We are pleased to have one of her lovely paintings.

I want to thank my publicist, Kathie Bennett, for staying after me to write this book. She was on board as soon as my first book was published. I also want to thank Pete Wellborn, who said to me when I mentioned writing this novel that it would be good for Gertrude to tell her story to Lizzie, the portrait painter. When I started writing, that is exactly what I did.

After I published my biography *Suffer and Grow Strong*, I wrote a murder mystery set in the world of football titled *Sudden Death* (2022). Since my husband Bill Curry and I have spent our life in that world, the story just came to me and was fun. I didn't know anything about writing fiction, so it was also a learning experience. But one thing I learned was that I loved writing fiction, and historical fiction was a natural outcome.

On my journey to learn to write fiction, I must thank my friend and writer, Ann Hite. She read my first draft of this book and made suggestions. She would remind me to "write scenes" instead of telling folks what had happened. I had to be reminded over and over. I appreciate her candor and sense of humor. More than anything, I appreciate her encouragement that this is an important story that needs to be told.

Also, I give a special thanks to my friend of many years, Dianne Baughan, who knows more about primitive American antiques than anyone I know. I wanted to make sure I described Lurany's heart pine "woven oak splint" seats correctly.

Mercer University Press published both of my earlier books, as well as this one. Director Marc Jolley gave excellent guidance and was always patient. Marsha Luttrell, Publishing Assistant, was always ready with good advice and a smile. Mary Beth Kosowski, Director of Marketing, was knowledgeable and answered all my questions. When called on, Jenny Toole in the business office was always helpful. I also want to thank my excellent copy editor at the Press, Kelley Land, who caught my mistakes and asked helpful questions. The small cadre of five people who staff Mercer University Press do an amazing job each year, putting out an outstanding collection of books. I am grateful to them all.

I also want to say thank you to my friends and readers who

are always asking if I'm writing another book. I appreciate their interest and even their many questions. They have encouraged me to stay the course and keep writing.

I must thank my family members, who put up with me and my love of women's history. Our daughter Kristin, her husband Bob, and her daughters Evelyn and Claire are always supportive and share my love of women's fiction. Perhaps Bob not so much, but he is supportive nonetheless. Our son Billy and his wife Kelly have five boys—Alex, Elliot, Brett, Jack, and Jamie—who are enthusiastic as well but are much more into sports. Again, Kelly is the one into women's history on that side of the family, and she always wants to know when my next book will come out.

But the one I live with must put up with the most from me: my husband Bill. He knows when I go into my little office space and begin to write, he is going to need to run errands and explain to folks where I am. He has been wonderful and has made more trips to the grocery store than he could have ever imagined. I give my sincere love and thanks to him and all my family. I am blessed.

I have spent years studying history with an emphasis on women who had to survive in a world that treated them as second-class citizens. Many of their stories have been forgotten. I am happy to tell another one of their stories, which is half fact and half imagined. But I believe it certainly could have happened this way!

Notes

9 – "Rochester, September 29…"

Carolyn Newton Curry, *The Life of Ella Gertrude Clanton Thomas, 1834-1907* (Macon, GA: Mercer University Press, 2014), 30 (hereafter cited as SAGS).

41 – "now considered one of the foremost painters in the South." *The Constitution* (Atlanta) 31 May 1899.

60 – *"Life size, $100, $300, $500.* Pictures in little $50." *The Constitution* (Atlanta) 19 May 1899.

90 – "The Lord giveth and the Lord taketh away…" SAGS, 62 & 63.

95 – "Our precious Anna Lou is dead…" SAGS, 63.

97 – "I hope I am grateful…" SAGS, 64.

100 – "All women in their condition should be favored…" SAGS, 66.

113 – "The fact is my nervous organization…" SAGS, 83.

119 – "Southern women are I believe all at heart abolitionists…" SAGS, 68.

135 – "Tears gather, it is only with an effort…" SAGS, 120.

136 – "I have been so proud a woman…" SAGS, 122.

138 – "Why, this is infinitely worse than Sherman…" SAGS, 127.

138 – "On 21 October 1872 in case of The National Bank of Augusta…" SAGS, 136.

155 – "Dr. and Mrs. Patrick for sixteen dollars per month…" SAGS, 146.

159 – "Since I have attended the convention…" SAGS, 153 & 154.

255 – "I look forward to attending your address at Atlanta University…"

Adele Logan Alexander, *Princess of the Hither Isles: A Black Suffragist's Story from the Jim Crow South* (Yale University Press, 2019), 144.

265 – "Woman was not taken from the head of man…" *The Atlanta Journal* (Atlanta) 29 November 1899.